If Only

BOOKS BY ANGELA MARSONS

ANGELA MARSONS

If Only

bookouture

Published by Bookouture in 2021

An imprint of Storyfire Ltd.
Carmelite House
50 Victoria Embankment
London EC4Y 0DZ

www.bookouture.com

ISBN: 978-1-80019-623-0
eBook ISBN: 978-1-80019-622-3

This book is a work of fiction. Names, characters, businesses,
organizations, places and events other than those clearly in the
public domain, are either the product of the author's imagination
or are used fictitiously. Any resemblance to actual persons, living or
dead, events or locales is entirely coincidental.

This book is dedicated to Kim Nash. A working woman, a mother, an author and one of the strongest women I know.

CHAPTER ONE

'Please, Mr Williams, I need to leave work on time tonight. I did mention it yesterday.'

Cher could hear the pleading tone that had crept into her voice, but she wasn't proud.

'That's unfortunate, Cher, but I didn't know then that Mr Hunter would want to see me this evening.' He smiled without regret. 'I might need you after I've seen him. He may have something urgent for me to do.'

Of course, a memo that would ensure world peace. An email that would end famine in Africa. Or, more likely, a fax to one of the retail tenants in the shopping centre, she thought.

She sighed deeply, just so he'd appreciate her sacrifice. Thanks to him, she was now going to be late for her own girls'-night-in party. Sarah and Deb would be chuffed to bits. She was host this evening to a night of pasta, wine and a dose of Tom Hardy on Netflix.

'I'll just wait here until you get back then, shall I?' she asked miserably.

'Umm… no, Cher, Mr Hunter is coming down here to see me.' The self-importance was as clear as the widening dark blue circle peeping out from beneath his armpit.

'He… he's what… but… he can't,' she protested, surveying her appearance. She glanced down at her chunky boots – suitable for a spot of fell walking. Her hastily applied lip liner had long since attached itself to a crusty baguette. If she'd known Michael Hunter was to make a royal visit, she'd have worn heels and mummified herself in Spanx.

'As the centre manager, he can go wherever he chooses, and I'm not sure the opinion of a secretary would deter him.'

The false nails on her right hand dug crescent-shaped indentations into the flesh of her palm. He knew she hated the term *secretary*. It always provoked a vision of short skirts, nail polish and sitting on the boss's knee.

'Hello, Cher. How are you?'

'H-Hello, M-Mr Hunter,' she blurted out, feeling her cheeks turn Christmas red.

She pushed back a clutch of unruly black curls to gaze up into eyes that were like smoked glass, set in olive skin. His fringe rested untidily on eyebrows that arched attractively. He walked towards the door into Mr Williams's office. It was good to watch that perfect, sporty bottom go.

'Black, no sugar would be wonderful,' he said with a grin as he closed the door.

Cher gazed after him and remembered *Indecent Proposal*, a film her mother used to watch. She pictured Michael Hunter as Robert Redford, but younger, and herself as Demi Moore and prayed he would offer her an indecent proposal. Would she sleep with him for a million pounds? More accurately, would he sleep with *her* for a million pounds and would her bank manager sanction the overdraft?

It wasn't just his physical attributes that she admired, although there was a lot there to admire, but his whole demeanour. He exuded confidence and control with a take-charge attitude that was reassuring. Yes, she knew some of the guys called him cocky and arrogant, but she didn't see him that way.

Her own mini crush on his good looks had developed into something deeper, and it was all down to Peppa Pig. Just a couple of years earlier, the popular children's TV character had been touring shopping centres during the school holidays. So popular were the events that crowd control failed completely when fights broke out due to parents jostling their kids to the front of the throng. Every member of staff had been called to the event to assist, but only when Michael Hunter appeared, standing at a safe distance, and uttered the words, 'Shut it down,' did things start to calm down. Peppa Pig left the stage, the crowd dispersed and catastrophe was averted. There were some that thought he should have helped with the crowd control and the complaints that other staff members had to deal with, but she understood that wasn't up to him. He was paid to make the big and unpopular decisions and he had done that, and she respected him for it.

She reluctantly dragged herself back out of the twilight zone and scrambled up from the chair. Coffee. He wanted coffee, she recalled, as her right leg brushed against a splinter of wood protruding from the edge of her desk.

'Shit,' she cursed, surveying the damage. A ladder ran the length of ankle to calf, pausing to create a crop circle before disappearing beneath the fabric of her skirt. *Could I look any worse?* she wondered.

She checked that no coffee granule had found its way through the filter into his cup as it so often did into her own. 'Shoulders back, chest out' she recalled from an assertiveness book she'd bought on impulse. 'Improve the demeanour, get noticed' it said on the first page, which was all she'd read before accepting the fact that it bored her rigid. The first act of assertiveness was to throw the bloody thing in the bin.

She raised her chin and stretched her neck to create the illusion that she was taller than five foot three in socks and inched, crab-like, into the room to avoid attention being drawn to the gaping hole in her tights. *God, how can he resist me?* she thought ruefully as she inched back out, ignored by them both.

Back at her desk, a couple of words that she'd inadvertently heard came back to her. *Downsizing* and *Audit. This is not good news*, she realised as laughter erupted from the inner sanctum. Oh good, everything was okay then. Unless he'd come down to fire her, she realised. That would explain why Mr Williams was laughing.

She switched the computer back on and considered typing the three memos that had landed on her desk during the last two hours, but decided against it. Despite advances in technology, Mr Williams remained old school. He wrote letters, memos and emails longhand and then plonked them on her desk to type and send. Given that he was unlikely to produce a mountain of work the following morning, they would keep her occupied for the first twenty minutes of a day that was sure to be no different from the rest.

She clicked on the Solitaire icon that provided a shortcut to the most used program on her computer. The cards unfolded and she began the psychological game that she always played. If she won the game, her legs would suddenly look great in Lycra or the clothes in her wardrobe would miraculously come back into fashion.

She decided to give the game more of a challenge. 'If I win this hand,' she whispered to herself, 'Mr Hunter will ask me out for a drink.'

She began clicking on the cards, eager to find out if the prophesying game was on her side. She snatched her hand away from the mouse as voices sounded close to the other side of the door.

'She's not PA material, but she's loyal,' she heard Mr Williams say quietly and knew instantly that he was talking about her.

She'd tried to convince herself that Mr Williams liked her, until he admitted that she managed to irritate him much of the time. While she was busy trying to arrange a hurt, offended expression, he'd explained that she was too argumentative and that he wished she'd never been taught to ask 'why', as it was the most overused word in her vocabulary. She had almost mentioned that there were a few others that she used in relation to him but had closed her turbo mouth just in time.

Michael Hunter swaggered past her towards the lift. She smiled in his direction, but he'd already stepped inside.

'It's okay, Cher, you can go now,' said Mr Williams quietly from the doorway. She was out of her chair on the word 'can'.

She paused. 'Are you okay?' She cursed herself for asking after what she'd just heard.

'I'll be fine. You go home.'

Alarm bells rang immediately. Mr Williams didn't like her going home very much. He was like a stick of rock: if you cut him open, he had the company name running right through him. And he didn't approve of people who came to work just for the money.

'Can I help?' she asked, stealing a furtive glance at the clock on the opposite wall.

He deflated and sank to the leather couch.

'The Tenants' Committee is commissioning an audit of the management team.'

'Why? Is the rent too high?'

He smiled at her like a tolerant uncle. She tried not to be irritated. If she knew little about the running of the department, it was only because he didn't involve her.

She resolved to look for another job the following morning. This was not new: the same thought occurred to her almost every day, either while she was filling the percolator or unjamming the decrepit printer.

This was not the dream that had pulled her through her business admin course at college. She had never wanted to create, like Sarah, or dominate, like Deb. She craved organisation.

The order of the nine-to-five workforce had appealed to her all her school life, ever since she sat watching the school administrator while waiting for the nurse to bandage her grazed knee.

She had gazed with awe as Mrs Johnson answered telephones while clicking away on an ancient PC. The sound was sharp and efficient. She fielded enquiries, found paperwork for the headmaster, lesson plans for the teachers and timetables for the students. She remained calm and friendly while people swamped her desk – all needing something before the bell signalled the next lesson – and everyone smiled and thanked her. She was one person but necessary to everyone around her.

When, years later, Cher was given the opportunity to spend her Work Experience period at a multinational steel company in the city centre, she chose, instead, to spend it with Mrs Johnson in the school office. Watching how the entire school seemed to revolve around and rely on that one person strengthened her own resolve. She wanted to be that one person. She wanted to be the hub. She had focused her qualifications towards Business Studies and Commerce, imagining herself as the indispensable aide to the director of a thriving, international business. Instead, she typed letters about overflowing rubbish bins and faulty automatic doors.

'No, Cher, the rent from the shops has nothing to do with us. That goes directly to the landlord. It's the additional service charge which covers cleaning and maintaining the premises.'

'Oh,' she said, purely because he paused.

'We're being audited next week, to ensure that, as the managing agents, we're providing value for money.' He shook his head, causing his glasses to move from the bridge of his nose. 'They'll go through all our documentation, asking all sorts of questions.'

'But there's nothing to hide, is there?'

'Heavens, no. There are no shady dealings or anything like that. It just places me in a precarious position, that's all.'

'But as the operations manager you co-ordinate all aspects of each department. How could they do without you?' she asked, even though she wasn't sure exactly what he did except redirect paperwork all over the building. Her desk often resembled a Royal Mail sorting office.

'Oh, Cher,' he said quietly. 'During an audit, one of the most dangerous people to be is middle management. The top brass look after themselves, and the workers are in no danger: they keep the place open.'

'Umm… Mr Williams, do I need to update my CV any time soon?' she asked, trying desperately not to be selfish and failing miserably.

'No, I don't think you have anything to worry about at the moment. The auditors will be more interested in what Mr Hunter called the "fat management". If they can cut a salary or two, it'll be a job well done.' He paused, growing older before her eyes. 'They won't worry about people like you. Your salary doesn't warrant their attention.'

She smiled, unsure whether she was pleased or offended.

'They're just trimming fat,' he said absently.

'Send them my way first.'

Mr Williams laughed at her poor attempt at humour. Yes, he was definitely worried. He never laughed at her jokes.

'I'm… umm… I have to…' She felt awful, but she could hardly expect Deb and Sarah to wait long for the luxury of cheap wine and frozen meals.

'Of course,' he mumbled, without looking up. 'You get off home.'

She retrieved her helmet from under the desk slowly, so he could see her hesitation in being forced to leave him alone. He wasn't too bad really. She didn't blame him for his old-school outlook. But it did mean that she remained unchallenged and uninspired.

'Hi, Cher. How's the bike?' asked Dan, the engineers' foreman, as he passed her at the door. His sandy-coloured hair was ruffled on the right side of his head, as it often was by the end of the day, after many passes of a hand that swept it every time he was deep in thought.

Dan had joined the department a year earlier when the previous foreman had retired. Mr Williams had felt that none of the engineers had enough experience to consider them for promotion, and so he had recruited externally, directly into a supervisory position. Any hostility from the team of plumbers, carpenters and electricians had quickly dissipated when Dan had turned his small office into a mini break room and donned a tool belt. She heard his chatter all day over the radio as he moved from one job to the next, supporting and assisting his team.

From the very first day, when he'd taken the time to come and introduce himself, they'd fallen into conversation easily, especially when he'd noticed the card game she was playing on her computer and had suggested others that were free to download.

Over time, he'd started to share the odd joke with her, and she had been happy to reciprocate. On other days, he popped his head around the door to tell her that the wind speed outside was increasing. Crucial information when commuting on two wheels.

'Fine but don't call it a bike: you'll have people think I own a proper one instead of a hairdryer on a frame.'

'If it ever breaks down' – he laughed, holding the door open for her; toned muscles pressed against the fabric of his shirt sleeves, and his tie hung loose beneath his open top button; he leaned forward conspiratorially as she passed – 'I've got an old lawnmower you can borrow.'

'Ha, bloody, ha,' she replied.

She laughed off the numerous jokes at her chosen mode of transport. Some day she would take driving lessons again: once her pathological fear of the three-point-turn manoeuvre had subsided. That was one of the things she liked about her moped – if it needed turning she could just pick it up.

Dan's low chuckle followed her into the lift. She wondered if he'd be one of the unlucky ones, but Mr Williams had said the workers were okay and she hoped Dan didn't lose his job. He made her laugh.

It felt awful, knowing that people's livelihoods were on the line and she couldn't even warn them, although she wasn't sure what she had to feel guilty about. With the new voice recognition systems, she could be replaced for fifty quid so she had enough problems of her own. The current one being that the cheesecake would never be defrosted in time for when her friends arrived.

She just hoped that Sarah would be late for a change, just like Deb was sure to be.

CHAPTER TWO

Sarah fingered the luxurious silk as it slid over her moisturised skin and hugged her curves perfectly. David loved sexy lingerie. Refined, not tacky, he always said.

She appraised her reflection and nodded appreciatively. This dusky pink teddy accentuated her small waist with a subtle gathering around the middle. The delicate lace edging teased her breastbone before dipping invitingly into her cleavage.

A swell of excitement churned her stomach. It would drive him wild when he found her waiting for him at the weekend, wearing this hot little number, covered only with an Indian-print silk kimono that brushed the top of her knees temptingly.

She smiled at herself as she pulled her blonde hair back, leaving only a couple of tendrils resting on her cheekbones. She would adorn her face with little more than foundation and a flash of tinted lip gloss. David liked her to look fresh and natural. Huh, if he thought that the natural look could be achieved without any help from Boots cosmetics department, he was seriously mistaken. She was twenty-seven, for God's sake.

She admired herself openly with honest acceptance of her own sex appeal. Her eyes were big and innocent like a frightened deer, and even in anger they remained doe-like. Her favourite feature was her lips. They were heart-shaped and luscious and revealed a Hollywood smile. She knew that the whole combination was a killer as far as men were concerned, but she was becoming a little worried. Time, however fervently she fought against its onslaught, was leaving its mark on her. Shadows were appearing beneath her eyes, in spite of the eight hours' sleep she enjoyed without fail.

Two very faint lines ran beneath her bottom eyelashes that refused to diminish underneath the creams and lotions she applied every night. They weren't yet trench-like, but she knew they were there.

She turned to the side and examined the reflection in minute detail. Satisfied that the all-over tan accentuated the teddy to maximum effect, she removed it and draped it over a lavender-scented hanger, ready for the following day. If that didn't win him away from his wife, nothing would. She knew every feminist that had ever breathed would be shaking their head in despair at the exploitation of her physical appearance to get what she wanted but, after so long waiting, she was desperate for David to make the right decision about their future.

She stepped into the shower, counting back to when they'd first met. Five years she'd been waiting for the day when he would realise that he belonged to her, that they had to spend their lives together. Five long years since he'd entered the book-shop where she worked.

She'd been instantly attracted to him. The first thing she'd noticed was his walk. It wasn't a swagger, but it was confident and self-assured. He was wearing beige slacks and a rugby shirt that showed off tanned, sinewy arms covered with sexy dark hair. For a few seconds she experienced every cliché she'd read about in books: the world simply stood still and everyone else disappeared; her heart started beating a little faster in her chest; her mouth dried up; and she felt an overwhelming need to be near him. It was unlike anything she'd ever felt before and had made her a little light-headed in its intensity.

She'd nudged Dora away slightly as he approached the counter. Her gaze was drawn directly to deep brown eyes that maintained contact with her own as he spoke. She appointed herself his personal shopper as he explained, with a charming smile, that he was shopping for books for his heavily pregnant wife. At that point, Sarah had immediately dismissed the fantasy that he would ask her out, though she allowed herself a little harmless flirtation as they shopped. Despite an obvious chemistry between them, she accepted that she wasn't going to feel those well-defined arms pulling her against his wide, muscled chest.

Later, after he left with a collection of books, Sarah couldn't even recall what they'd chosen. She only knew that for half an hour the book store had turned into an airless vacuum with no staff members, no Saturday-afternoon crowds and no pregnant wife. She tried to banish the thought of his athletic build and rugged good looks all day Sunday, but no amount of running on the gym treadmill eradicated the image from her memory.

The following Monday morning, he had appeared at the counter once again. Sarah almost swallowed her heart as it jumped into her mouth, and without asking she knew why he'd returned before he even spoke. His easy, confident smile sent blood rushing directly into her cheeks and frissons of electricity through her body. He invited her for coffee as a thank you. Internally, she'd fought the temptation and refused. The man had a wife, a pregnant wife. He wasn't free. He wasn't available. He belonged to someone else. He persisted though, and she felt helpless. Her whole being wanted to spend time with this man. She was drawn to him in a way she'd never been drawn to anyone else. *Go for coffee*, she justified to herself. *It's just coffee.*

They headed to the nearest Costa, where he regaled her with tales of his recent trip to Marrakesh.

She listened in wonder as he explained how they used the heat from the Turkish baths for cooking bread. David talked of the communal ovens in narrow, crowded streets used by the entire community, and the night markets, bustling with dancers, and food vendors offering snails, fish and peppers. Sarah had barely spoken, hypnotised by his low, velvety voice.

More coffees followed, then a dinner date or two. Sarah worked hard to convince herself that they were just friends: two people enjoying each other's company. The more she got to know him, the more she realised he wasn't happy in his marriage. She knew her initial feelings of lust were deepening and that she was falling in love with him. On their third dinner date, she revealed her true feelings and told him that she couldn't see him again. Much as she couldn't stand the thought of life without him, she had to try and do the right thing. To her surprise, he'd admitted that he too had fallen in love with her and that the thought of never seeing her again was unbearable. That was the night they'd returned to her flat and made love for hours. It had been everything she'd dreamed of and had cemented her view that the two of them were meant for each other and that his marriage to Bianca was some cosmic accident that had occurred when the fates had been looking the other way.

In the early days, she had tortured herself with thoughts of Bianca, and she had tried once or twice to break it off, but she couldn't imagine her life without David in it. She eventually reconciled to herself that Bianca got much more of David's time than she did. She lived for the brief snatches of time they spent together.

Throughout the football season, their Saturday afternoons were idyllic. It was easier to keep Bianca from becoming suspicious through his purchase of a season ticket to Wolverhampton Wanderers Football Club, which was inevitably followed by 'a few beers with my friends, darling', and so he wasn't expected home until after six. During the few months separating the end of the season and the beginning of the new one, he was forced to be a little more creative, which meant he didn't always make it.

He'd spoken proudly, once, of his own subterfuge, claiming that being the father of a girl, who would never want to share his Saturday afternoon football, it would work for years. It hadn't been until two days later that Sarah had realised what he meant. She'd questioned his long-term plan, as he'd always claimed he would break the news to Bianca when the time was right. He had kissed her lovingly, saying it was merely a figure of speech.

Now, she shivered with delight at their imminent Saturday afternoon together. He'd sit and listen to the football game first, claiming that he should at least know what had happened if he was supposed to have been there. He'd mentioned that Bianca had no interest in football, so Sarah doubted if she even asked.

But it didn't matter: Sarah loved their special afternoons. She pottered in the kitchen, cooking, while he sat with his ear glued to the radio. From the kitchen she would hear the occasional 'Whoa' or 'Nooo' and she could normally follow the game from that. But what she loved was, for that short time, she could play the part. For one brief afternoon each week, she could hum to herself and pretend that it was real, that this was *her* life and it was *her* husband cheering and booing at electrical appliances.

When the game finished, she would feel his presence behind her. His hands would rest on her shoulders before sliding down her back to her waist. He loved to hold her waist. He would lean forward, pressing his body against hers. Her hands would support her weight on the worktop as his mouth kissed lightly at the hairs on the back of her neck, occasionally nipping her sharply, sending flashes of desire through her.

His hands would slowly, deliciously, travel from her waist around to her stomach. His fingers would trace lines across it while his thumb teasingly touched just underneath her breast. She would squirm and try to face him to feel his mouth on hers, but he would hold her firm while his thumb worked its way higher, until it was lightly brushing against granite-hard nipples. At the very second that he felt her body begin trembling, he would turn her around and kiss her searchingly, and they would be lucky if they made it to the bedroom.

Afterwards, they would lie in bed. David would massage her from head to toe, guiding her to an almost hypnotic state of relaxation. She'd pretend that they would sleep in the same bed that night, wake up and have breakfast together: the Sunday-morning type with tea, toast and newspapers. She could pretend that he wouldn't, on the stroke of six, get dressed, kiss her lightly and leave, abandoning her to face the worst time of the week.

Saturday nights were torture for her. After he'd gone, the flat seemed bigger, emptier without his presence. She normally lay on the sofa and cried, trying desperately to fight off images of him driving home to his wife, while still able to feel the imprint of his hands massaging her back.

Only one thing was worse than his leaving and that was when he failed to turn up. Occupational hazard of being 'the other woman' Sarah realised, but there was nothing crueller than waiting for their brief time together only to be disappointed, sometimes minutes before. She pushed that thought away force-fully. It only drew her attention to the loneliness that didn't always live in her stomach but never seemed far away.

If she ever questioned why she continued to live her life this way, she only had to recall that one magical afternoon each week when the world ceased to exist and she was treasured and desired like a rare wild flower and the doubts fell away.

She glanced at the dusky pink teddy and smiled ruefully. She was under no false illusions that a slip of fabric would bring David to her forever. She wasn't that naïve. Her plans were bigger than that.

She entered the spare bedroom and closed the door behind her. One side of the room was given to ugly black bookshelves crammed with an eclectic selection of fiction and factual books. The far corner was dominated by a curved mahogany desk that she had fallen in love with just before she met David. She remembered that period of total immersion in writing and the hope that maybe one day she would make it. The sensation hadn't lasted long, and the desk now stood accusingly bare, except for a paper tray holding a couple of newspaper clippings. The dilapidated PC had been replaced by a laptop and an iPad.

She extracted a folder from the bottom drawer of the desk and lowered herself onto the single bed reserved for drunkenly incapacitated friends. The ring binder was sectioned off with coloured dividers labelled 'Charts', 'Diary', 'Articles' and 'Aphrodisiacs'. It was like a project folder she'd had at school for a study on food groups.

She fingered the red line, drawn that morning with a felt tip and ruler. A perfect line, an inch long, demonstrated the increase in her temperature. The graph looked like a company chart detailing the peaks and troughs in sales revenue.

The diary section hadn't been touched for two weeks. David's daughter, Chelsea, had cut her head open the previous Saturday and had ended up in hospital with stitches. Sarah's immediate reaction had been concern for both David and his child. He must have been terrified, and she'd had to remind herself to be a nice person when her second thought had been 'Why Saturday?' It wasn't that she blamed Chelsea, but the days between their time together seemed endless enough without being cancelled at the last minute, leaving another empty week ahead.

In the diary section, she recorded the intimate details of her sex life in an effort to identify any links with whether or not she reached orgasm easily, with difficulty or not at all, just in case. She'd read somewhere that a woman couldn't conceive if she didn't have an orgasm. If she was perfectly honest, she didn't believe that, but she didn't want to leave anything to chance.

She leafed through the next section idly, knowing most of the articles by heart. She'd read all about oestrogen levels, sperm count, fertility drugs and IVF.

The last section listed, in alphabetical order, the name of all aphrodisiacs known to man and beast, ranging from 'Absinthe' to 'Yohimbine'. The first created images of the Parisian artistic communities at the turn of the century using absinthe to add fervour to their ardour. The second was used by native tribes in South America and West Africa; its erotic potency was rumoured to produce an effect on the brain and stimulate the nerves of the genitalia. In spite of their romantic histories, she had yet to find anything in the freezer section of Sainsbury's that listed them as ingredients.

She closed the folder and placed it back into the drawer. David never came into the spare bedroom but she hid it anyway. The lingerie was the icing on the cake, but she knew that with his child inside her, the temptation of their life together would bring him to her forever. That plan had formed three months ago and she'd been trying ever since.

She returned to the kitchen to check the cupboards for the items she would need for the weekend. Deb would be proud of her efficiency. Where David was concerned, everything had to be just perfect. On Saturday morning, she would shop for fresh ingredients that would be fried, baked, roasted and grilled into a meal. Unlike Cher's habit of throwing a lasagne into the micro-wave, vegetarian cooking relied on many different ingredients.

She knew people laughed at her meat philosophy. It wasn't that she disagreed with animals being eaten when she shopped as organically as she could: death she didn't have a problem with, figuring that everyone would succumb to it eventually. What she didn't like was the fact that the animals didn't get to lead a long and happy life first. Until the supermarket wrappers stated that no animal had suffered unduly in the making of the food and that it had died of old age, she would not eat meat.

She checked the ingredients off one at a time: chopped and ground nuts, onions, garlic, celery, peppers, mushrooms and soya source. Her hormonal eye took a cursory glance over the contents to ensure that there were a couple of aphrodisiacs present. Satisfied that the garlic and celery would aid her plight, she made a mental note to throw in a little artichoke and fennel just to be sure.

She dressed quickly, realising that she was almost late for Cher. Still, she was happy that everything was in order for the weekend. She had the definite feeling that their lovemaking against the dying teatime sunshine would produce the one thing that would bind him to her forever.

With the promise of the following day, she knew that even Deb would not bait her tonight.

CHAPTER THREE

At seven fifteen Deb's phone rang.

She was poised at the front door, a night of fun and relaxation almost within her grasp.

And, of course, Margie had some way of knowing that.

She looked around for the tracking device but could see nothing obvious. She wondered if her future mother-in-law had an entire satellite at her disposal.

As usual Deb stared at the phone, wondering if she had the courage to ignore it. She could find an excuse: there were hundreds, ranging from 'I was working late' to 'I was having oral sex on the doorstep with the milkman'. Margie would believe either one.

Her feet began moving in the direction of the car, but her thumb aimed towards the answer button.

Why couldn't she just ignore it? It wasn't like this daily conversation added a lilt to her walk or made her more pleasant to be around. But she couldn't ignore it. She was like an addict. *Just one more fix and then I'll stop*, she thought as the ringing became impatient and, she could swear, louder.

'Hello,' she answered cheerfully. Start as you mean to go on, she thought.

'Hello, Debra, it's Mum…'

Deb cringed twice: she hated the full use of her name and this woman was not her mother.

'Hello… Margie.' She couldn't bring herself to say it. She'd never had much use for the word and it felt alien on her lips.

'I picked up some of that Irish Cream you like yesterday. Shall I pop it round at the weekend?'

'Umm… I think Mark is coming round to see you on Saturday morning,' Deb said, trying to think quickly. He hadn't been but he would be now.

'I gather you're not coming with him then?'

'No. I'll concentrate on cleaning the house while he's gone.' There, that should earn some brownie points.

'It wouldn't hurt for one day surely. I could do with your advice on some paperwork I've had from the gas company. They want to sell me electricity, I think.'

Deb hesitated. Did she really need advice or was there some ulterior motive?

'I'll see if I can—'

'Oh good. I want to show you some invitation samples I got from the stationers in the high street. We should try and keep our business local, Debra, and Ernest is such a nice man.'

Deb cringed inwardly. Ernest was not a nice man at all. He'd been as subtle as a sledgehammer, peering and almost salivating at her V-neck sweater. He was an odious little shit with squinty eyes and extraordinarily long fingers, which had given Deb the creeps.

She preferred to order the invitations herself, as she worked for a stationery company and could get a fantastic discount, but that was apparently against the law. Deb had, at one point, considered going to WH Smith and grabbing a pack of brightly coloured invitations, decorated with balloons, jelly and ice cream, to send to a handful of people whom she would genuinely have liked at her wedding.

Margie had favoured invitations with rainbow swallows set against summer skies, with ornate calligraphy decorated with golden swirls. Deb had found them to be a little too showy and opted for rose blossoms embossed onto the card, with silver wording.

'And you'll need to get the cake ordered. It's only three months.'

'I doubt that every local baker will be too busy to produce one given a couple of months' notice and, if so, Tesco do a nice line in party cakes featuring Thomas the Tank Engine and Homer Simpson.'

Margie remained silent for a few seconds. 'Really, Debra, it's hard to know when you're joking sometimes,' she huffed.

Fifteen to love, Deb thought.

'Well at least the church is booked.' Margie sighed. 'But you really need to develop a sense of urgency. And we really need to decide on the inscription for the Bibles for the bridesmaids…'

'Margie, I've told you a hundred times that I'm not giving Cher and Sarah Bibles as presents. I'd like to buy them a piece of jewellery, probably gold pend—'

'But it's traditional, Debra. Some things have to remain sacred.'

'I'm not doing it, Margie. They wouldn't thank me for them, so I'm not spending money on bloody Bibles.'

Margie's fixation on the Bibles was beyond Deb. It wasn't as though she was particularly religious.

She knew she had to hide her resentment of the woman's interference. Maybe then she would actually get married this year.

She recalled the previous year when the date had been set at the local registry office. No pomp, no ceremony, just a few close friends and a cold buffet at the local pub later. But absent-minded Margie had forgotten the date and arranged to go on a last-minute holiday to Tenerife with one of her WRVS cronies that she couldn't possibly get out of. She'd felt awful about them postponing their small affair until her return.

After discussing it with Mark, Deb had decided on a simple ceremony in Ibiza, again with a few close friends. She loved the simplicity of a romantic setting, with toes touched by the warm sand, reciting her vows in a cool white dress beneath the sunshine. She could imagine nothing better than sand, sea, sun and as much tequila as she could drink.

Three days before the wedding, Margie had been struck down with a mystery virus that had forced her to retire to her bed in a fit of eighteenth-century swooning. Amidst her hollow insistence that they should do it without her, Deb had been sorely tempted, but she wouldn't have done that to Mark.

Once Deb had cancelled the plane tickets and grudgingly decided on a full-blown church wedding, Margie's virus had suddenly disappeared. The woman insisted on helping her plan the wedding, claiming that she was sure nothing would go wrong this time, and convincing Deb of what she already suspected: that the virus had never existed.

Since that day, Deb had been bombarded with information on serviettes, serviette rings, bridal favours, printed menus, corsages, bouquets, photo albums, photographers, dresses, veils, champagne and wines. Her head spun at night as she lay down to sleep. She'd glance across at her future husband – his short black hair tufted, his good looks relaxed with a half-smile, the small scar on his shoulder from a football injury – and wonder if it was all worth it.

Then she would lean over and kiss his cheek lightly. Yes, it was.

Deb couldn't wait to be married to Mark. They had moved into their house after the first failed wedding attempt, due to the start of the mortgage payments, but she wanted it to be official. She wanted to declare her love for Mark openly, and it rankled that Margie had managed to get her own way with a convoluted church affair when a simple pagan ceremony in a nearby field would have been enough for her.

Deb recalled Mark's theory about their thorny relationship. He believed it was because Deb had had no practice with mothers and didn't know how they acted. Deb thought that was total bollocks. She didn't need to have known her own mother to see that his was a controlling, manipulative witch. Her own mother had died before she was two years old. One day, while hanging out washing, she had collapsed with a ruptured brain aneurysm that had been undetected yet fatal. Deb had grown up without a mother and also without the memory of a mother.

Throughout her school days, she had watched longingly as her classmates had been dropped off at the school gates by mothers fussing that they were warm enough, that their uniforms were arranged correctly, that their hair was tidy. She had watched those same mothers hide the hurt as their children had grown and had squirmed away from the farewell hugs and kisses. Had it been her, she would not have been so eager to get away.

There had been no warm and fuzzy aunts onto whom she could transfer those feelings, no relatives with whom she could form a substitute parental bond. By the time she reached high school, she listened only to the kids who were rebelling against their parents, the ones struggling to maintain a relationship. She focused only on the negative mother and daughter relationships to help her feel better about being excluded. By the time she reached college, she had tried not to think about it at all.

None of the above made Margie any less difficult to handle. She was manipulative, controlling and any hope Deb had fostered of building any kind of relationship with the woman had been quashed when Margie had insisted on talking about one of Mark's angelic ex-girlfriends during their second meeting.

She had not allowed that hope to resurface again and had reverted back to her 'not a relationship I need' stance.

'I'm sorry, Margie. Dust and dog hairs wait for no one, but I'll pop round soon.'

Margie sniffed. 'If you must. Oh, I almost forgot, I bought a lovely pink bathroom set for you from Marks & Spencer.'

Deb rolled her eyes and shook her head at the same time. Firstly, she hated fluffy bathroom sets and, secondly, she detested the colour pink. It was a washed-out tone of her favourite colour: burgundy. There was nothing pink in her house. She preferred the dignified strength of the deep red. Oh well, something else that Mark was going to have to sort out on Saturday. Fluffy pink wasn't going anywhere near her pristine white ceramic.

She held the phone away from her ear as Margie droned on about centrepieces and seating plans. Why did she subject herself to this every time? What the hell was she hoping for?

Deb realised that the earpiece had fallen silent. A faint wave of hope turned her stomach. Maybe she'd talked herself into a heart attack. Deb instantly felt bad for the thought, but not as bad as she should have.

'Anyway, Margie, I must go. I'm on my way to Cher's.'

Margie humphed and Deb could visualise the eye-roll.

'As I was saying, I'll have to go. I'll speak to you soon. Bye.' Deb replaced the receiver before she had chance to argue.

Deb always finished the conversation with the words 'I'll speak to you soon', as if that would discourage her from further phone calls.

The harassment didn't stop when she was at the office. When the phone calls had started at work, Deb had taken great delight in recognising the number and pressing the button marked 'Voicemail'. Being shrewder than Deb had given her credit for, Margie had quickly learned to hide her caller number so that the screen remained blank. With so many companies now adopting the same practice, Deb couldn't take the chance of ignoring what might be a very important call.

And then there were the evening calls and the polite enquiries as to what she was cooking for tea. Deb normally taunted her with the names of herbs and spices like chervil and sorrel. A sniff of disapproval would emanate through the phone line as she'd decry the need for 'normal': basic foods like chips, stew, dumplings, sausages and mash. Apparently, there was no problem in the world that a good potato couldn't solve.

Deb put the car into first gear with more force than necessary, causing the gearbox to squeal out in protest.

Before she pulled away she heard a muffled ringing sound from her handbag. Margie's number screamed accusingly from the LED display.

Cher, you'd better have a damn good supply of alcohol by the time I get there tonight, Deb thought as her thumb moved towards the answer button.

CHAPTER FOUR

Cher was fairly smug that she wasn't too late getting home after all. The journey had passed quickly, in spite of the rush-hour traffic, thanks to her fantasies about Michael Hunter. On the way home, she had received the finger twice and a few grumpy horns when she failed to move on a green light. She responded to their irritation by honking her horn back, which only amused pedestrians, as it sounded like a bad case of flatulence, and had no effect on motorists attempting to reduce her to roadkill.

She had already tidied up her living room, which was spacious and fashionable, although parts of it were not strictly hers, more inherited from a previous long-term boyfriend, Richard, who'd found it necessary to indulge in a little overtime with a barmaid at the local pub while Cher was at the gym. She'd accepted that the relationship was pretty much finished when the idea of losing the surround-sound TV upset her more than the fact it was over.

She'd taken his clothes to his office in a bin liner and emptied them all over his desk, including his unwashed boxers, then hysterically informed him that he could collect his electronic gadgets if he knew how to reassemble them, following their untimely encounter with a baseball bat. He never came back.

It had been her most serious relationship and, to her knowledge, the only time she'd been cheated on. There was no question it had made her feel like shit and had left her comparing herself to the apparent perfection of her rival, Cazzy Mosley, who she'd tracked down on Facebook with just a few key details from Richard's page before he blocked her.

Cazzy did Callanetics. Cazzy did yoga on the beach in a leotard. Cazzy posted pictures of exotic meals she'd prepared. Cazzy had long hazel hair with an attractive natural wave. Cazzy also seemed like a nice person, which didn't help: she couldn't even claim superiority in that department.

There was no doubt that single experience had left its mark on her, and yet it wasn't the reason she questioned her ability to find and keep a boyfriend. When she looked back on relationships either before or after Richard, she was aware that all of them had simply fizzled. There had been no clear reason for the break-ups. No pops or bangs, just fizzles. The calls, texts and messages had simply slowed and then stopped. It wasn't her experience with Richard that caused her to view herself so critically. That had been a case of him eating a sandwich when a cream cake walked in the door. He just couldn't resist. More concerning was her inability to hold the interest of a potential boyfriend for more than a couple of weeks before they simply meandered away with no strong feelings either way.

She pushed the thoughts aside as she lit the candles that would fill the room with the clean, fresh aroma of vanilla. The scene was set for a great night in, which they tried to manage a couple of times a month. The wine chilled in the fridge, the cheesecake thawed by the radiator and the lasagnes were ready to go into the microwave.

Sarah was the first to arrive, bringing with her more wine and a cheery expression.

'You dressed up then?' she asked, surveying Cher's faded jeans and vest top. The large white handprints that were supposed to cover each breast stretched halfway down Cher's torso.

'And you look as gorgeous as ever,' Cher said truthfully. Sarah smiled but didn't disagree. Her friend looked cool and fresh as always. Her floral-print wrap dress suited her figure perfectly, but then again, Cher thought, a potato sack would make Sarah's figure look great.

'You're not actually cooking for a change, are you?' Sarah asked suspiciously.

'It's lasagne and salad, so I guess it'll just be lettuce for you.'

'Late from work again?' she asked, surveying the defrosting dessert.

'Yep, I was too busy drooling over Michael Hunter to give you a thought.'

Sarah tipped her head. 'Why don't you ask him out?'

Cher almost choked. 'Yes, why don't I? I'll ask out a bloke who dates designer bread sticks to go for a cheap curry with me. However will he contain himself?'

'I just thought…'

'How many times do I have to tell you that Cinderella was a fairy tale? Just because it was made into a movie doesn't mean it was a true story with the names changed to protect the innocent.'

'I see – you're scared.'

'Get lost.'

'At last, Deb's here,' observed Sarah as the door almost caved in. 'Oh dear, how many pedestrians did she score tonight?' Road rage was not so much an occasional occurrence for Deb: it was the way she lived her life.

Cher opened the door prepared for the scowl and deep, grating voice that would greet her.

'I swear to God that I am going to seriously maim that woman if she tries to invade my wedding one more time. Hello,' she snorted as an afterthought.

'Oh well, Cher, at least you'll be able to thaw the cheesecake. Just ask Deb to breathe on it.'

Deb threw herself into an armchair. 'Come on, furnish me with some of that cheap Asti you keep in unending supply.'

As Cher poured a generous measure, Deb burst out laughing. 'What's that crap on your toes?' She peered a little closer as Sarah wiggled them for her benefit. 'You look like a walking astrology chart.'

'Don't condemn what you can't comprehend.' Sarah smiled sweetly.

Cher placed the wine glass straight into Deb's hand. 'Hey, Deb, I saw Michael Hunter today. He is just so—'

'I'm going to ignore the phone. It's simple,' Deb interrupted.

'Is that it?' Cher asked, unable to believe she'd been interrupted for that.

Deb tried to explain. 'Don't you understand? That phone call is like a drug. I have to know what she thinks about me. I need to know what snippet of evil she has to dispense on a daily basis; so, if I can just break the cycle, I feel that life would be much improved.'

'So by ignoring the phone calls you'll become a better person?' Cher asked.

'Exactly.'

'But aren't you just fixating your own subconscious fears and anxieties onto the persona of Margie? Thereby apportioning blame for your own—'

'Jesus, Sarah, how much have you had to drink?' Deb interrupted.

Sarah blushed as Cher stifled a chuckle. A glass of wine unlocked Sarah's vocabulary. It would cease after another two glasses.

The pinging sound of the microwave drove Cher to her feet. Heating a few frozen meals hardly constituted gourmet cooking, but Cher wished she'd ordered a pizza instead.

She could just make out something Deb was saying about a meeting at work, and she was missing it while she scraped crusty tomato puree from the sides of the cardboard container.

'Sorry, but you're going to have to repeat that,' Cher said, kicking the kitchen door shut behind her. She had a plate in each hand and a third balancing precariously on her forearm.

'There's not a lot to tell,' Deb said, refilling their glasses. 'Imelda has called a meeting for Monday morning, which is bad enough, but with the added irritation of Pricky Stone being there.' She frowned as she took the balancing plate from Cher's arm. 'I've been playing various scenarios in my mind all day, and the only one that makes any sense is that he's being promoted for some unfathomable reason.'

'But why has she only invited the two of you? Wouldn't the rest of the sales team be present if that was the case?' Sarah asked, reaching for the crusty piece of garlic bread that Cher had been eyeing up.

Deb shrugged. 'We're the top two performers in the team,' she said without conceit. 'Our gross sales have been evenly matched for the last seven months.'

'Have you heard any rumours?' Cher asked.

'There's a whisper about Imelda being promoted. She's been taking a few extended lunch breaks recently.' She thought harder. 'And I suppose she has spent a little more time with the big chiefs, but there was talk of it more than a year ago which didn't amount to anything.'

'Have you even considered that it could be good news?' asked Sarah, the eternal optimist.

Deb shook her head fervently. 'You must be joking. Imelda worships the ground that Pricky slithers over.' She sighed heavily. 'And it's just like that damn woman to be so secretive and make me worry over the weekend.'

'Are you going to let her?' Cher asked.

Deb reached for her glass and downed it. 'Fuck her,' she cried, refilling her glass once more.

Sarah and Cher elected to consume their pasta sitting on the floor around the rectangular coffee table that separated the two sofas, much to Deb's despair. She chose to eat 'like a civilised person' at the table, until she missed a brief conversation, which prompted her to plonk herself between them.

'Watch the bottles,' Cher cried. Her concern was more for the wine than herself.

'Who the hell has drunk this much anyway?' asked Deb, surveying the empties.

'You, I think. Ooh, I feel all woozy.' Sarah giggled as she finally made it to a vertical position. Her food was barely touched, but Cher didn't take offence. The microwave had reduced the meals to a liquefied mess. Cher pushed her plate away at the same moment as Deb.

'Your command of the English language once you've had a couple of drinks is second to none. What's woozy mean, for goodness' sake?' Deb asked, rolling her eyes.

'Woozy is when someone has a few drinks and actually lets their hair down a bit, Deb. You might have read about it somewhere.'

'If you're trying to say I'm no fun, just watch this.'

'Deb, don't,' Cher warned as her head began to spin slightly.

Deb picked up a half-full bottle of wine and downed it without pausing for breath.

Cher sat back against the sofa and let her head rest against the cushion, enjoying the total relaxation that had invaded her body. Never again, she'd said after the last time but, God, it felt good.

'I knew you'd do that, Deb. You're so predictable,' Sarah said, laughing from beside her. She nudged Deb in the arm and offered a challenging expression. 'But what wouldn't be predictable is you ringing up that mother-in-law of yours and telling her what you really think of her.'

'Oh, if only I could,' Deb cried as she sprawled in her seat.

'I can't believe how much you let her get away with. You're not normally concerned about what you say to anyone. You've got more balls than the Wacky Warehouse. Why do you let her taunt you so much?'

Deb thought for a moment with her eyes closed. 'Every time I get close to breaking point with her, Mark manages to calm me down. He thinks she's wonderful and helpful. He doesn't see the interfering, manipulative bitch that I see.'

Cher and Sarah tried to remain serious but couldn't after so many bottles of cheap wine.

'It's not funny. I just want to get married, but I know she's lulling me into a false sense of security. She's planning some type of famine or drought this time, I'm sure of it.'

'Okay, while we're moaning, what about you, Sarah – has lover boy decided to leave his wife and kid for you yet?' Cher asked.

Sarah sighed and reached, searching for a bottle that still held any liquid. They were all empty.

'Once I get pregnant, he'll leave her,' she said with intoxicated bravado.

'Do you think?'

'Absolutely. I know how much he loves kids. He'd love us to have one. So would I.'

'He already has one,' Cher muttered before she could stop herself. Luckily, Sarah didn't hear, and Deb expertly steered the conversation away.

'What about you, Cher? What do you want?' asked Deb as she attempted to place one leg over the other. It fell back down.

Cher pulled her attention away from the lava lamp that was sending her into a hypnotic trance. 'I want Michael Hunter to fall so deeply in love with me that he can't bear to be more than fifty feet away.'

'And when the pigs cease flying, what would you really like?'

'Thanks for the vote of confidence,' she said miserably. She didn't need any confirmation that he was way out of her league. He was Premiership League while she was a Sunday morning kickabout in the park.

'Well let's be honest,' Deb said, sitting forward. 'None of us is going to get what we want. My mother-in-law is probably never going to allow me to marry her precious son; Sarah's married man is not going to leave his wife; and Michael Hunter is not going to whisk you away in his white Maserati.'

'We'll just see about that, shall we?' Cher said, trying to keep the petulance out of her voice. It was one thing knowing herself that Michael Hunter would never look twice at her, but being told it so confidently by her best friends was another matter.

'I don't see either of you any closer to getting what you want. Has your Minoan dance with the snake deity done you any good, or your Katrina fertility doll?'

'Kachina doll, if you must know, and the Native American Hopi tribe swear by it,' Sarah defended hotly.

'And I'm taking positive action with not answering the phone,' Deb added.

They looked at each other and laughed – hard. 'We're pathetic,' Sarah said.

'Ooh, ooh, hang on,' Cher cried intelligently as her eyes searched the crowded bookshelves that occupied an entire wall of her lounge.

A vague recollection of a rainy Saturday afternoon in a cheap bookshop came to mind. Books being sold for pennies. She'd brought back as many as she could carry, feeding her thirst for knowledge in books due to the fact she received no stimulation from work. Most days she could send her fingers to work on the bus. Her brain need not attend. A chuckle broke free from her lips. The vision that the entire sum of her as a person was a bunch of fingers was depressing in the cold light of day but quite amusing when she was pissed.

'Christ, what's that?' Deb asked, scrunching up her eyes at one book. She reached for the square-framed spectacles she used for reading. They were old-fashioned, with plain black frames which looked surprisingly stylish on her narrow face and emphasised her green eyes.

Deb read the title of the book she'd been scrutinising. '*Life's Dominion – An Argument about Abortion and Euthanasia*.' She guffawed loudly. 'Bloody hell, I bet this is just a laugh a minute.' She placed it back and surveyed a collection of pocket-sized books Cher had purchased ages ago.

'Cher, did you buy these all together?' she asked.

'Umm… I think so. Another bookshop was closing down.'

'You know, that's the trouble these days. Nobody reads anymore,' Sarah moaned.

Deb rolled her eyes. 'I was only asking because there's one on *Relaxation*; *Managing Anxieties*; *Controlling Panic Attacks*; *Overcoming Depression…*'

'Yeah, so what?'

'I just wondered if the shop assistant offered you the number of the Samaritans on your way out.'

'Here we are,' Cher cried, locating the book she was looking for. Although she was sure her eyes had passed over it a few times without actually seeing it.

'A spell book. What the hell are you thinking?' cried Deb.

Sarah took the book from her hand and started leafing through it.

Deb lit a cigarette. 'Come on, Cher, you have to be joking. You know all that stuff is hogwash. Put it away.'

'Live dangerously, Deb. And anyway, what are you worried about? If it's rubbish, then you have nothing to fear.'

'Count me out.'

'It's just a bit of fun, Deb,' Sarah mocked. 'You're being predictable again. And what if it worked and your mother-in-law finally allowed this wedding to go ahead?'

Deb snarled. 'Okay, you pair of children. Anything to shut you up.'

Sarah giggled excitedly as Cher leafed through the book. 'Here we are. This one will do. It's a general spell called the "Four Winds Wishing Spell"; what you wish for dictates which herb you use, umm… or the other way round.'

'Ooh, what are the choices?'

Cher read a little further, shaking her head to encourage her eyes to focus. '"Success and prestige, promotion and advancement, power, general, love and prosperity": which one do you fancy, girls?'

'All of them,' said Deb, getting into the spirit a little.

'Umm… I think I'll have to go for general. Are you sure there's not one for fertility in there?'

Cher looked again but there was nothing. 'What about you, Deb?'

'Power,' she stated. 'The power to make my wedding go ahead without Margie putting a hex on the day.'

'And I'll go for love, of course. I'm going to wish that Michael Hunter becomes so obsessed with me it's going to take a restraining order for me to fight him off.'

Sarah stared dreamily into space. 'And I'm going to wish for David's child.'

'Aaah,' Deb and Cher chorused.

'Get stuffed.'

Cher threw Sarah the book and struggled to her feet. She felt as though someone had turned her around in circles before removing the blindfold. She spotted three kitchens and headed for the middle one. 'Sarah, have a look at what we have to do while I get the herb rack.'

She was pretty sure that she had all the ones listed. Her mother insisted on buying her obscure foods to entice her away from frozen meals.

'Here we are then. It's cinnamon for Deb, verbena for Sarah and cardamom for me. Now what?'

Sarah passed the book back to her. 'Here, you do it.'

Cher read quickly. 'Okay, girls, the spell needs to be performed outside. Come on.'

Sarah jumped up and instantly regretted it, while Deb moaned about getting mud on her heels.

Once outside, in the darkness, Sarah began to make spooky, haunting noises. Deb joined in. A light went on in the flat above Cher's, reducing them all to fits of laughter.

The garden was a sloping square of unruly wheat-like grass, except for the far corner. The middle-aged couple in the other ground-floor flat had laid claim, like gold prospectors, to a portion that was exactly one quarter of the whole.

Metal stumps joined together by hanging steel chain, a foot high, segregated it from the rest of the area. Inside, the grass was short and tidy, like plush green carpet. A white plastic patio set with a Heineken parasol was guarded by two wooden decorative wheelbarrows that looked like miniature cannons. Entry into that section of the garden was by invitation only.

'Come on, you two, we need to be sensible,' Cher cried, before stumbling over her shadow cast by light from the kitchen.

'But it's freezing out here. Couldn't we do this inside?' moaned Sarah.

'No, you have to be outside and, anyway, you're not throwing the herbs all over my carpet unless you're coming back tomorrow to vacuum.'

'Okay, what do we have to do now?'

Cher moved towards the kitchen window in an attempt to read the writing more clearly. It made little sense to her.

Deb nudged Sarah and pointed at her. They both began to laugh hysterically.

'What?'

'It helps if you've got the book the right way up,' Deb roared, again nudging Sarah, who fell to the ground.

Cher immediately saw the funny side. 'Oh, I just thought it had changed to Swahili,' she cried, turning the book the right way up. 'Okay, have we all got our herbs in our hands?'

'Yes,' they replied together.

'Right, hold the herb to your mouth and breathe onto it, trying to force your wish through the herb itself.'

They paused for a moment as Deb breathed a little too hard and lost half the herbs.

'Do you think it'll still work?' she asked seriously.

'Now we have to turn to the north and say: "King Boreas of the North Wind, by the powers of earth, I call to you to carry my wish to the northern quarter, and by the powers of the gnomes, I ask that you bring me success."' The word 'gnomes' brought forth more gales of laughter.

'I can't believe we're enlisting the help of Sneezy and his mates. I mean we've already got Dopey over there.' Deb laughed, pointing at Sarah.

'They're dwarfs, you stupid woman,' Sarah replied.

Cher instructed them to blow a quarter of the powdered herb from their palms in the direction of the north.

'Now turn to the east and say: "King" whatsisface, blah di blah di blah, "by the powers of air, I call you to carry my wish to the eastern quarter, and by the powers of the sylphs, I ask that you bring me success."' Cher was getting fed up with the long paragraphs that were difficult to read.

'Now blow a quarter of the herb from your palm in the direction of east.'

They all did so once they'd established which way was east. Cher reckoned it was over by the conifers.

'Now turn to the south and say: "King Notus" yada, yada, yada… I'm so bored… "by the powers of the salamanders, I ask that you bring me success."'

Deb added a few more Ss than necessary onto the word salamander.

'Is that a speech impediment or are you just pleased to see me?' asked Sarah, which wasn't funny but made them all laugh anyway.

'Now speak your wish into the herbs left in your hand.'

'I wish for David's child,' Sarah said.

'I wish Margie would just disappear,' Deb whined.

'And I wish for my boss to fall in love with me,' Cher said dreamily.

She sighed heavily and returned her gaze to the book.

'Blow the rest of the herb to the south,' Cher instructed. 'Now turn to the west and say… Oh bollocks, say what you like but I'm off back inside. I'm bloody cold.'

'Yeah, me too,' said Deb, blowing the rest of the herbs at Sarah.

'What now?' Sarah asked.

'What do you think happens now? We wake up tomorrow and our lives have changed beyond recognition,' snapped Deb. 'Or we're all down with the bloody flu.'

They huddled back inside and switched the fire on to full heat. The icy wind had numbed their cheeks and sobered them up.

'Okay, what now, do we raise demons from the dead for an encore?' Deb asked.

Sarah giggled. 'I'd rather have another drink.'

'I think we all look rather pathetic,' Cher observed of them lying around in varying states of disarray.

'No, us standing on your lawn blowing condiments around was pathetic. Oh well. Time to go. Share a taxi?' Deb asked Sarah.

'Need any help to tidy up?' Sarah asked.

Cher surveyed the room. 'No, it'll wait until tomorrow. I'm off to bed. See you soon,' she said, closing the door behind them.

The room really was a mess, but she stifled the guilt and walked through it to her bedroom. The numbing effect of the alcohol had worn off, leaving only a desperate need to crawl into bed, sleep and dream of Michael Hunter.

CHAPTER FIVE

This is not good, Cher thought as she walked into her office twenty minutes late, awaiting a chastising glance from Mr Williams and his cold shoulder for the rest of the day. He only had one opinion on coming in late – don't.

She slid into her chair and tried to appear as though she'd been there for hours, but something was wrong. There was a strange smell: coffee, that was it. A full pot steamed away in the corner. Spooky. No one made coffee except her. Mr Williams didn't even understand the intricacies of a temperamental percolator.

She shrugged and reached for a cup. Her system was crying out for caffeine, having had no intake after seeing the LED on the alarm screaming LATE when she finally surfaced from a comatose state.

'Ah, Cher, you're in. I'd love one,' said Michael Hunter as he came out of Mr Williams's office.

She struggled to hold on to the slippery mug. 'B-But…'

'Mr Williams has called in sick today, and my office is being decorated so I thought I'd use his.'

Cher tried to close her mouth to a more fitting circumference. Why had no one told her that Santa really did exist? Michael Hunter must have made the coffee, she realised as he closed the office door. Her feelings of lust blossomed into lifelong devotion. He was a senior manager but not above performing a menial task like preparing a pot of coffee.

She poured him a drink and tapped gently on the door before entering, then placed the cup on the silver-plated coaster and retreated. She hadn't expected any acknowledgement from Michael Hunter. He was a busy man, talking into his mobile phone while keying into the computer.

She closed the door quietly and surveyed the contents of her desk. It was empty. There were no loose-leaf sheets of A4 lined paper with Mr Williams's tidy handwriting, but that was okay. It meant she could be ready for anything that Michael Hunter wanted to throw at her. She began to visualise herself as Julia Roberts in *Pretty Woman*, where she tells Richard Gere that he won't ever want to let her go. That's how Michael Hunter would feel about her.

'Cher… Cher… are you okay?'

She turned and coughed, twice. It was just Dan, the engineers' supervisor. 'I'm fine, thanks,' she mumbled, trying to hide her embarrassment.

'You seemed in a world of your own,' he said, smiling. 'Is he in?'

'Mr Williams is off ill today. Mr Hunter is using the office in his absence.'

'Umm… I really need to see someone. The overtime has been messed up again. I need to get it sorted.'

'Oh, Dan, don't worry. I'm sure it will work itself out… over time.'

Dan groaned at her poor attempt at humour. 'You write your own routines or what?'

She chuckled at his pained expression. 'Yeah, I'm here all week.'

Dan laughed.

Cher sobered. It wouldn't look professional if Michael Hunter came out of the office and found them laughing. 'Do you want to see Mr Hunter?'

Dan thought for a moment and loosened his tie slightly. To distinguish him from the engineers, Dan was instructed to wear trousers and shirt and tie instead of the polo shirts worn by the guys. His discomfort was obvious.

'I'll have to. It can't really wait. The men are relying on that money to start booking their annual holidays. There's no way I'm going back down with bad news. I'd have a better chance with a pack of lions on meth.'

She rang the extension. 'Mr Hunter, Dan is here – Dan Rickman, the foreman. He'd like a word… yes okay… thank you.'

She replaced the receiver. 'He'll see you in a minute, if you could just wait.'

Dan nodded. 'How's the coffee?'

She frowned. 'The what? Oh the coffee.' She smiled. 'You made it?'

Of course Michael Hunter hadn't had the time to make coffee. What had she been thinking? But of course it was the kind of thing Dan would do. She remembered one time when her bike had a slow puncture on the way into work. She'd spent a few hours worrying about getting it to the garage, but then Dan informed her he'd called a mate who worked at a tyre place, who had come out and fixed it. His thoughtfulness and her sense of relief had earned him a proper coffee and a doughnut from the bakery down the road.

'I know how I feel if I don't get my first cup of coffee. I thought you might be the same.'

'I am, and thanks.'

'Any plans this weekend?' he asked.

'Not really, you?'

He raised his eyes upward. 'I'm taking my son to the cinema to see the new Star Wars film. I don't suppose you'd—'

'Oh, excuse me,' she interrupted as Michael Hunter buzzed her extension. 'Okay, I'll send him in. He'll see you now,' she instructed, replacing the receiver.

Dan nodded and left her alone with her thoughts.

Fifteen minutes later, the door to Michael Hunter's office slammed behind Dan. He stormed past Cher's desk with a curt nod before taking the stairs. Most unusual. She'd never seen Dan in a bad mood.

The door opened again.

'I'd love a coffee, Cher.' He sat on the leather sofa next to the percolator.

She tried not to stare at his easy demeanour as he relaxed back. His suit jacket had been removed to display a dark grey shirt that had been loosened slightly around the neck. His hair was ruffled, and he'd never looked sexier.

She poured the coffee with slightly trembling hands as she envisioned a scene she'd seen in a film once, where the hero takes the coffee cup from the likeable female and then takes her in his arms to kiss her passionately.

Michael Hunter looked at her a little strangely as a low groan escaped from between her lips. She coughed as she held the cup forward with the handle towards him. Her fingers recoiled from the heat of the cup. The hot coffee, followed by the mug, fell between them as she gazed after it in horror.

He jumped up from the sofa. 'What the hell are you trying to do, scald me? You stupid—'

'I'm sorry, oh God, I'm sorry. I don't know what I was thinking. Please, let me help.'

He grabbed a paper towel from beside the coffee machine and dabbed at the three spots of coffee on his trousers as he headed back into the office.

'No, thanks. You've done enough,' he said, slamming the door.

She sat back in her chair and didn't try to stop her head as it fell forward and rested on the desk. Great, she'd really shown the man her efficiency so far. So far, she'd almost given him second-degree burns. Even she couldn't wait to see what she had planned for an encore.

He remained safely in his office for the remainder of the day, appearing only to issue her with some cash and a lunch order of chicken pasta and bottled water.

Two minutes before five the door opened again. He walked out looking even more dishevelled than earlier. He glanced at the empty coffee pot.

'Would you like me to make more coffee before I go?' she asked.

A slow smile began to spread across his slightly tired features. 'No thanks, I think you've had enough fun with the percolator for one day.'

'I'm sorry about that, I—'

He waved away her apologies. 'Don't worry about it, no permanent damage. I'll live – just,' he teased with a crooked smile.

Be still my heart, she cried inside as those expressive grey eyes gazed intently at her with a hint of a question. Please let him be wondering why he'd never noticed her slaving over a computer before. Why his only interest in her was the speed of her fingers. Let him be questioning why he had, until now, been blind to the smouldering passion that lay unignited between their very souls.

'Cher, can you get decaf tomorrow? That coffee has got me wired.'

'Of course, Mr Hunter,' she mumbled, removing her helmet from beneath the desk and returning to planet earth. She headed outside and pulled her thoughts back into line. Michael Hunter was never going to notice anything more than the speed of her fingers or the quality of her coffee.

Her moped refused to start on the first two attempts, confirming to her that it knew exactly where they were going: the weekly tea ritual at her parents. It refused to start every Thursday. Either it was a very intelligent vehicle or a vessel for her subconscious.

A noise that was half moan and half groan escaped her lips as she parked outside the terraced house. A glance at the Lexus told her that Marlon and Patricia, her brother and sister-in-law, were there. Not Patty or even Trish – the name was pronounced *Patreesha*, but Cher delighted in calling her Pat, just to witness the pent-up rage that showed in her thin mouth that twitched like a hamster's nose.

Her amusement subsided as she realised what that meant: the children from hell were also there. She undertook a swift inventory of what was in her handbag to ensure she would leave with the same contents.

The door was flung open by a twelve-year-old devil wearing an army uniform.

'Peon, peon, you're dead – I shot you. Your guts are all over the floor,' he hollered, brandishing a silver pistol at her.

'Hello, Jeremy,' she managed through gritted teeth as she searched for the hidden swastika on his suit.

Cher's mother bustled through from the kitchen to greet her. Her long black hair, far too long in Cher's opinion, hung straight at the sides, with a fringe cut just above her eyebrows.

'You watched *Cleopatra* last night then?'

She hugged Cher tightly, as though she'd been away for months instead of a week.

'Hi, Pat,' she said, popping her head around the living-room door to find her in her normal spot. As usual, she was squeezed into an area no more than two inches wide at the very edge of the sofa, with her bony elbow making indentations in the green velour.

'Good evening, Cher,' she replied with a slight nod before her attention reverted back to the television screen. Her job as a researcher for the local television station instilled in her the responsibility to watch every edition of the news as though it were her personal project to find flaws. Either that or she just liked to pretend to be important.

A swift, sharp slap on her behind told her that Philip, the ten-year-old version of Satan, had realised her presence.

'Gotcha,' he screamed with glee.

'Philip,' Pat cried in horror.

Cher's head whipped around. Surely not. Oh please, let her be about to exert a little discipline.

'What sort of word is that? If you look in the dictionary, I don't think you'll find the word gotcha.'

He shrugged, slapped Cher again and cried, 'Got you.'

Her teeth were already hurting with the force of her fused jaws.

She joined her mother in the kitchen. Only she could keep Cher calm enough not to string Philip up by the ears, paint a bullseye on his jumper and throw darts at him.

Elaine Paige crooning show tunes from the radio and the sweet aroma of freshly baked chocolate muffins calmed her immediately. There was enough to feed the local community. Cher had long ago labelled her mother a bakeaholic because she just couldn't stop.

Being the last one to leave home, Cher had worried that her mum would struggle with life in the absence of any children to nurture. Her dad would be fine, she'd convinced herself. He would simply lavish more attention on his pigeons.

But as soon as Cher had left home, her parents had bought a rickety old camper van for weekend trips and joined a weekly formation dancing club. Her worries had been in vain. They had a better social calendar than she did.

'Where's Dad?' she asked, placing two muffins in greaseproof paper beside her handbag.

She motioned towards the back door. 'He's showing Marlon his new pigeon. He's named her Carol after Carol Vorderman.' She chuckled. 'He's got a real crush on her, you know.'

From the noise in the garden, Cher guessed the kids were out there too. She pushed the door shut with her foot.

'What's cooking?' She sniffed the air trying to discern one particular aroma out of the mixture of savoury and sweet. One meal at her parents' forced her to calorie count for the rest of the week.

'Beef roast, your favourite, and hot chocolate fudge cake for afters.'

'Umm lovely.' The waistband on her skirt constricted at the thought of it. But her mother was right: it was still her favourite. In her opinion, you couldn't beat a home-cooked roast dinner: a huge joint of beef that had been cooking slowly for a couple of hours, with an occasional loud spit as the meat juices around the base of the joint exploded; roast potatoes that were brown and crisp after being turned every fifteen minutes. Her stomach grumbled at the thought.

'Any man on the scene yet?' asked her mum pointedly.

'Nah, I think I put 'em off on the first date when I declare that I want to marry them and bear their children.'

'Cher, you don't, do you?'

Cher laughed at her expression. 'Why, do you think that's why they never call?'

'Get away with you. You'll kill me you will, Cher. The other two safely married with kids of their own. Only you left to worry about.'

It was the same conversation every week. 'Mum, why worry about me? I'm a grown woman with my own home, a decent job. Worry about something else, like how to stop Jeremy signing up with any terrorist group that will take him.'

'You don't think—'

'For goodness' sake, Mum, I'm joking. He's twelve.' She visibly relaxed. 'They don't take them until they're at least fifteen.'

'Don't be like that, Cher. They're nice kids. They love you to death. You're their favourite auntie,' she said, placing two coffee mugs on the table.

Cher groaned. 'Don't say that, Mum. I don't want to be anyone's favourite auntie. That means I'll never settle down and have kids of my own. Favourite aunts never do. They become destined to a life of solitude, spinsterhood and lots of pets.'

The force of an explosion blew the kitchen door open.

'Here, Auntie Cher, we brought you a present,' said Philip, the youngest of her nephews. She trusted him slightly more than Jeremy, who would have no doubt passed her a live hand grenade.

'Close your eyes, it's a surprise.'

Her mother's tolerant smile, which comes only with grand-motherhood, begged her to play along.

As she closed her eyes and held out her hand, she realised that she was gambling with her life. She instantly recoiled at the sensation of the cold wetness that slithered across her palm and began working up her hand.

Her eyes opened to find three obese worms entangled in her palm. Her look of horror produced screams of delight and enjoyment as she quickly threw them back outside.

'Ouch,' she cried as a sharp object whipped her behind. She turned to find Jeremy in possession of a peashooter.

'Mummy wants you,' she lied, wondering what deranged person had furnished that child with such a deadly weapon.

'Oh, they're so boisterous,' her mum enthused as she returned her attention to the boiling vegetables. There were many words for those two, Cher decided, but boisterous was not one of them.

'They're the best case I've ever seen for the theory of total sterilis—'

'Cher.'

'Where's Laurence?'

'Oh, he's not coming tonight. Paula's ill.'

What, illness? No way. There was no illness severe enough to keep them away from the weekly tea. She'd tried it herself a few times. Flu, bubonic plague, E. coli, she'd tried them all. Even the story that aliens had abducted her and she was calling from the planet Zog had failed. How come Laurence could get away with it?

'Hi, sis,' Marlon greeted as he came in, shivering, from her dad's shed. For the end of June it was an unusually cold day.

Cher quickly appraised him as she did every week. He was the oldest and looked it. At thirty-six, his receding hairline aged him by ten years. His gaunt face, brought on by diet food all the time, didn't help either. Pat was currently on a health kick, which meant that Marlon hardly ate, except on a Thursday night.

'Is tea done yet, woman?' asked her father gruffly as he made for the sink to wash his hands.

As usual, Cher was shocked by how cramped the kitchen became once her father was in it. His huge bulk seemed to be everywhere at once. The vision of her father guiding her mother around the dance floor had provoked visions of a rhino in a tux. She'd accompanied them one night and couldn't believe the grace with which he hauled his trucker-type frame around the dance floor.

Her mum silenced Elaine Page. 'Just dishing up. Gather the troops,' she chimed happily, enjoying having her family around her.

Marlon went to let Pat know that dinner was served. Not that Patricia would join them. Allergies, she claimed, kept her away from the dinner table. She was forced to maintain a strictly controlled diet, so she remained in the living room, analysing the news.

'Hey, Cher, what's that place of yours planning to do about the congestion on the roads?'

'Don't start, Marlon,' Cher pleaded. This was another conversation she was sick of having. Each week there was another objection to the place where she worked. Her dad had once said he'd prefer her to work for the Mafia. She'd explained, sarcastically, that most crime families didn't exactly advertise in the local press, but once they did, she'd be sure to give them a call. As usual, her facetious comments were met with a slight frown and a brief headshake, which often made her wonder who was the nuttier: him or her.

'You know it's killing the trade in the high street, don't you?' Marlon asked.

Here we go, she thought. 'Marlon, I work there. I don't own it.'

She awaited the inevitable and was not disappointed.

'Couldn't get the car out the street the other day. All cos of the traffic going to that place,' her dad groaned as he salted his plate into a winter scene. The roast potatoes resembled snow-topped mountain peaks. 'They should pull the bloody monstrosity down.'

Her mother took the salt shaker from his hand and placed it out of reach.

Cher knew she was going to bite. She just didn't know how long the bait would need to be dangled. Another mouthful of comfort food did not soothe her growing irritation.

'All those shops it's forced to close down. All those jobs, lost.'

'Fred, leave her alone. It's not her fault that people have lost businesses they've had for generations,' her mum defended, doing her no favours at all.

'Dad, where do you think those people work now?' That was it. She'd bitten.

'You take a walk along the high street on a Saturday morning and you'll see the effect it's had.'

'For goodness' sake, it's only given people the choice. If they still wish to trawl around countless shops with heavy bags in the freezing cold, paying the highest price, then that's their choice. If not they can come to The Keys. It's progress. What's the problem?'

'Progress, is that what you call it? You don't watch enough films, my girl. Haven't you seen what progress will do to us? Before you know it, we'll have a lawless society, run by groups of thugs and terrorists, where any decent folk will have to live underground in fear of their lives because of the looting and pillaging above.'

Cher tried to pinpoint the exact film or television programme he was quoting, but decided it was probably a mixture of a few.

'Somehow, I don't think improved shopping facilities will prompt the end of the world, Dad,' she said wearily.

'Well I still don't like the place,' he grumbled, as he always did when he ran out of argument. The rest of the meal passed in silence. He'd always argued that talking over the dinner table buggered up the digestion, and that was why all them posh folks who rattled their way through six courses looked so thin and pale. Following his logic, Cher had tried talking to the television whilst eating a bag of Minstrels, but she still felt her Donald Duck pyjamas getting tighter.

'Everybody out,' she ordered as Marlon finished last. 'I'll do the dishes.'

It was her way of getting a little peace after the Spanish Inquisition.

She emptied the pedal bin and took the bag outside. The door slammed behind her to squeals of 'Auntie Cher's got worms, Auntie Cher's got worms.'

She let out a deep breath that got swallowed by the cold. *The only worms I know are at the other side of that door*, she thought as she started to bang on the kitchen window in the hope that someone would hear her. Ten minutes later, Marlon let her back in, finding his children's antics hilarious.

Her spirits started to lift as she placed the last dish into the sink. She was on the home straight. One cup of coffee and she'd be over the finishing line and on her way back home to a small flat that was quiet and peaceful and all her very own.

'Ouch,' she cried again as a low-flying pea caught her in the thigh. That was it. She'd had enough. She grabbed the offending child by the collar and lifted him up so that his chocolate-smeared face was level with hers. His toes dangled two feet from the floor. He looked like he'd seen Freddy Kruger.

'Now listen here, you little shit, I've had a bad day at work. I'm tired, pissed off, probably frustrated and I have PMT. That won't mean much to you now, but trust me, it will when you're older. I've smiled pleasantly while you've popped me with that thing all night, and I've had enough. Once more and I'm going to shove it so far up your nose, you'll have a built-in snorkel. Get it?'

A slight trembling nod was the reply, yet still she was loath to let him down. Shame on her. She was having fun.

Philip came running into the room. 'Auntie Cher, I want a go. Pick me up.'

She placed the shaking child back on the ground. He backed out of the room, taking his younger brother with him. She smiled at his departure. She'd get no more trouble from them for a while.

One cup of coffee later and she was on her way home.

The tranquillity of her flat welcomed her as much as the double brandy warmed her. Once again she returned home a little sad after being surrounded by couples. Her parents were a couple that existed in their own fantasy world that would have challenged any psychiatrist, but they were happy. Marlon and Pat were a strange, distant couple but an occasional look would pass between them and hold for a couple of seconds. Even Jeremy and Philip were a couple – a couple of little shits.

Maybe I should get a cat or something, she wondered as she sat with her legs tucked under her, watching an episode of *Real Housewives*. At least the flat wouldn't be so empty, she reasoned. Oh no, it was happening. She was considering buying a pet. She was becoming the favourite auntie.

She snuggled down into the sofa, hand clamped protectively around the brandy glass and fantasised about Michael Hunter. Maybe the spell had worked. She laughed. Yeah, sure. It would take a lot more than blowing herbs around the garden to bring

Michael Hunter her way. Maybe if they were the last two humans on earth, but knowing her luck, he'd discover a long-lost need for celibacy or a stray sheep.

She pushed the thought away and wondered idly what Sarah and Deb were doing.

CHAPTER SIX

The bistro was dimly lit, exuding a low dark atmosphere even in daytime. Situated in a quiet backstreet, it offered seclusion and privacy and was the only place David felt comfortable taking her to dine. Stacey had asked for the address twice, this not being a part of town her sister frequented all that much. The very reasons that Sarah and David liked it were the reasons that Stacey hated it.

Sarah had deliberately booked the table she and David used, as though she could wrap herself in the memory of him to protect her from Stacey.

At least their mother was appeased by the monthly lunches she endured with her sister, and Sarah had to admit that was the only reason she continued. Why else would she spend at least three days after the event buying expensive cosmetics and making full use of her gym membership?

Sarah checked her appearance in the mirrored glass opposite. Her hair was freshly washed and feathery after drying naturally. Her face looked healthy and tanned, with a tiny amount of blusher to emphasise her cheekbones. Her lips were coffee-coloured and slightly glossed. Her stone-coloured waistcoat showed off her lightly bronzed arms and titivated her breasts into a cleavage that defied gravity and was definitely not all her own. She smiled at her own pensive reflection. A lot of effort had gone into her natural appearance.

She didn't need to look to the doorway to know when her sister arrived. The rest of the diners did it for her. There was an unmistakable squeak of fabric on upholstery that signalled Stacey's arrival. Sarah couldn't stop herself from watching as Stacey moved towards her in a perfected catwalk swagger. With her head held high, she paid no attention to the people around her. They were of little importance and not people that she socialised with.

She looked stunning in a black jumpsuit that hugged her breasts, emphasised her tiny waist and enhanced her five foot nine height.

Sarah could feel herself sliding down in her chair as she looked at the shiny, glossy hair that didn't budge an inch as she moved. As usual, Sarah felt like the paler, washed-out version of her older sister. It was as though on the second attempt the mixture had been formed but a vital, vibrant ingredient was missing.

'Been waiting long?' Stacey breathed, sitting gracefully.

'Just got here,' Sarah said shortly. Stacey delighted in making people wait, and Sarah didn't want to admit to the twenty minutes she'd been chewing on breadsticks.

Sarah had no idea what could possibly make Stacey late. She didn't work, although she constantly claimed that it was such a responsibility overseeing the local economy, which basically meant shopping.

Sarah recalled one time that Stacey had invited her on a shopping trip to London. At her mother's insistence she agreed to go, thinking it might be fun after all. Within two hours of arriving, Sarah understood her role. She was the pauper who got to watch humbly while Stacey tried to choose between two Chanel jerseys that cost a month's salary for Sarah, before deciding to take them both; but Sarah told her mother that she had a wonderful time and showed off her little beefeater statue to prove it.

'Sorry, sweetie, I'm going to have to rush. Dinner party this evening. We're having some friends over to see our new indoor pool.' She rolled her eyes. 'It's gooooorgeous. The terracotta tiles were imported from Mexico especially.'

'Oh, I didn't know you'd had—'

'We'll be arranging a family type thing soon. I'll let Mum know,' she said with a flick of the hand.

Sarah nodded. Other than this monthly lunch, neither of them contacted each other directly. All communications went through their mother like a telephone exchange. She could have been offended that, as family members, they weren't allowed to socialise with Stacey's friends, and if Sarah had thought that Roger shared her sister's snobbery, she might have been, but Roger was the most inoffensive, sweet man she'd ever met. He'd just been unfortunate enough to become bewitched by Stacey after knocking her to the ground whilst rushing from the offices of the chain of furniture stores that he owned. Stacey described their meeting 'like a scene out of *Notting Hill*', but knowing her sister, Sarah seriously doubted that the fateful incident had been accidental.

'And anyway, I need to get a little relaxation in before the caterers arrive,' she whispered as the waiter approached.

'I'll have a salad of avocado, basil, feta and tomato please' – she touched his bare forearm with her manicured nails – 'but no mustard, thanks, sweetie.'

'Mixed grilled vegetables,' Sarah grunted, even though he hadn't even looked her way. His face was flushed and his legs had turned to stone.

'Thank you,' Sarah said harshly to get his attention. He wandered away awkwardly, checking his notepad.

'Why must you always do that?'

Stacey laughed. 'You're no fun at all. You should learn to lighten up and enjoy life a bit more.'

If I had a team of accountants to pay my mortgage and a limitless Gold card, I might, Sarah thought.

'And what did you mean by relaxation?'

Stacey smiled coyly and flicked imaginary fluff from her trousers.

'You're not still doing the gardener?' Sarah asked, although she'd seen the Italian stallion, Giovanni, who had not been employed for his green fingers.

'Oh, don't be so crude. It's not exactly a meeting of the minds, as they say, but he burns more calories off me than my personal trainer.'

Sarah shook her head knowing that she had no right to judge. Maybe it made a difference that she knew Roger.

'People in glass houses shouldn't throw stones, sweetie.' She cast a glance over Sarah's stomach. 'Any luck yet?'

Sarah regretted telling her sister about her plans to become pregnant with David's child. Even at that she was failing. She tried to divert the question.

'Have you considered trying?'

Stacey chuckled. 'Roger thinks we are, poor love, but I quite fancy getting one of those cute Chinese babies. They're so adorable. Apparently, you can get them on the internet with your credit card. Isn't that just marvellous?'

Sarah could think of a few words for selling babies on the internet and marvellous wasn't one of them.

'But wouldn't you want one of your own?'

Stacey chuckled and shook her head. 'Some friends of ours have just adopted a little Vietnamese boy, and it was so quick and easy and totally pain-free. This way, the only thing that'll feel the pain is Roger's wallet.'

Sarah had to wonder what type of mother her sister would make if she wasn't even prepared to sacrifice a bit of pain and a few stretch marks. Just how much of herself would she be able to give to a child?

Sarah was saved from making any type of reply as the waiter placed Stacey's dish before her and almost threw Sarah's across the table.

'No mustard,' he murmured with pride, as though he'd achieved world peace.

Sarah watched as Stacey pushed the feta cheese to the side of her plate. She had yet to find anyone who had witnessed her sister eat solid food in the last two years.

'I don't know why you're trying to land yourself with David's child anyway. If you think it'll make him leave his wife, I think you'll be disappointed.'

'He loves children. You should hear the way he talks about Chelsea,' Sarah defended hotly. Criticism from Stacey was just too much to bear.

'My point exactly. He already has that life back home with his three-bed semi, librarian wife and devoted daughter. Why would he want it again?'

In spite of herself, Sarah found herself listening to her sister's words, if only to prove her wrong.

'On the day he met you, he was attracted to something and I don't think it was your child-bearing hips.'

Sarah looked self-consciously at her hips.

'He saw another life that he could lead. He's a typical man and is under constant pressure to reassure himself that he's virile and exciting and that he can still attract female attention. That's where you come in. You are as close to a strong, independent woman as he's ever going to get, so you represent a different life to him. There's no point offering him more of the same. Yes, you might get him for a while, but then he'll be after that special something from someone else.'

'He wouldn't do that to—'

'Don't be so naïve. That's exactly what he's doing to his wife now. Do you really think your relationship would have lasted this long if you were a single parent with three screaming kids? I'm telling you that any attraction he has to you at the moment will be severely injured when he smells dirty nappies in your flat and sees baby puke on your shoulder. You need to offer him something else, something dangerous, something that will make him feel like a nineteen-year-old stud again. You need to give him a fantasy.'

'But I don't want to be a fantasy. I want us to be a normal couple, cooking Sunday lunch, dining out with friends, going to the theatre once in a while, snuggling up in bed together.'

Stacey snorted and pushed her plate away. 'Yes, but you've got to get him first.'

Conscious of continuing to eat alone, Sarah speared a round of courgette and followed suit. She was determined to move the conversation away from her and David. Her sister's words were sounding quite sensible in a Stacey sort of way.

'How's Roger?'

Stacey waved away the question as she glanced at her Cartier watch. 'He's okay.'

'Mum said he had an angina attack last weekend. Is he working too hard?'

'Don't feel sorry for him: he's fine. What do you expect if you spend all your spare time hitting a ball for yards and then walking after it? If you want someone to feel sorry for, just look at this bloody manicure: it's scandalous.' She held her left hand in the air, exhibiting nails as red as an eagle's talons after a kill. 'I asked for Whispering Rose and this is definitely Plum. Honestly, I could sue them for this.'

Sarah stopped the foot tapping beneath the table before it reached up and kicked her sister sideways.

'Anyway, sweetie, must dash. I'll let Mum know about the family get-together, and you must bring that luscious chappie of yours. I would sooooo like to see him again. Ciao.'

And with that she was gone, leaving Sarah with two barely touched meals, an inferiority complex and the bill.

Sarah wandered home slowly, dejected by yet another stilted lunch with her sister. Her home loomed up in front of her, empty and silent. There would be no visit from David, due to Chelsea's involvement in a Sunday school pageant, he'd told her proudly. Sarah pushed away the picture of David and Bianca watching proudly as their daughter quoted a few words on stage in her best Sunday dress. She tried not to imagine their proud glances and shared chuckles.

The only sound that met her was the ominous ticking of the pendulum clock in the hallway. Throwing her handbag and jacket into the corner and opening the door to her study, she faced the computer and sighed, remembering the days that she'd sat in this same spot and written with freedom and sheer abandonment. She had filled long, lonely hours creating characters and developing storylines for her own amusement, getting lost in the story and becoming a part of it until darkness would prompt her to move stiffened muscles. The room had been a safe place where nothing could touch her, hurt her, because she was in another world, one that she had invented; and she'd been happy, until the day that Deb had urged her to send a story to a magazine.

Sarah recalled the excitement and anticipation of emailing the story. Her fear had been overshadowed by the pure joy that something she had created from nothing was winging its way to London. It was like offering up your newborn child to the world for approval, and for the first time in her life Sarah had felt as though she was actually a part of something, that she was finally doing something to realise the dream that she'd harboured since she was a child.

It was a dream that she'd tried to explain to her parents when it became time to choose her best subjects at school.

'But you should learn to type, dear, just in case.' Whereas Stacey's love of painting had been encouraged. Sarah had loved to watch her paint effortlessly, mixing vibrant colours, and even then Sarah had known that her sister had a gift.

Sarah remembered writing a short essay for English homework when she was around nine. She'd spent hours forming a short piece that was open and honest about her fear of the sea. She couldn't wait to show it to her teacher. The next morning she found it discarded by the bin covered with paint splodges of different colours, where Stacey had cleaned her brush. Hot tears had stung her eyes as her mum had held it up to the light, but it was ruined.

'Just write it again at lunchtime,' her mother said, and she had tried but all the time aware that the second piece had lost something that had been present in the first draft – something raw that had spilled out while examining her fear.

Sarah's fingers trailed over three shelves of reference books that she dusted almost obsessively and, every time she did, a familiar hunger gnawed in her stomach to sit and write with the abandonment she had before, but since her first and only rejection, she had been unable to lose the invisible censor that looked over her shoulder, mocking every word that she wrote. Cher had thought it was a good rejection because they'd taken the time to write something personal on the rejection slip. They had *liked the characters but little emotion was evident.* Those words were emblazoned on her brain every time she tried to form a sentence.

She turned away from the inert computer screen and reached for her 'Baby Folder', recalling her sister's reasons for wanting a child. It seemed that Stacey wanted a child as a fashion accessory.

She shifted uncomfortably in her chair. Were her reasons for wanting a baby so different from Stacey's? She pushed the thought away. She would love her child and give it the best possible life she could. But a nagging voice at the back of her mind, which sounded unmistakably like Stacey's, tormented: 'But you still want it for a reason.'

Sarah slammed the folder shut and placed it back in the drawer. Other words that her sister had said began to come back to her, and a slow smile spread across her face as the seeds of an idea began to take root.

At eleven thirty, Sarah was trembling slightly but she was ready. She pulled the belt of her calf-length rain mac tightly around her waist and closed the door behind her. The air had turned cool after a warm June day and circled her bare ankles. The roads were quiet as people stayed home and prepared for their first day at work.

She reached her destination in ten minutes flat and parked the small Peugeot around the side of the building. A few other vehicles littered the car park. She paid for one ticket and entered the cinema.

Her eyes located David sitting where she'd instructed: in the lonely area at the far right of the cinema where the view of the screen was slightly obscured. A group of five sat immediately before him, and a middle-aged couple sat a couple of rows back. Perfect, she decided. A few people close by but not too many.

She stood for a moment, her figure bathed in the light from the lobby, and breathed a sigh of relief. The message she'd left on his mobile had told him where and what time and nothing else. She hadn't been prepared for the fact that he might not turn up.

She took a deep breath before slowly approaching where David sat and slid into the seat next to him. He turned to face her, his brow slightly furrowed, his mouth shaped in the form of a question. She placed her index finger over his lips and gently turned his head to face the screen. Her right thigh brushed against his as she crossed her right leg over her left. Her ankle swept against the soft velour of the seat in front, prompting the occupant to turn briefly. Sarah's heart rate increased as she realised what she was about to do and that strangers sat only inches away, in front and behind.

Her coat opened slightly to reveal the smooth bare skin of her calves and knees. She could see David watching her from the corner of his eye as she trailed one red fingernail suggestively from her knee to her inner thigh and back again. She reached over to his left hand that lay slightly clenched in his lap and ran her nails teasingly along the length of the finger that was no stranger to the very centre of her.

She burrowed her hand beneath his so that his palm rested on the top of her hand like a shield and gently guided him towards her breast. Her own hand caressed her left breast with his hand on top, leaving him in no doubt as to what she was doing. Every movement was slow and deliberate, sensual and erotic. She gave a low murmur as her nipple began to harden beneath the touch of her own fingers.

David shifted uncomfortably in his seat. He moved his hand slightly to take over from her, but she held fast, pinching her nipple between her thumb and forefinger, sending exquisite jolts of pleasure through her body. She was in no rush to quicken this erotic encounter and allow David to take control. She sensed his impatience to remove her hand and caress her breast himself, but she continued to stroke herself with lazy, sensual movements, forcing his hand into the role of observer.

She could see that David's breathing had quickened. She smiled to herself in the darkness as they both continued to stare ahead at the French subtitled movie playing on the screen. Her right hand left her breast and travelled down, taking his with her, over her taut stomach and lower. She caressed herself lightly while David's hand continued in its role as an idle onlooker. She splayed her hand so that it covered the centre of her and writhed against it. She heard David's sharp intake of breath before she took his wrist in her hand and guided his finger inside her.

A low groan escaped from her lips as David's finger moved rhythmically inside her with the familiarity of someone who knew her well, but with the added excitement that came with fear of discovery. She felt her body losing control, wanting to give in to the temptation of letting him continue until he brought her to climax, but she regained focus just before the point of no return and shifted slightly, removing his finger from inside her. She allowed it to rest against her thigh as her right hand reached over and expertly opened the button on his trousers and slid the zip down, exposing a bulge in his boxer shorts. Every natural urge inside her begged her to lean down and take him in her mouth, but she resisted; that would come later, she hoped.

She reached for his hand and guided it inside his trousers. He resisted slightly, but she maintained her journey and found herself flaming inside as he caressed himself with her hand lying on top of his. Never had she felt so erotic as she did, watching him touch himself. His long fingers trailed up and down the hardened shaft, forcing it harder within his hand. His breathing matched hers, and his eyes were wide. Sarah wanted to straddle him and ride them both to climax, but she resisted. She had a plan in her head which she had to stick to in order to get the desired result.

She moved his hand aside and continued to touch him slowly and teasingly, moving up and down with deliciously slow, tender movements. His head rolled backward slightly, and he swallowed deeply. Her own mouth was dry and her breathing like a marathon runner. She watched his facial expression closely and experience told her when he was close. She removed her hand, pulled her jacket tightly around her and walked out of the cinema without a backward glance.

The cool night air hit her as she paused in the entrance doorway, locating her car. A few stragglers were leaving from the other screen that had just finished. She stepped off the bottom step and felt a hand grab her roughly on the elbow. She felt herself being pushed around the side of the building towards the wall of blackness behind the cinema. The hand was splayed possessively on her elbow and gave no opportunity for manoeuvre.

Sarah gasped as David threw her against the wall. He pulled the jacket from her shoulders and pushed her back roughly against hard brick that punctured her skin. She cried out, but David didn't hear as he buried his teeth into the tender skin rising up from her collarbone. His hands found her wrists and pulled them above her head, holding them there with his left hand. His right hand moved down and squeezed her breasts roughly. Sarah could feel herself panting with desire, willing him to enter her and take away the grinding ache that had spread all over her body.

His head lowered and he bit her nipples, sending ripples of desire through her entire body. His hand reached down and found the centre of her easily, his fingers sliding inside her, producing an explosion that had Sarah writhing against him. She started to moan his name, but his lips silenced her. His teeth ground against hers in an act of possession. Her legs started to tremble, and she fell against him, but his hand continued to hold her wrists above her head in a vulnerable position.

His hand slid out from inside her and expertly undid his trousers, releasing his hardness against her bare stomach. Sarah groaned, aching for him to be inside her.

He released her arms and pulled her legs around his waist before entering her. Sarah's head fell back against the hard brick as David pounded into her. She came again and again and could barely breathe. She looked deep into David's eyes and saw a wildness, a possessiveness that she'd never seen before. He was like a caveman, claiming, almost branding his woman forever. Behind the wildness Sarah saw an intensity, an excitement that wasn't familiar to her and had never made itself known during their lovemaking in her small flat. His eyes burned into hers without love, without tenderness, without compassion and Sarah knew that if he wasn't hers now, he never would be.

CHAPTER SEVEN

'Hey, stop worrying. Probably a bonus for all your hard work,' Mark said, passing his toast crust to the dog, who took it and gulped it without chewing.

'You must be joking. They don't offer bonuses but it's been on my mind all weekend, which is probably just what that bloody woman wanted.'

'But if you've done nothing wrong, you don't have anything to worry about. You know you're responsible for at least a quarter of their total sales. They know how lucky they are to have you.'

Deb smiled. 'But you're biased.'

Mark kissed her lightly on the lips. 'I love you,' he whispered.

'Mmm… you too,' she replied, enjoying his lips against hers. It was a ritual between them to say it every morning. It was also Mark's logic that they never sleep or leave the house on an argument: because if you truly loved the person, you wouldn't sleep anyway, and if you left the house and something happened, you'd always regret it. She smiled, remembering how they'd met. Deb had been sitting on the steps at college, revising for an economics exam, when a twig landed a foot away from her big toe. She looked up, straight into the eyes of one of the boys in her history class.

'What are you doing?' she snapped.

He sat down beside her. 'According to the Choctaws, I have just made my intention of marriage clear to you. In a couple of days, I should stop by and ask your parents formally for your hand in marriage.'

Deb tried to stifle a chuckle, but his lopsided grin was having a strange effect on her stomach.

'So it would be handy if you could give me your address, so that I might inform them of the upcoming nuptials.'

'And what if I don't agree?'

'You simply stand up and walk away, but beware: I would be ostracised by my entire tribe and sent to the mountains to live out my existence in solitude. You wouldn't want that on your conscience, would you?'

Deb laughed. 'Would they settle for a coffee and a doughnut?' she asked.

He'd smiled widely and helped her to her feet and, from that moment, she'd been in love.

For the four years after they left college, Deb saw very little of Mark while he was off building a reputation for himself as a historian, travelling to Egypt to study hieroglyphics or to China to study the Mahayana Buddhist scripture, the *Lotus Sutra*. Deb occasionally saw other men while Mark was away travelling, as a sort of defence, in case he returned and no longer wanted to be with her. None of them ever came close, and her love for Mark deepened every time he left her. On the morning he was due to leave for six months to study the Hebrew *Torah*, he arrived on her doorstep and admitted that he couldn't leave her again. Within days, he'd landed a job working for a research company that was like a firm of solicitors, with all employees specialising in different subjects. Mark specialised in beliefs and customs and was called upon by writers, publishers, corporations and MPs. His job occasionally called for overseas trips, but not as often or as prolonged.

'Okay, time to pull out the big guns,' Mark said, putting his breakfast plate in the sink. 'Stand up.'

'Why?'

'Trust me,' he said, pulling her to her feet. 'Now stand beside me facing the patio window.'

'What the hell are we doing?' she asked, following him.

'Stand with your feet apart like this and stretch your arms up and out as far as you can. Go on, reach up.'

'For what?' she asked, copying him.

'There's a small tribe in Papua New Guinea called the Midloins, who follow this ritual every morning to induce positivity. Go on, stretch.'

She did so.

'Right, now bring your arms down and bend them over in an arc in front of your chest, so the tips of your fingers meet at your breastbone.'

She did so.

'And reach up to the stars again and then bend them in front of your chest one more time. Now put one arm up like this and—'

'Mark,' she said as she burst out laughing. 'Are you making me do the YMCA dance?'

His eyes danced with devilish amusement.

'There is no Midloin tribe in Papua New Guinea, is there?' she asked.

'No, but I reckon we've just given Mrs Webb opposite a chuckle or two.'

'Come here,' she said, feeling some of the tension ease out of her body. Every day she was thankful to have Mark in her life.

He wrapped his arms around her and kissed the top of her head. 'You'll be fine and, if not, I know a really creative tribe in Haiti that will hex the house of anyone—'

'Go on, get off to work,' she said, moving out of his embrace, even though she could have happily stayed there all day.

He reached for his jacket and briefcase before blowing her a kiss.

'Well, Tess, it's just you and me,' Deb said as the door closed behind Mark. 'Are you ready for the call from the queen of doom?' she asked as she heard his car pull off the drive. Tess wagged her tail, which brushed against the linoleum of the kitchen floor and produced a cool draft across Deb's feet. 'But you know what, girl, today we're not going to answer it.'

Deb realised that she could just leave the house early before the landline rang, but somehow it wouldn't be the same. She had to physically hear the phone ring and purposely ignore it to prove to herself that she could.

She busied herself making the house doggie safe, as she always did. With that job done, she glanced at the clock that was ticking ominously towards twenty past. Late this morning, Deb thought, feeling a sting of annoyance. She wanted to prove herself. She had to show that the woman's opinion meant nothing to her.

She washed the breakfast dishes that normally waited until later. Tess remained by her side with her ears pricked in anticipation. The annoyance started to burn. Eight thirty and no call. Deb checked that the ringer was switched to the 'on' position. She and Mark often switched it off if they didn't feel like talking to anyone. The ringer was fine. *Hurry up, woman, you're never this late and I have to go to a bloody meeting*, Deb thought.

By eight forty she had no choice but to leave the house, and her mood wasn't good. How could Margie know that today of all days there would have been no reply? It was one thing having a hidden camera somewhere, but a direct line to her inner thoughts was a little too intrusive for Deb's liking.

She calmed slightly as she recalled one time when this had happened before: before nine thirty, her mobile phone had rung, and there was Margie dispensing her infinite wisdom on the social decline of the family unit due to the invention of the microwave.

Deb ran two amber lights on her way to work. The meeting was booked for 9.15 but she didn't want to be late. She was sure that Ricky Stone wouldn't be.

'Is she here yet?' Deb asked breathlessly as she rushed past Willow's desk.

'Running a little late, but Ricky Stone has been ensconced in the boardroom since eight thirty.'

Deb grunted as her mobile started to ring. She answered hurriedly.

'It's Mum, I'm sorry to have missed you earlier but I've been looking at venues—'

'Margie, can't this wait? I have an important meeting to go into.'

'Well not really, Debra, because I think that judging by the cost of the venues to supply food, it might be more cost-effective to—'

'Margie,' Deb screamed down the phone, 'I haven't got the time at the moment.'

'But I just need to tell you that I've arranged for—'

'I'll give you a call once I'm finished. Bye.' Deb pressed the 'off' button before Margie had the chance to press redial.

'Sorry I'm late, Debbie,' said Ms Stringer with a tight smile. 'But I'm glad to see you haven't been waiting too long.'

Deb pulled a face at Willow as she followed Ms Stringer into the boardroom. She removed her coat and scarf and hung it on a coat stand without breaking her stride.

'Good morning, Ricky, how was your weekend?'

Ricky nodded towards Deb before turning the light of his sales smile onto Ms Stringer, who didn't have the sense to know it was false.

'Well I tried a weekend at that spiritual retreat you told me about. Such wonderful countryside; the surrounding woodland simply took my breath away, just as you said.'

'Take anyone special?' Ms Stringer asked, tipping her head slightly.

'Still waiting to find her unfortunately.'

Ms Stringer blushed. 'I'm sure you will.'

Deb stifled a chuckle and almost told them to get a room.

Ms Stringer took the head of the rectangular board table, and Ricky sat on her immediate left. Deb took a seat a few places down the table.

'Firstly, I'd like to congratulate you both on the work you have done for the company and tell you that it has not gone unnoticed, as has your commitment to moving this company forward.'

Deb noticed that she seemed to be speaking directly to Ricky, who was nodding so hard he should have had four paws and been in the back of a Reliant Robin. Deb remained still, although her foot was twitching slightly beneath the table.

'Debbie, you have worked for the company for seven years, and Ricky you have been a member of the team for five, and both of you are highly valued.'

Deb tried not to analyse each word, but that previous sentence had definitely sounded off balance to her. And why keep calling her Debbie? She loathed it. Why shorten a name to something that was longer than the original? Deb just wished she'd get on with it. The air in the boardroom smelled of marker pens, hot coffee and bad news.

Ms Stringer began talking in a low monotone voice about her own ascent from office junior to sales manager, and Deb took a moment to analyse her. Her face was long, with a small nose that would have been attractive on a smaller face. The small round glasses she wore emphasised the nose by giving the impression that they were about to fall off. One constantly wanted to reach over and push them higher on to the almost non-existent bridge. Her eyes were large and quite attractive, but her irises never seemed to stay still. Their constant movement made Deb want to look behind to see who had just walked in. Her hair was pulled back sharply off her face and had been every day for the last seven years, as far as Deb knew. She wore a high-necked white shirt buttoned to the top. The sleeves were long and cuffed tightly around her wrists. Deb stole a glance along the table and saw that Ms Stringer's one concession of femininity was a gold chain that circled snugly around her ankle. Deb also noticed that she had her legs crossed beneath the table, with her right leg pointing towards Ricky Stone.

'So, my appointment as sales director, while appreciated and greatly deserved' – she paused to issue a brief, tinkling laugh; Ricky nodded his absolute agreement – 'leaves us with a little issue of who is going to replace me as sales manager.' She opened her hands expressively, as though it were an impossible task.

Deb's mouth opened as the door sounded to herald the arrival of the croissants. Willow placed them on the table and gave her a subtle wink before closing the door behind her. Deb reached for one immediately; it was probably best to fill her mouth with something if she was about to learn that Ricky Stone was her new boss. Deb bit into the croissant and tasted nothing. The very idea that this idiot could be her boss was too much to bear. She glanced at him leaning back in his chair with one foot resting on his knee, as though he was in the local coffee shop or at home watching a football game. His top shirt button was open, giving him a relaxed, nonchalant demeanour that would have been extremely attractive in a man with less arrogance.

'I think anyone who was tasked to fill your shoes could only hope to be half as good,' he said.

Deb almost choked on a crumb of warm pastry that had gone down the wrong way.

Ms Stringer sat back, as though trying to infuse a little relaxation into the tense atmosphere. 'So what do you both do in your spare time?'

Ricky leaned forward and brushed a crumb from the crotch of his trousers, inevitably drawing Ms Stringer's attention to that area of his anatomy. 'I like to keep fit, weights, stretches, the occasional eight-mile run. I play squash to release a little aggression, and I've just started to play golf. My colleagues wondered how I might fit in on the golf course,' he grunted derisively, 'but obviously that wasn't a problem.'

Deb hadn't yet fathomed what this meeting was about, but realised she needed to get into the conversation as soon as possible or else leave the room. The question about their social lives was so far away from Ms Stringer's goalposts it was like playing on another pitch.

She coughed lightly. 'I like to spend time with my friends, read, take the dog for long walks along the canal.'

Ms Stringer nodded vaguely in her direction. 'So tell me, Ricky, what is your handicap?'

Deb ripped another piece of croissant, glancing at Ricky's neck as she did so. What exactly was her part in this discussion?

Ms Stringer dabbed at the corners of her mouth and pushed her plate away, signalling the end of breakfast.

'Down to the business at hand. My replacement will need to be committed to the company, with an extensive knowledge of the job and the priority of those all-important figures. The person will need to assume the role of manager and offer guidance and support to his – sorry, Debbie, figure of speech – to his or her staff and be ready to take the flak when things go wrong. The person will be directly responsible to me – pretty much how it is now,' she said a little imperiously. 'They will be expected to attend conferences, board meetings – when I'm not available of course – and basically be a middle manager who, unfortunately, has very few friends.' She smiled brightly at Ricky but the smile had dimmed by the time it reached Deb. 'Being a middle manager means that you're not privy to the most confidential information and therefore not a member of the senior management team, and as the manager you're not really part of the sales team; so it's not an easy role to fulfil, but we have every faith in you, Ricky, and of course you, Debbie.'

Deb's ears began to prick up. Finally, it was getting interesting.

'It's a difficult decision to make between the two of you. Having researched and analysed your figures for the last two years, there is barely a percentage point between you. On the whole, Ricky has, at times, had much higher figures and, at times, lower figures,' she said as though admonishing an adorably errant child. 'But yours, on the other hand, Debbie, have been consistently steady.'

Deb smiled radiantly as she realised that Ms Stringer had struggled valiantly to say those last few words.

'As I said, it is a very difficult decision to make and therefore I'm not going to. You are.'

'What?' they said together. Ricky was frowning, forming his two bushy eyebrows into one long one that was not attractive.

Ms Stringer smiled. 'Basically, my promotion doesn't begin for three months, and in that time your performance is going to be judged on a number of criteria and a decision will be made at the end.'

'Sales figures?' Ricky asked.

'That will form the biggest part of the decision, but there will be other factors like commitment to the job, number of new contracts and other criteria that you don't need to worry about.'

'So basically, you're setting us against each other?' Deb asked, incensed. She felt like a gladiator being sent into the coliseum. She wouldn't piss on Ricky Stone if he was on fire, but somehow the ethics were all wrong. For years they had been urged, trained and moulded into working as a team, with a little healthy competition initiated by themselves, but this was for promotion. This was a step up the corporate ladder, and it made Deb feel like a puppet.

'Is this the fairest way to decide the best person for the job?' Deb noticed that Ricky was staying quiet, but his look of unease confirmed that his feelings mirrored her own, though he was letting her do all the talking. 'I mean, do you expect a certain amount of backstabbing in our efforts to get the best sales leads, and how can we be judged on criteria that you're withholding from us?'

'I think you're being a little short-sighted, Debbie. There is nothing wrong with a little healthy competition and, in all fairness, we could have done this over the next three months without your knowledge, but at least now you can give it your best shot knowing what's at stake.'

As far as Deb was concerned, it was a way of squeezing every last morsel of effort out of both of them for no extra money and no reward at all for one of them.

'Do you have a problem with the selection process, Ricky?'

He shook his head and looked down at his Gucci shoes. Deb could have jumped across the table and throttled him. It wasn't a selection process; it was a dolphin exhibition, and the one to jump through the highest hoop got the fish.

'If you'd like to pull out at this stage, I'm sure Ricky would have no problem with—'

'No,' Deb said emphatically. One look at the slow smile that was beginning to spread over the moron's face convinced her that she couldn't give it to him on a plate. The long-term ramifications of that action would be to report to Ricky on a daily basis, and that was something she couldn't do in this lifetime.

'I'm in,' she said, raising her chin defiantly.

Ms Stringer nodded her approval. 'Good. The three-month period starts today, so we will have a decision' – she looked at her watch as though she was starting a race – 'the second week in September.' She pushed her chair back to signal the end of the meeting. Ricky jumped up and opened the door for her.

Great, Deb thought, a week before her wedding she could be out of a job. She knew that really her job wasn't at stake, but there was no way she would be able to continue to work for Ricky Stone. She'd have his head on a platter with an apple in his mouth before the first month was out.

Ricky grinned openly at her from the doorway. 'May the best man win,' he said with a mock salute. Deb waited for him to leave the room and gave him a salute of her own.

'So give us the goss,' Willow said as Deb returned to her office.

'You really don't want to know.'

Willow rose and poured Deb a coffee. She had the sensitivity to know when not to push.

Deb closed the office door behind her and slumped into her chair. What the hell had she let herself in for? If today's performance was anything to go by, she didn't have a hope in hell of landing that job, but Christ, she wanted it. She hadn't realised how much until there was a possibility of getting it. She loved the job she did and had done for seven years, but it was time for a change. The mornings didn't hold the same promise of challenge that they once had. She didn't get the same amount of excitement about closing a deal these days. The chance to move the department forward and be in a position to set realistic targets, to offer training courses, conferences, seminars for the staff, to encourage their talents to yield better results, to find ways to motivate a team of people who received no recognition for the job they did. To introduce bonus and reward schemes. Her mind buzzed with ideas on how to improve the department. Yes, she had to admit that she wanted the job, and she would work damned hard to get it.

'Deb, just a reminder to phone your mother-in-law,' Willow said, popping her head around the door.

'Cheers, but do you want to do it for me?'

Willow began to writhe with mock convulsions. 'Not on your life.'

Deb sat up straight and dialled the number. 'Margie, Deb. What was so urgent earlier?'

Margie humphed on the other end of the phone. 'Anyone would think you're not interested in your own wedding. I'm only trying to help, you know. If it was left to you, you'd walk down the aisle in your birthday suit, clutching a handful of dandelions, with a cold buffet—'

'Margie, what did you need to talk to me about?' Deb interrupted. Margie could whine on for hours and Deb did not have the time, especially now. She had to focus on her three-month-long plan of achieving the best sales figures she'd ever had.

'As I was saying earlier, I've been looking at the cost that the venues put on for food and it seems to be extortionate, so I got to thinking about just hiring the room and bringing in our own caterers. I've done the figures for the hundred and fifty who are coming and it does work out considerably cheaper.'

Deb frowned. That was fifty more than she and Mark had agreed. Maybe he'd recalled some long-forgotten relatives. She'd check with him later.

'Will The Swallows allow that?' Deb asked. She'd thought that it was a package deal.

'The hire of the hall increases minimally, but it still works out a couple of hundred pounds cheaper and the selection is impressive.'

'Can't grumble at saving a couple of hundred quid, I suppose,' Deb conceded, about to congratulate Margie on her findings.

'Good, I thought you'd be pleased so I've arranged for the caterers to give us a demonstration of the dishes at two o'clock this afternoon. I knew you'd agree with me.'

Deb closed her eyes. 'Margie, I can't leave work just like that. I have appointments, clients that I can't possibly let down. I need to—'

'You need to relax and have a lunch break, young lady. It won't take long, and it is the most important day of your life.'

'Margie, it's impossible for me—'

'You could always trust me to make the right decision on your behalf.'

'I'll be there. Shall I collect you on my way home?' Deb offered grudgingly.

Margie paused. 'Umm… no dear, they're coming here, to my house. It seemed easier, you know, for directions.'

Deb's fingers gripped the phone tightly, and she chewed back the barrage of insults that itched to travel down the phone lines. The damn cheek of the woman, inviting the caterers to her own home instead of Deb's. Who the hell was this wedding for? Deb wondered but immediately knew the answer. It was for Margie, but she just had to play along if she wanted to get married at all. If the plans didn't suit Margie's purpose, there would be no wedding. She issued a curt reply and slammed the phone down.

She opened her diary and groaned. Harper & Williams was a publishing house that occupied three floors of Tower Buildings in the centre of Birmingham. This was her third visit and she was sure an order was to be issued, so sure that it had been included on her projections for this week. She groaned again. She could have done with this order to put her straight into the running for promotion.

'Margie, I am so going make you suffer for this,' she said to herself, her active mind filling with visions of thumbscrews and stretching machines and any other ancient torture treatment she could imagine.

She pushed her chair back and went in search of Willow and was surprised to see Milton in the office next door to hers, staring at the computer screen. She liked Milton, even though he was a bit of a drip. Until a couple of months ago, she had merely tolerated his bumbling good nature, finding it too difficult to have a conversation with him. He was a rounded man from the bald patch on his head to his generous belly. Poor old Milton normally did badly on the sales figures. Charisma wasn't his strong point, but good old plodding and hard work was. He'd been a salesman all his life, twenty years at office stationery. A couple of months ago, Willow had informed her that his wife was tragically dying of a rare blood disease. With no children to help him through the heartbreakingly short time they'd had left, his absence from work had plunged his sales figures even lower and he'd returned to work a different man. No longer jolly and bumbling, just tired and stooped.

'What's Milton in for?' she asked Willow, who was punching her keyboard efficiently. The sales staff were out on the road every Monday morning. She was only in the office to attend the meeting arranged by Ms Stringer.

'Called in by Imelda to check his figures for last week.' She slid a copy of his report surreptitiously along the desk. 'Apparently, there must be some mistake.'

Deb skipped the details and read the bottom line which showed an increase of less than two per cent. His projection for this week didn't look much healthier. Deb felt sorry for what he'd had to deal with, losing his wife and constantly having to measure himself against people younger and keener.

'I can't make my two o'clock, Willow. Something has come up.'

'Bugger, they must be about ready to order by now.'

Deb nodded.

Willow started leafing through the diary. She stabbed Thursday. 'I'll see if I can postpone—'

'Give it to Milton. Ask him to take it,' Deb said, glancing to where he was shaking his head vaguely at the computer screen.

Willow followed her eyes. 'But this one will be worth quite a bit of—'

'Just do it,' Deb instructed before returning to her office.

Deb was mildly surprised to see Margie scrubbed and dressed in her Sunday best when she opened the door. She looked like a child on Christmas Eve. On first inspection, Margie appeared to be the type of mother-in-law that any girl would wish for. Her round face was warm and homely, with a full head of once-black hair that was being allowed to age gracefully. She had succumbed to middle-aged spread, but wore stylish slacks and long shirts that took a stone off her weight. Her only jewellery was the engagement and wedding ring that she still wore, and a fine belcher chain around her neck that Mark had bought her. At five foot three she was four inches shorter than Deb, although Deb was no longer fooled by her appearance. Poison bottles were small and compact but undoubtedly deadly.

'It's a man,' Margie exclaimed excitedly, as though they were in short supply. 'I expected it to be a woman but he's very nice.'

Deb removed her jacket and threw it over the stair bannister. 'Something smells good,' she said as a multitude of aromas drifted into the hallway and assaulted her nose.

'He's got one of those hotplate trolley things that I always wanted for dinner parties when Jack was alive.' She clasped Deb's hands. 'Oh, this is going to be such fun.'

Deb instantly recoiled. She withdrew from contact with people other than the people she chose, and Margie was not one of them. If Margie noticed, she didn't show it as Deb followed her into the kitchen.

'Deb, this is Derek Mason who will be demonstrating his range of dishes for us today. Derek, this is my soon-to-be daughter-in-law but already one of the family.'

'Pleased to meet you,' he said, offering his hand.

Deb shook his hand warmly, trying to ignore the posh tone that Margie was trying to adopt, as she always did with anyone who spoke nicely. Unfortunately, it ended up sounding like a parody.

Deb sat down opposite Margie and thought how unlike a catering consultant he was. A rather heavy-set man in a navy suit who looked more suited to selling double-glazing, but his smile seemed friendly and genuine and Deb warmed to him immediately.

'I was just explaining to Marjorie—' He blushed slightly. 'Sorry, Margie, that we have three main menus, samples of which I have brought for your appraisal this afternoon. Some of the dishes are of Asian origin, but if you want a beef roast I'm sure we can accommodate that too; these days though, young couples like yourself prefer to go for something a little more adventurous.' He laid his hands on the table as he pushed himself to a standing position. He had the cleanest fingernails Deb had ever seen on a man.

'I would imagine that you need to get back to work, so will I begin to tantalise your palettes straight away?'

Deb nodded, tensing her stomach muscles to stop the noise echoing around the paisley tiled kitchen. She liked Derek immediately. He didn't try to oversell his products but was prepared to let them speak for themselves – in her mouth.

'I'll lay out the starter, main course and dessert of each selection at one time, so that you may sample any of the three dishes, and I'll tell you a little about the dishes as you taste. All of the dishes are served with the relevant wine, ranging from Chablis and Chardonnay to Tokay-Pinot Gris and Gewurztraminer. Ready?'

Deb nodded and picked up a fork.

'This is our basic package called "The Tasty Bite" and begins with an attractive salad comprising edible flowers such as chive, lavender, fennel, marigold, and the leaves are chervil, tarragon and flat-leaf parsley.'

Deb took a bite but found the whole idea of eating flowers indigestible. Margie speared something that looked like curly lettuce and placed her fork down. *Yes, this is going to be fun*, Deb decided.

The main course was a Vietnamese dish called *suong nuong*: grilled pork chops with baked new potatoes. Deb detected ginger and garlic in the sauce, which was tasty but a little bland after a couple of bites.

The dessert was called *akbari shahi turkri* and originated from north India. Deb bit into it to find it was a glorified bread and butter pudding, with the addition of saffron and cardamom. She took a second bite. Hmm… that was definitely a winner, but she wasn't sure about the other two courses. She stole a glance at Margie, who seemed to be trying to get into the spirit of things but hadn't stopped sipping water since the pork chops.

Deb wiped her mouth. 'Is that commonly known as the pauper's surprise?' she asked with a smile.

Derek's mouth twitched. 'It is our most economic choice, yes.'

He removed the plates as Deb smiled brightly at Margie. Her mild discomfort was obvious. Her eyes had lit up when he'd mentioned the beef roast earlier, but Deb was in the mood now and was dying to try more.

Three more plates appeared, all looking more colourful than the last. 'This selection is "Divine Delicacies". The starter is *salade cauchoise* and is made up of new potatoes, ham strips, celery, double cream, spring onions and black olives.'

Deb bit in greedily; she adored black olives and the cream mixed with the other ingredients was delicious. There was enough garlic to flavour but not dominate.

'The main course is Andalusian chicken with sherry from Spain. A truly delightful dish, if I do say so myself, served with long grain rice flavoured with saffron and shallots.'

Deb speared a pieced of chicken. The taste hit her immediately. There was lemon, tarragon, not to mention the sherry.

'Is there crème fraiche in the sauce?' Deb asked, going in for seconds.

Derek nodded. 'The name of the dish comes from the small Andalusian town of Jerez de la Frontera. The young wine is matured in oak barrels for a year then fortified with brandy before being blended to produce a range of sherries.'

Deb felt the assault on her senses with the second mouthful and would have been happy to polish off the lot. Margie poked tentatively at a piece of chicken that hadn't touched the sauce.

'The dessert in this selection is *gula melaka* from Malaysia. It is a type of sago pudding with palm sugar and coconut milk.'

Deb liked the presentation of the dessert. It was the shape of a small Christmas pudding but orange, with tiny little jewels draped in a waterfall of coconut milk. It was cold and fresh and not too heavy after the chicken and rice dish. Deb nodded her approval to the second selection.

'It looks like a mound of fish eggs,' Margie said as he removed the plates.

'The third selection is "The Palate's Delight".'

Deb tasted a morsel from the Thai lobster salad. The main course of *char kuey teow* may have been the most luxurious choice, but Deb wasn't struck on the pork and prawn relationship. The lacy *roti jala* pancakes were light and tasty and suited the dish perfectly. The dessert was the Italian *panforte di* Siena.

Deb found the third selection a little too rich for her taste. She didn't completely agree with the way lobster was cooked. In the main course, she felt that the soy sauce, oyster sauce and garlic was a little too overpowering, and the honey and nut cake a little too heavy to round off such a meal.

Deb pushed away the plates. Margie had barely said a word, and Deb found herself becoming rather fond of this muted Margie.

'I'd like to hear your prices, especially for "Divine Delicacies".'

Derek didn't make any pretence of reaching for a price list. As Deb would have expected, he knew his prices by heart. He named a figure per head that was marginally cheaper than the cost at the hotel without their cost for the evening buffet.

'What about the buffet?' she asked, hoping that this opportunity was not going to be too far out of her price range.

'Our buffet is an enticing mixture of exotic and not so exotic finger dishes that would suit anyone. I could send you a selection by courier for testing.'

'And the price?'

He smiled widely. 'That's the nice part. The buffet comes free with either "Divine Delicacies" or "The Palate's Delight".'

Deb smiled gratefully. 'I'll give you my address.' By her reckoning, she was about three hundred quid under budget for a meal that was a little more exotic than the fare that the hotel offered, but not too weird that people wouldn't give it a try.

Margie stood and held out her hand. 'Well thank you for your time, Mr Mason. We'll be sure to contact you when we've reached a decision.'

Deb shot daggers at the woman who was none too gently guiding him out of the kitchen.

'Hold on a moment, Derek,' she said pointedly. 'You seem to have forgotten something.' She reached into her handbag. 'My deposit cheque. Is fifteen per cent agreeable?'

Deb ignored Margie's rude harrumphing as she handed over the cheque and bid him goodbye. She swallowed her irritation with Margie's assumption and tried to focus on the fact that, for once, she had her own way and had finally made one decision about her own wedding herself.

Margie returned to the kitchen as Deb was putting her jacket on. 'Well done, Margie, for arranging that. Another thing sorted, eh?' God help her, she was trying to be nice, but Margie looked as though she was going to explode.

'Auntie Mavis will never be able to eat all that rich food. It'll bring on her angina in a flash, and one of Mark's second cousins can't touch chicken; it gives him hives.'

'We can sort something out for them,' Deb said to mollify her.

'Well I'll take a cheese sandwich to the reception.'

Deb pulled her belt tightly. 'Margie, you arranged it. What on earth did you expect?'

'Soup, prawn cocktail maybe, tiramisu at a stretch.'

Deb sighed. There was no pleasing the woman. 'Well it's one less thing to worry about. That's what you wanted, isn't it?'

Margie turned from the sink. 'I suppose so but I wish there'd have been roast potatoes.'

Deb checked her watch. 'I've got to go. I'll talk to you soon.' Maybe this restrained Margie would be a godsend. Maybe if her nose was just slightly out of joint, she'd back off a little and let Deb do it in her own way.

Margie solemnly walked her to the door, and Deb couldn't help but hope that this would herald a change in the dynamics of her wedding planning.

'At least that's one less thing to worry about, eh?'

Margie brightened visibly. 'Yes, of course it is. I'll get on to arranging the flowers tomorrow, shall I?'

Deb sighed and closed the door soundlessly behind her.

CHAPTER EIGHT

By the time Mr Williams had been off work for three days, Cher was growing mightily suspicious. This was not a man with normal, fallible body organs. This was a drone that had given up all rights to a personality for the good of the company.

Unwanted visions of him floating in a lake somewhere swam before her eyes, but she forced them away. He was probably enjoying a well-earned rest while his body parts were serviced.

She'd enquired about his health with 'the dolls' in the executive suite, but her request had been met with frosty glares and dismissive shrugs. Cher was aware that they had little idea who she was, but surely Mr Williams was higher up the corporate ladder – or food chain as she preferred to call it.

The environment up there had never appealed to Cher. It was where the executive managers and their trinkets lived. The atmosphere was both snobbish and superior, and she didn't want to live there.

The offices occupied by Mr Williams and her were situated on the other side of the shopping complex and ran along the same corridor as the janitor's stores. Mr Williams had smiled slightly once when she'd made the idle comment that 'they're in first class and we're in steerage'.

She'd thought about going up there again today, as she drove in, but she could feel her courage ebbing away. Michael Hunter was still occupying the office that she guarded and wasn't due in until the afternoon. Maybe she'd ask him later. Doubtful though. She avoided any direct contact with him unless specifically addressed after her assets had been suitably demonstrated. She now knew he liked decaf, and she fetched his lunch without being asked. These being the two most challenging aspects of her job.

'Hello, Cher, how bin ya?' asked Nellie as she pulled a vacuum cleaner into the office behind her.

'You're limping a bit there, Nellie. You okay?' Cher asked, trying not to fall into the Black Country slang.

'Just my toenail. It'll be all right when it's better.'

Cher frowned. She seemed to be in serious pain. 'Shouldn't you be at home resting that foot?'

She guffawed loudly. 'Oh are, and I could tell me old mother that she ain't getting her slice of boiled ham this week.'

Cher nodded. The cleaners didn't get paid for days off sick. Another luxury Cher didn't appreciate. She looked closely at Nellie's lined face that tried bravely not to grimace as she bent down to unwind the vacuum flex. Her hair was completely grey and stuck out at the sides. Her hands were wrinkled and plastered with hard skin that looked like peeling paint. How old was her mother? Cher wondered.

'Nellie, have a seat for a minute. It won't hurt you.' Cher took the concertina pipe from her hands.

'No, no, ooh no, I couldn't,' she cried, looking towards the office door.

'It's okay, he's not in yet. Go on, rest that foot a bit.'

Nellie lowered herself cautiously onto the sofa. She couldn't contain the groan of relief as the pressure eased off her toe.

'So God's not in yet?'

'God?'

'Yeah, Mr Almighty, that's what we call him. Walks round like he created the bloody world, that one.'

Cher chuckled as Nellie's face creased into total disgust. It was no use trying to explain Michael Hunter's position to her. She'd typed the memo informing all cleaning staff that overtime was on hold for the time being, but Nellie would never understand the sort of pressure he was under.

'It wasn't so bad with old Willy. He was a bit stiff but he knew how to treat the staff.' She sighed deeply and shook her head. 'Well, them days are gone.'

'He'll be back when he's better.' Cher smiled, trying to placate her. 'And then everything will return to normal.'

She huffed. 'I wouldn't be too sure of that.'

Cher's antenna picked up immediately. 'What have you heard?'

'If only you knew the things I hear up in those offices, it'd make your toes curl. Of course I'd never divulge anything. Primitive information it is.'

Cher tried not to burst out laughing at her serious expression and the fact that she meant privileged. She couldn't possibly know as much as she wanted her to think she did. She sensed Cher's disbelief.

'You know, I was thinking the other day, as I heard 'em talking about Mr Williams, that I was like all the three wise monkeys rolled into one. I go up there, after most of 'em have gone home and it's like because I don't speak, they think I can't see and that I've got no ears. It's like I'm invisible, you know.'

'What were they saying?' Already a pebble was forming in Cher's stomach.

'Well I couldn't really say, you know,' she said imperiously.

'Oh go on, Nellie. How else will I find out all the way down here? I know it's difficult for you and I don't wish to question your integrity, but you know far more than I do.'

Her feathers visibly puffed. 'Well only cos it's you. There's some folks coming in to look at everything that goes on, you know, like a test or something…'

'Auditors, is that what you mean?'

She nodded. 'That's him. Anyway, at first I thought they were talking about somebody's weight when I kept hearing the words top-heavy, which could apply to a lot of 'em to be honest, and I don't mean in the brains department. But I heard them mention Mr Williams a few times…'

'But someone's got to do the job,' Cher mumbled as she switched the vacuum cleaner on.

'Cher, no, stop it. You can't do that. You'll have me sacked. It's not right.'

She made a move to get up, but Cher gently eased her back down. It wouldn't hurt her to run the vacuum over the office. She was still trying to deny the communal ten pounds that had become hers.

Sarah and Deb had both laughed when she'd voiced her theory that a weight of ten pounds gets passed from woman to woman. It's the ten pounds that creeps on during a comfortable relationship. It sneaks on while you no longer pay attention to the fat content and kilojoules on the back of the lasagne box. It takes you by surprise when you miss the odd night at the gym or forget to decline the last jam tart. That ten pounds was currently hers and it had to come off. Although it was hard, looking at her parents: her father being a hefty fourteen stone, carrying most of it on his stomach and her mother not that far behind, but leading in the even distribution category. A little of the guilt had left her when she'd read somewhere about weight and shape being hereditary, and she realised that she wasn't only fighting cravings and a love of good food – she was fighting genetics.

She was just vacuuming the pieces of crusty baguette from under her desk when Nellie stood quickly with a frightened look on her face. Cher turned, fearing Michael Hunter's early arrival. She sighed with relief.

'It's just Dan,' she reassured Nellie and saw his open smile cool slightly.

'Obviously *he's* not in then?' Dan said, nodding towards the office door.

Cher shook her head as she handed the vacuum back to Nellie. She slunk out of the office with the vacuum in tow.

Cher sat down quickly, aware that a few dark curls were welded to her forehead with sweat. Christ, she really needed to get fit.

'About an hour,' she replied and heard the slight breathlessness.

'I won't even ask,' he said, grinning as he pointed to a retreating vacuum cleaner.

'What's wrong with you?' It was unusual to see Dan with a frown, although it had happened more in the last few days.

'Just him again.'

'What now?'

'I received an email this morning summoning me up to the heavens. Those people don't even know I exist, so it has to be something bad, and it has to be the work of him.'

'He's okay really, Dan, honest. He gets just as much hassle as the rest of us.' Cher had no idea if that was true or not, especially with the amount of joviality she usually heard coming from the office. But as his temporary, unofficial PA it was her duty to protect him. And the fact that she was madly in love with him.

Dan shook his head. 'Well you would say that. What else would I expect from his office wife?'

'Uh?' she asked, blushing at his reference to the word 'wife' in any capacity.

'It's your job to defend him, isn't it? You have to remain loyal and impartial, and I respect you for that so I won't put you in a difficult position by saying any more.'

Oh great, if there was gossip to be had, she'd just talked herself out of being included on the mailing list.

'I might be loyal to my boss, but I can always be trusted not to—'

'Great.' Dan laughed heartily. 'Now you sound like a German shepherd.'

'Gee, thanks.'

His eyes smiled and she was pleased to see some of the tension leave his face. 'I meant that in a good way.' He paused as though he wanted to say something.

'Speak,' she commanded.

'Don't you think there's a weird feeling around here at the moment, like it's unsettled?' He shook his head and perched on the edge of the desk. 'Maybe it's just me, but I get the feeling that the lads are aware of it as well.'

Cher loved the way he always referred to them as 'the lads'. Some of them were in their forties and fifties yet answerable to Dan. Somehow he managed to get the best out of them while still earning their respect and enthusiasm.

'I don't know, to be honest, and I'm not being coy or secretive. I really have no idea what's going on.' She chose not to repeat Nellie's observations, partly because the woman had spoken in confidence and partly because she was unsure of the accuracy.

He nodded as though he believed her. 'It's just, if there is talk of redundancies or job losses, I'd like to be able to warn some of the lads who have children. Things like this can drag on for months. Some are already looking and I'd hate them to pass up a good offer if there are plans to reduce the workforce here.'

Cher noticed that so far he hadn't mentioned anything about himself and his own job, only the guys.

'That reminds me. Have you been attacked by any wands of foil recently?'

He looked puzzled.

'The new *Star Wars* film,' Cher reminded him. He'd mentioned taking his son to the cinema a few weeks earlier.

His jaw tightened slightly as he glanced towards the door to Michael Hunter's office. 'I've had to put him off for a couple of weekends, thanks to him, but I've promised faithfully that if he leaves the kitchen utensils alone, I'll take him in a couple of weeks.' He smiled engagingly. 'I've been meaning to ask if you'd like to—'

'Daniel, how nice to see you. Been waiting long?' Michael Hunter asked as he breezed past. His navy suit was loose-fitting and perfectly cut, as usual.

Dan followed him into the office without waiting to be asked. Cher caught Michael Hunter's surprised expression. His tolerant voice was being affixed as he closed the door.

Cher found it hard not to be curious about Dan's irritation. In a way it was quite refreshing to see someone fight back. Many people had passed her door gathering their wits to stand up to Michael Hunter, but they all came out the same way: red-faced and hunched.

The need to know what was going on distracted her from the two reports on her desk. It was no use – her new professionalism, brought on by the presence of Michael Hunter, was dissolving before her eyes. How coincidental that fresh coffee was needed and the percolator was close to the office door.

'Oh, darn it,' she cursed as she opened the bag of perky coffee and showered the blue carpet tiles with grains of Colombian decaf. She was forced to clean up the mess with a dustpan and brush.

The coarseness of the floor covering scraped at her knees, which found no protection from her gusseted tights with added Lycra.

A magazine article she'd read had proclaimed that darker tights made legs look slimmer, but they only made hers look like stumps. She made a mental note to herself to take more care as to what magazine articles she should take seriously.

She'd tried to improve her reading matter the previous weekend. Her hands had been forced away from the popular weeklies with true stories, which confirmed that her own life wasn't so bad after all, towards one of the many *Good Housekeeping* glossies. She'd always wondered how these magazines could be so thick. How much was there to say? But as she picked up the magazine, her pleasure was immediate and unexpected. She trailed along the magazine rack with glossy in hand, ensuring that the title was visible. No more gazing at cures for hangovers and surveys on the best low-fat mayonnaise. This magazine would give her things to talk about at parties. This single, glossy magazine had the ability to change her life.

That was until she idly leafed through it and found not one article that interested her. She didn't need stacking storage cases for the kids' toys that cost as much as the rent. She didn't want to make quilts and curtains from material that could be acquired for extortionate prices. The feeling of pretentiousness left her as soon as she binned the offending article.

She smiled wryly. It certainly hadn't contained any articles on throwing beverages all over the floor and then crawling on all fours to listen at your boss's door.

She swept at a couple of granules and tried to hear what was being said.

'I have no idea why you've been summoned upstairs,' Michael Hunter protested. Cher doubted that was true, yet he sounded offended and genuine.

'I find that hard to believe. Where do you lot get off playing with other people's lives? My men have families, responsibilities…'

Cher moved a little closer. How could Dan speak to him like that? It wasn't Michael Hunter's fault.

The silence lengthened into a few seconds. 'Well it's obvious that you've as much integrity as a sewer rat, so I'll get out of your way.'

Cher realised much too late that the volume of Dan's growl had increased. He stormed out of the office and almost fell over her.

He straightened quickly, regaining his poise.

'Coffee…' she offered lamely. He gave her a look that was a mixture between preoccupation and amusement.

She scrambled back to her desk and wondered again what was going on. The feeling that it affected her just wouldn't go away.

'Cher, I wonder if you could assist me with these boxes,' Michael Hunter called from the doorway.

'Of course. Where do they need to go?'

'Back to my own office. I'm afraid I'll be leaving you today.'

Cher nodded and felt a crushing disappointment that could only be compared to the Christmas Eve that she saw her father, clad in reindeer antlers, carrying her presents down the stairs.

There were only two boxes that needed transportation, so they'd make that last walk together.

'Only take one at a time. I'd hate you to strain your back.'

Cher nodded: as ever, he was thoughtful.

He perched on the edge of her desk as she did a lift and jerk movement with the first box.

'It must have been quite an experience working for a senior manager for a while. If I could take you upstairs with me, I would.'

Oh God, she was melting. He'd take her if he could. Damn the powers that stopped him.

'But you're just too important where you are. We need you here on the ground level.'

Cher understood that. He needed someone he could trust. The thought warmed her.

'And we'll still see each other, sometimes, won't we? It's not as though I'm leaving the country. Who knows when we'll bump into each other?'

Her knees started to tremble as she caught a glint in his eye. Her heart soared. Everything was becoming clear to her now. He returned her feelings but couldn't act on them, at least not yet. The professional relationship was far too precious to tamper with. Dan had been correct: she was his office wife and that took priority. But all that was about to change. He was returning to his proper office wife: the one that nagged him about keeping his appointments and writing correspondence. He knew that by leaving her he was removing any ethical obstacle to their love.

Oh, how would she contain herself until the day he declared his undying love for her? she wondered as she almost dropped the archive box.

CHAPTER NINE

Cher arrived at the community centre to find the others already waiting.

'About time. I was just beginning to think I was to be denied the sight of you in Lycra,' Deb said, chuckling.

'Hey, if we get bored we can always pop to the AA meeting next door,' Cher murmured to Deb.

'Oh no you won't,' Sarah commanded. 'This is exactly what we need. Although, you could visit that room on another night. I'm sure they'd take you.'

'Is everyone ready for the sight of me in upward dog position?' Cher asked.

Deb shook her head as Sarah corrected her.

'Downward dog, you idiot.'

It had been Sarah's idea to attend a yoga class. She felt they all needed to limber up and, in the absence of any recent sexual gymnastics, Cher had to agree.

She watched as the other six women changed into their yoga attire and felt self-conscious at the lack of privacy. Sarah peeled off jeans and T-shirt to reveal that she was the only one with the foresight to have her outfit on underneath.

Cher and Deb used each other as shields against the rest of the room, which worked well until Cher's foot got caught in the lining of her bodysuit, sending her thundering to the ground.

Sarah laughed loudly, and Deb politely covered her mouth with her hand.

Sarah was listening intently as Cher tried to push herself to the back of the group, so that no one would be forced to stare at her backside. The instructor, a woman in her early twenties with legs as smooth as breadsticks, gestured for them to form a circle in front of coloured rubber mats. She spoke quietly with a toneless, flat voice that Cher thought came only after a full-frontal lobotomy.

She spoke of positions like the cat, tree and triangle. Cher glanced sideways at Sarah on her left, who was listening to every word.

'The main two components – the asanas, which are the physical postures and the pranayama, which is the controlled breathing – come together and work simultaneously. They stretch all parts of the body and even massage the internal organs and respiratory system.' She paused as if expecting a communal gasp of surprise at this revelation.

'Yoga is beneficial for cleansing the body of impurities…'

'D'ya think it'll work on a doner kebab?' Cher muttered.

'From this day, you will be known as a yogi which is what all practitioners of…'

'Wasn't there a cartoon about him?' Deb muttered towards Cher, who stifled a giggle. It was Deb's turn to receive a chastising glance from the instructor.

She managed to follow the instructor's directions of the cat position, which was basically getting on all fours, arching the back and lowering the head, forcing her to look a little too closely at the pendulum effect of her breasts. Cher quickly raised her head, relieved when they moved on to the tree. The motion of her hands stretched high above her head forced some of the tension out of her shoulders.

Cher found that she was fighting the absolute boredom of the whole exercise during the simple twist. Just as she was coming to the end of the ten-second hold of looking over her shoulder, a dramatic shriek startled her.

'Shit, I've got cramp,' Deb cried, looking like a disconsolate owl. Cher could fight it no longer and collapsed into a fit of giggles, before reaching over to help her friend, who was clutching her neck. A few exasperated sighs convinced Cher that they'd be better off at the coffee shop across the road, drinking cappuccinos and gossiping.

She helped Deb to her feet, glancing apologetically at the rest of the group, who looked relieved that they were leaving, then guided Deb towards the door, grabbing their belongings on the way. Once they were safely in the corridor, Deb straightened up without any trouble or discomfort.

'Christ, I couldn't stand another minute—'

'Sarah's coming.'

'Oh shit,' Deb cried as she repositioned her neck.

'Are you okay?' Sarah asked with concern. Cher looked away.

'I think I'll be okay but I need to walk for a while.'

Sarah nodded and guided her towards the stairs. Cher held back, smiling at Deb's duplicity. She couldn't wait to tell them about Michael. Michael – his name sounded strange in her head. Lonely somehow. Until now he had always been either Mr Hunter or Michael Hunter, but never just Michael.

'Michael Hunter nearly asked me out,' she blurted as they crossed the road towards the café.

'He didn't?' screamed Sarah.

'No chance,' claimed Deb doubtfully.

'Well he said that, even though he's moved offices, there's no reason why we shouldn't bump into each other again sometime.'

'And that's it?' Deb spluttered. 'That's all he said?'

She looked to Sarah for support. She'd understand the undertones. She shook her head. 'Sorry, Cher, I'm not sure that would classify for almost asking you out.'

'Don't either of you understand what he was trying to say?'

'Yeah, I'll see you again when there's no one else around to make my coffee or fetch my tuna salad.'

'Chicken,' she corrected. 'Come on, it's possible he's going to ask me out, surely?'

'About as likely as this chocolate muffin not heading straight for my hips,' Deb said, pulling the cake onto her tray.

'Christ, Cher, if you think he's actually keen, you need to get a life,' Sarah said as they sidled into a corner booth. 'Sorry to sound brutal, but all this mooning over Michael Hunter is turning your head from other potential opportunities is all I'm saying,' she said, shrugging.

'Oh yeah cos they're just lining up outside my office door and, for your information, I have got a life,' she replied tartly, hoping she wouldn't be questioned too deeply or be required to offer proof.

Deb guffawed. 'Yeah, to everyone else junk mail is bin food. You actually take the time to read it and reply to it, before logging on to sadtart.com.'

'Piss off. I know he's going to ask me out. I can feel it.'

'I think I may have some news on that score myself quite soon,' Sarah offered coyly.

Deb bit into the chocolate muffin, sending crumbs flying everywhere. 'What gives?'

Sarah smiled widely. 'Well let's just say I remembered a scene out of *Sea of Love*, but instead of going grocery shopping I went to the cinema.'

Cher had seen the film and found that to be a powerfully erotic scene. She only wished she had the confidence to do something like that, but knowing her luck, the poor, unsuspecting male would laugh his bloody socks off and ask her to fetch the popcorn. Sarah was assured enough to know that no red-blooded male would find anything humorous in her taut, tanned body.

'What happened?' Deb asked.

'Christ, it was like nothing I've ever experienced before. I've still got the bruises on my back. He punished me for teasing him and then took me home and made love to me for hours.' She tipped her head sideways. 'I have no idea how he explained it to his wife.'

'How romantic,' Cher said, trying not to be jealous.

'And I managed to make a decision about my own wedding which infuriated Margie.' Deb raised her cup. 'So, girls, it looks like our lives are looking up.'

Cher clinked her cup against Deb's. After their earlier comments about Michael, she wasn't so sure, but she smiled cheerfully regardless.

Cher drove into work cheerfully on Monday morning. The distinct aroma of freshly brewed coffee was unexpected as she entered the dungeon that was her office. The airless space without windows imprisoned any smell that was powerless to escape. Cher's heart lifted. Maybe Michael had returned because he just couldn't cope without her, but then again he hadn't made the coffee the last time. Dan had.

At that second, Dan materialised before her. He looked different as he smiled engagingly. Of course, he was wearing a proper suit instead of his usual supervisor's attire. It took a few seconds longer to realise that he'd come out of Mr Williams's office.

'But why… who… when…?'

'If you hang on a minute, I'll try to answer all of those questions,' Dan replied as he took two cups from the shelf. Was he expecting company?

'Milk no sugar, right?'

She nodded numbly. Nobody made her coffee. Was he stupid? She was the coffee maker – her and Morphy Richards.

Dan placed the coffee on her Chris Hemsworth coaster and took a seat on the leather sofa, just as Michael had done. She couldn't help wishing it were him that occupied that space, with his effortless grace and confidence, unlike Dan who looked totally out of place in a suit jacket. He reminded her of the dressed chimps that used to advertise the teabags.

'I'll try and answer your questions, but this was just as surprising to me as it was to you. I think you should know that Mr Williams has been made redundant.'

'What?' she cried, sending red-hot coffee sliding down her throat before it was ready to go. She tried to disguise the choking as a cough.

Dan nodded. 'I know, I'm just as angry as you are, but—'

'How could they do that to him?' she moaned indignantly on his behalf. How could they make him redundant? A man who had given everything he had to the company. She imagined him at home, wandering around the garden aimlessly, trying to come to terms with the acute sensation that he should be somewhere else. A vision flitted through her mind of him shuffling, hunched, to his favourite armchair that would now suck the very reason for living from his bones. One day he would sit in that armchair, stare at a television screen and never get up again. They hadn't only fired him – they'd killed him.

'I spoke to Harry last night, right before he was due to board a flight for Bermuda. He's taking a well-earned holiday with Vera.'

It infuriated her that he referred to them on first-name terms. And so what if he was taking a holiday? It didn't mean that he wasn't destroyed by the news. The full realisation might hit him in Bermuda, and they'd be reading an article about him walking out to sea.

She peered suspiciously over her coffee cup. Dan was no better than the suits upstairs. How had he engineered it so that Mr Williams wouldn't be coming back?

'Why you?' she asked sharply.

He shrugged. 'Your guess is as good as mine. I told you about my summons up to the executive suite. Well this was the reason.'

'You should have refused. Then they would have brought Mr Williams back.' She wasn't sure if that was true, but as the words left her mouth, an expression of unease tightened Dan's mouth.

'I was hoping that we'd be able to work together quite well.'

Had he really? Well she was just about sick and tired of playing Musical Managers. She never knew who was going to land in the office next.

'Of course we'll work together…' Her words trailed off. It didn't feel proper to call him Dan anymore, but the words 'Mr Rickman' wouldn't come either. 'You will have my professional support at all times.'

'Of course, thank you,' Dan said quietly as he removed himself from the sofa. He paused at the door, as though there was something he wished to add, but he changed his mind, closing the door behind him.

Cher was a little surprised at her own frostiness. It wasn't as though Mr Williams and she were soulmates or anything; in fact, they'd had more than a few disagreements. She wasn't particularly fond of the old stickler, but a vague feeling of disappointment wouldn't leave her. For some reason she'd expected Dan to fight for Mr Williams's rights. To refuse the job on principle, rather than jump into someone's grave. He'd always been the focal point for the feelings of the engineers, their spokesperson, but now he was no longer one of them. He'd sacrificed them to climb the corporate ladder and that disappointed her for some reason.

She busied herself with the filing that she always left for Monday morning, so that the worst job of the week was over straight away. Having had Michael Hunter in the office, there was little to be filed.

'Cher, I'm going down to the workshop for a while. I won't be long,' Dan offered as he walked past the desk. She nodded but noticed that something was different. He'd removed his tie and opened the top button of his shirt.

'It's just not me,' he admitted with a smile as he caught her glance.

She coloured slightly and looked away. Who was he trying to kid? He was going to see the troops who would probably knife him if he went down there trying to be the big man. It occurred to her that Daniel Rickman was very clever, playing both sides of the fence. He could be the manager when the people upstairs summoned him. He'd learned enough of their political backstabbing games to jump into another man's grave, yet he knew how to act like one of the lads.

'Cher, have you ever been downstairs?'

She shook her head. Mr Williams had said it wasn't necessary. In fact, she only recalled him going down there a few times.

'Do you want to come?'

She glared, enraged by the image he was trying to present to his 'lads'. 'I'm not a trinket, Mr Rickman, to be brandished as your new possession. It is not necessary for me to follow you around. I'm sure that the new car and mobile phone are the only status symbols you need.'

A look of thunder forced his eyebrows together as she wondered where the hostility was coming from, but every time he opened his mouth he offended her more.

'I can assure you that my only reason for asking was to increase your awareness of the department for which you work, as many of the engineers have never met you,' he rebuked as he turned and strode away.

Christ, what was wrong with her? It didn't matter how she felt about his promotion. Maybe he had worked hard and deserved it, but she'd have to be careful how she spoke to him. She straightened her back and posed herself into her very best professional stance, ready for his return. Up until now, they had been friendly and pleasant to each other, sharing jokes and banter, but that relationship had now ceased to exist. He would get her total support and loyalty, that was only right, but it didn't mean they had to speak to each other.

'Has he started yet?' Nellie asked, pulling the vacuum cleaner behind her.

Of course, Cher marvelled, even Nellie had known before her. 'Yes.' She nodded.

'Old Willy was okay but Dan's a good bloke.'

'Even if he is ambitious.'

'Why do you say that? I'd have thought you'd be thrilled to bits to have a young, good-looking bloke like him to work for,' she asked, emptying the paper recycling bin.

'I just don't think it's right, that's all.'

'How's that then?'

'Oh, you know,' she moaned, flustered at her own negativity. Dan was a nice bloke, as Nellie said, but she'd have unreasonably expected something different from him, something better.

'Well, to be honest, I don't see what else he could do. It wasn't like he was given the choice.'

Her interest was piqued. 'Huh?'

'Well it's not like he could afford to take the other option.'

'What other option?'

'Didn't he explain anything?'

Cher wasn't about to admit that she hadn't given him the chance. 'No,' she said shortly.

'Oh well, it's not really my place to divert any information, if he hasn't—'

'Nellie,' she warned.

She sighed deeply, as though she was being forced to reveal a secret military operation. 'Well I work on Friday nights, up in them offices. It's not like down here where I can do it during the working day. Them snobby cows wouldn't have a cleaner around while they're busy comparing hemlines and heels. Anyway, I heard the whole conversation, I did,' she claimed dramatically.

Cher nodded, wishing she'd hurry up.

'Anyway, the big boss man told Dan that if he wasn't prepared to try and do two jobs, then he might as well pack his bags because they couldn't afford to pay the two wages. He asked if he could be demoted back to engineer status, and they said there were enough engineers but a supervisor and manager wasn't necessary and it was his choice. Have a go or get stuffed.'

'Oh my god,' she moaned as her head fell onto the desk. Dan had been placed in the unenviable position of having to choose between his loyalty to the engineers and the necessity of earning a living, and she'd talked about trinkets and status symbols.

The booming noise of the vacuum didn't rouse her from her deflated position. After the way she'd spoken to him earlier, he was probably in the executive suite at this very moment, demanding the termination of her employment, which she deserved. Her head lolled from side to side. Oh, God, she groaned inwardly, what had she done this time?

CHAPTER TEN

Sarah rearranged the display of 'new talent' books and fought a tidal wave of envy: bitterness at people who were doing what she could only dream of. She'd hankered after a dream that had seemed impossible. As long as she wasn't trying, she had no possibility of failing. That had been until the early hours of Monday morning when David had left her. She'd felt wide awake with a fresh hunger to record every single emotion she'd experienced.

For the four days since, she had ignored his phone calls in an effort to whet his appetite further, and it had worked. Her exploits on Sunday night had unlocked something inside her and, except for the yoga night, she had spent every spare second in her room, either scribbling away or punching the keyboard. Ideas for stories had flooded into her mind, and she had recorded everything for fear she might lose one valuable thought.

The part of the seductive mistress that she'd played that night had made her realise that on the blank page, she could be anyone she wanted to be, go anywhere she chose. The voices in her head were louder, the words clearer, urging her to use her hands, her head, her heart to produce sentences that would express personality and individuality. She had fallen asleep each night thinking about the stories that she'd love to write, the characters that she ached to create.

Last night, it had been almost grudgingly that she had climbed into bed. Fatigue had drawn her towards a darkness that she wanted to fight, but as three o'clock approached, she knew that she had to rest. Thoughts, ideas and lines of dialogue flashed through her tired mind, forcing her to lean over and scrawl barely legible reminders onto a notepad. She forced the crowds of thoughts to disperse but couldn't wait for the morning to come when she would have a fresh head, fresh ideas and fresh eyes.

Earlier, during her shower, she had found herself wondering how much of her time and energy had been used for a couple of occasions each week; if she wasn't planning and preparing for them, she was crying and mourning their end. She was a little conscious of wishing her life away.

'Till, please,' Sarah heard from halfway down the shop. Her teeth ground and clenched. For a manager of a bookshop, his sentence structure left a lot to be desired. She'd seen thirteen managers in her time, and one thing they had in common was a fresh idea for the window display.

The unfortunate thing about the shop was its shape. The long, narrow store afforded hardly any window space, limiting the hooks to bring people inside. Posters were sent through daily from head office, half of them binned. If they'd all been placed in the windows, it would have been goodbye to natural daylight completely.

This manager was a first. Not just because he was young, even younger than she was, but because the ink on his degree from business college was not yet dry. He'd had no experience with books, but maintained the logic that a good manager could manage anything. 'I would apply the same drive and determination if this were a supermarket,' he'd claimed during his first huddle: ten minutes each week where the staff were free to voice any queries or complaints, which had swiftly become a rostrum for his own instructions.

Sarah wasn't sure if she agreed with his theory. Surely a manager had to know the business to manage it efficiently?

She entered the serving area without looking at the customer. 'Hello, Sarah.'

Her head snapped up. 'David, what…?'

'Here, put this through for me. I don't want to get you into trouble.'

Sarah looked around self-consciously before turning her attention to the book. She almost laughed. *Time Management* it screamed in red, angry letters. She wondered if the irony of the book was lost on him.

'Good choice,' she mumbled.

'It's the first one I picked up. I just needed to see you.'

He spoke in hushed tones, even though there was no one around. The shop had only been open for twenty minutes and didn't get busy until at least ten.

'What's wrong?' He looked preoccupied but his eyes sparkled. Sarah held her breath.

'I'm going to tell her tonight that it's over. I have to be with you, Sarah, and it has to be now.'

Sarah's heart turned. At last he felt the way she did. He finally understood what she'd been trying to tell him for years. They were meant to be together.

'How are you going to tell her?'

'I'll wait for Chelsea to go to bed, and I'll just explain to Bianca that I don't love her anymore. She wouldn't want to be in a one-way relationship so she'll be okay, but I just wanted to warn you to be ready. I don't know what time it will be but it will be tonight.'

Sarah nodded eagerly. He looked like they were about to embark on an adventure.

He reached over and squeezed her hand. 'I'll see you tonight.'

Sarah leaned forward to kiss him. 'Not here,' he said. She smiled; old habits die hard. What did it matter now? They would soon be free to do whatever they wanted. She watched him leave the store, checking each way, like a child crossing the road. Sarah shook her head with disbelief.

At last, David would be all hers. The life that she had dreamed of for five years would finally belong to her. Her hands clenched in excitement. Everything was coming together. The hunger to produce sentences was once again alive inside her stomach, and she now had the man that she loved. She wanted to dance around the shop telling everyone her news. She wanted to ring Deb and Cher and revel in her triumph. She finally had him.

Damien passed by the cash till. Sarah switched off her hapless grin and coughed, twice. Damien turned.

'Everything okay?' he asked with a distasteful grimace. He possessed an unhealthy fear of germs or bacteria anywhere near him and, he was proud to extol to all his staff on a regular basis, had never had a sick day in his life.

'Just a cough,' she said, placing her hand over her mouth and coughing again. 'I'll be fine.'

He frowned. 'You really shouldn't be in if you feel unwell.'

Sarah had another coughing fit but waved away his concerns. 'Honestly, I'll be okay. I have to finish stacking these books.'

He took a step backward. 'I'll get Dora to do it. Get yourself off home. I don't want you to infect… passing your cold around to everyone else.'

'If you insist,' Sarah said, raising her hand to her mouth again; this time, to hide her smile. She grabbed her jacket and handbag. It was Thursday and Damien would not expect her in tomorrow, but she'd make a call with her best flu voice in the morning, right after she'd finished making passionate love to David.

On the way home, she stopped to pick up some supplies so that they wouldn't need to leave the house for a couple of days. She went into the newsagents to grab a golfing magazine that he read occasionally. In her mind she had an idea of the haven she was going to prepare, ready for his arrival. He wouldn't need to do a thing, only sit and relax and allow her to ease away all his tensions. She envisioned the night ahead; their first as a real couple. She smiled to herself as she spied the magazine he liked. She was determined to create utopia.

Her eyes travelled past a magazine with the word WRITING emblazoned across the top. Sarah paused. She'd never seen it before and as she picked it up and leafed through it, she felt an excitement begin to swirl around her stomach. A sales assistant had to physically nudge her to move her away from a shelf that needed filling. She walked guiltily to the checkout, feeling like a complete fraud for even buying the magazine. She awaited the woman's derisive smile at her purchase, but she swiped it with the gun disinterestedly.

When she got home, she placed the magazine on the coffee table, dying to open it, but other things had to be done. The next few hours were to be spent cleaning the flat from top to bottom. She wanted crisp, clean sheets on the bed for David's first night. She wanted to make space in her wardrobe for David's clothes. Every room had to be vacuumed, polished and tidied so he'd know he wasn't living with a slob, and she wanted to litter her home with scented candles ready for his arrival. A bottle of single malt whisky sat on the kitchen unit beside two glasses: David's favourite drink.

She had it pictured in her mind how the night would play out. The vision played in slow motion with misty edges. He would arrive and she would take him in her arms and lead him to the couch. She would place a generous measure of whisky into his hand and gently massage his neck and shoulders, then guide him to the bathroom, where he would lie surrounded by the white flame of flickering candles with a musky scent that would make him feel relaxed and sexy. She would prepare a light supper while he bathed and take him a whisky refill. She would wash his back and possibly join him in the warm, soapy water. They would towel each other dry before eating their light supper, and then David would carry her to bed and make gentle love to her in the darkness, no longer hurried by the clock. They would whisper to each other long into the night. He wouldn't go to work tomorrow, she was convinced of that, not after the break-up of his marriage. He would fall asleep in her arms, wondering how he had ever questioned where he was meant to be. And then tomorrow their life together would begin.

Sarah checked the time. It was almost four thirty. He'd be hours yet. She had plenty of time to do the jobs, she reasoned, reaching for the magazine. A quick browse wouldn't hurt.

The first page was about the movements of editors and snippets of news. Sarah read every word, frightened that she might miss something, whilst holding the magazine reverently, as though it were a delicate flower that could be crushed with one false move.

She read the magazine from start to finish twice, relishing every single word. One article she read, about a successful crime writer, explained that she'd always been writing in her head, and the hardest thing was getting started. Sarah nodded voraciously, feeling that maybe there was hope for her yet.

She took out a notebook and pencil and began to scrawl the first line of the magazine's monthly competition. The words looked good on paper. She carried on, writing the first thing that came into her head and found it beginning to take the form of a story. Her hand flew across the page, unable to keep up with the thoughts rushing through her head. Grammar and punctuation were completely discarded as she left her present state and wrote only what came into her mind.

The inability to see what she was writing forced Sarah to glance at the clock, which told her it was nearly ten. She removed herself from the sofa and did a couple of neck-stretching exercises, then threw away the herb tea and poured herself a coffee from the pot that had been standing for eight hours. It was a thick grey colour like old socks but she didn't care. She looked over what she'd written and found about three paragraphs that she liked. She discarded the rest and started again. At eleven thirty she forced herself again to read, through hooded eyes, what she'd produced. She frowned at some parts, smiled at others, felt a small glow of pride and knew that tomorrow she would start again.

She became aware of a soft tapping on the front door. She looked at her appearance in horror. She hadn't done any of the things she'd meant to. The flat was a mess, there were no candles, there were no fresh sheets and she hadn't even showered or combed her hair. She gathered up all the loose-leaf sheets of A4 paper and threw them into her spare room, catching a quick glance at her reflection in the hallway mirror. The whites of her eyes had more red lines than a road map. She smoothed her hair, but it made no difference to her unkempt appearance.

She opened the door and realised that she need not have worried about her own appearance: David looked worse.

He almost fell into her arms. He was still wearing his work clothes, which looked crumpled and stale. His eyes were red-rimmed and underlined by dark shadows. She guided him to the sofa, where he slumped backward.

'I'll get you a drink,' Sarah offered, at a loss with what to say. Any words would sound banal.

He took the drink with trembling hands and downed it in one gulp. She refilled his glass. He sipped it and placed it on the floor, shaking his head.

'Sweetheart, was it hard?' she asked and instantly regretted the question.

He looked at her but seemed to be looking through her. 'Of course it was bloody hard. Ten years of history is hard to discard in one night.'

It was on the tip of Sarah's tongue to remind him that he'd been seeing her for half of that time, but now was not the time.

She nodded and reached for his hand. He resisted slightly and then let her take it. 'Christ, Sarah, you should have seen her. She was destroyed. I thought she might have had an idea, you know, that something was going on, but I must have hidden it better than I thought.'

'Was she angry?'

He shook his head. 'It would have been better if she was, but she was just numb. It was like she was in shock. She just sat on the sofa, crying.'

'It's not your fault,' Sarah soothed. As far as she was concerned, it was no one's fault. From the moment she and David met, the fates had taken over and that was the way she explained it to herself.

'But watching her cry like that. It tore me apart. She wanted to know why I'd stopped loving her, and I couldn't answer.' He banged his fist against the arm of the sofa. 'I couldn't fucking answer her. I owed her that much.'

'Darling, it's for the best that she knows now. It would have been crueller to leave it any longer.'

He looked at her squarely for the first time. 'I hope I don't have it in me to be any crueller than I felt tonight.'

'But now she can move on with her life. She can meet someone else and—'

'Don't say that,' he snapped, pulling his hand away.

'You should want her to be happy, and if that means meeting someone else, then so be it.'

'No one else will be a father to my child,' he raged and then slumped back down.

'Does she know yet?' Sarah asked softly.

David shook his head. 'Bianca is going to explain it to her tomorrow.' He shrugged. 'How the hell she's going to do that I don't know, seeing as I don't understand myself.'

Sarah frowned. 'You fell in love with someone else. It's terrible, it's heartbreaking, but it happened and now we have to move on.'

'Chelsea'll be wondering where I am tomorrow morning. How will she concentrate at school? Do you think Bianca will tell her in the morning or wait until she gets home from school?'

'Probably wait,' Sarah answered, really having no idea when Bianca would tell her daughter that her father had moved out.

He stared straight ahead. His eyes looked haunted. 'I've never felt like a bad father, you know, even when I was here with you, because I knew that Chelsea wanted for nothing, that I spent every available minute with her. I've always taken the time to be with her, to take interest in what she's doing at school, her friends, her homework. Every night I've helped her with spelling. She never could quite get the hang of it. She's gifted in other areas. She loves sports, especially gymnastics. Her teacher really thinks she could have a future. I remember a few months ago when we went to watch her at the school sports day, Bianca thought—'

'David, stop torturing yourself,' Sarah said a little more harshly than she'd intended.

He nodded and took another slug of whisky. 'I always thought it would happen, you know. I never strung you along. I always intended to tell Bianca about you but, since that night, I just knew I couldn't be away from you any longer. It's as though you've bewitched me.'

Sarah smiled. This was a bit more like it. She understood that David would be hurting after seeing his wife so upset, but he was with her now and she was eager for their life together to begin.

'Do you think that feeling would have passed if I'd waited for a while?'

Sarah tried not to be hurt by the inference in his words, but it bit – hard. 'Did you want it to?' she asked, moving away from him slightly.

He shook his head and reached for her hand. 'Don't take it personally. I'm just mixed up right now. It was harder than I thought. Don't take any notice of what I'm saying. You know I want to be with you.'

Those last words held no conviction at all as his mind again began to drift. Sarah kissed his cheek and went to the bathroom. She sat on the edge of the bath as the water filled and the mirror steamed up. She lit musk candles to relax him. She sensed that the night wasn't going to go according to her plan, but he was here, that was the main thing, and if he needed tender loving care, then that's what he'd get. She took a deep breath and returned to the lounge to find him holding his wallet, hunched. His shoulders shook slightly.

'Sweetheart, I've run you a bath.'

He slipped his wallet back into his pocket and wiped his eyes quickly with the sleeve of his jacket. She glanced at the suitcase by the hallway door. 'Shall I unpack while you're in there?'

He shook his head as he brushed past her. 'No, I'll do it tomorrow.'

Sarah returned to the lounge and finished David's whisky. She would have loved a nice hot soak herself, but she guessed that David wasn't in the mood. She took a moment to psych herself, ready for more hurtful words. She wanted to be understanding, she really did, but sooner or later he had to accept that his future was here with her.

Once things had settled, she would meet Chelsea and, on their two-weekly Saturday visits, they could all go to the park and the zoo before coming back here. Sarah would cook tea for them and then David would take her back to Bianca and then come home, to her. She wouldn't try to be a mother to the child – that would be too patronising. She'd try to be her friend. Sarah knew she was a likeable person and couldn't see there being a problem with Chelsea. Once she saw how happy her daddy was, she'd be happy for them both.

She sighed. Of course David would be upset. It was all so fresh. Tomorrow would be a different story when he realised that it wasn't all that bad. Once he made arrangements to see Chelsea every couple of weeks, he'd feel differently. She would have to make sure that he understood that she had no wish to keep him from his child. She would urge him to make those arrangements with Bianca as soon as possible.

She tapped lightly on the bathroom door. 'Do you need someone to wash your back?' she asked, trying the door handle. The door was locked.

'I'll be out in a minute,' he said in a muffled voice.

Sarah frowned at the door, feeling as though she was being shut out of his feelings. 'Are you okay, David?'

'Will you just give me a minute?' he snapped.

Sarah sat on the bed, feeling like an interloper in her own flat. The door opened and David emerged dressed in the white towelling robe that she kept for him.

'I didn't mean to snap, I'm just tired,' he said, kissing her lightly on the forehead the way he might with Chelsea.

Sarah nuzzled her head inside his bathrobe, basking in the clean, fresh smell that radiated from his warm skin. His hair was wet and dripping onto the dressing gown. The hair on his arms was wiry and damp. Her arms rose to encircle his waist to draw him closer. He stepped aside. 'I think I'll just go to bed,' he murmured.

Sarah nodded and went to turn the rest of the lights out. She undressed in the darkness of the bedroom and spooned herself against David's body. She'd waited a long time for this. She arched against him invitingly, rubbing her breasts against his shoulder blades. He moved slightly forward, mumbling again about feeling tired.

Sarah lay on her back, staring at the silhouettes cast on the ceiling from the street lamp outside. A hot tear stung her tired eyes as the feeling of rejection coursed through her. It was new and it hurt. She glanced towards David's body and noted that his breathing had changed, but she couldn't help wondering if he was acting so she'd leave him alone. He had made her feel like a viper, a sex-crazed maniac, when all she wanted was to feel his arms around her, holding her tight.

She turned on her side and faced the wall. She pictured an image taken from an aerial view and realised how different this was to what she'd imagined. In her mind, they should have been entwined in a mass of limbs and joints, either making love or just holding on to each other. The reality was that a foot of space separated them.

Her eyelids grew heavy in the darkness, and she felt the pull of sleep tugging at her. He needed more time, she thought as she felt herself falling. And time was one thing they had plenty of now.

*

She slept deeply and woke at eight thirty, just in time to place a sick call to work. She reached over to feel David's body but found crumpled sheets in his place.

She threw on a dressing gown, hoping he was preparing breakfast for a lazy first day together, but the flat was empty and silent. A cup with the remains of instant coffee had been left on the kitchen sink drainer. She placed her hand around it. The mug was stone cold. He'd been gone for ages. She looked for a note but there was none. She breathed a sigh of relief when she saw his suitcase at the bottom of the bed. It was open. Maybe he'd packed his clothes away, she thought. But the suitcase remained as it had the night before: full, except for the fresh shirt he'd removed to wear for work.

Sarah bent to retrieve the suitcase to pack his clothes into the wardrobe. She stopped herself. No, that was something he had to do himself and she was beginning to wonder if he ever would.

CHAPTER ELEVEN

'I'm still not convinced,' Mark said dubiously as he placed his football boots into his Adidas bag. 'I'm not sure I believe that you left my mother safe and well after the food tasting. It's been a few days and she still hasn't phoned.'

Deb flicked some washing-up bubbles at him. 'Don't knock it, just enjoy it.'

He shook his head as he folded his shorts. A lock of black hair, damp from their joint shower earlier, fell across his eyes. 'I'm going to get a phone call later – I can hear it now. Mr Grant, I'm afraid your mother has been found dead. Stabbed, beaten, shot and trussed up like a turkey. We suspect foul play.'

Deb laughed at his poor impersonation of a police officer.

'And you know I won't be able to testify on your behalf. Spouses can't do that,' he continued, leaning over to kiss her.

'Ah, but you're not my spouse yet, so you could testify about the continued mental torture that I've sustained.'

'Yeah, but what's your friendship with Cher got to do with anything?'

Deb flicked a handful of water at him. 'Get out, and don't come back until your priorities are sorted.'

Deb wiped the kitchen surfaces and turned the radio off. Nothing was going to spoil her mood today. Margie hadn't contacted them by form of visit, telephone or carrier pigeon for a few days, and Deb felt as though she'd been freed on parole for good behaviour. Life looked good. The last few days had shown her how idyllic life with Mark could be without the intrusion of his bloody mother and, for the first time, she was looking forward to making a decision about her own wedding.

Tess sloped into her basket and curled up as Deb reached for the car keys. Deb stroked her head. 'See you later, girl.'

She arrived at the boutique, aware of the excitement that had grown in her stomach, imagining herself gliding down the aisle. Whenever that vision occurred to her she was always gliding alone. She had yet to ask her father if he would do her the honour of giving her away, but she wasn't going to let that spoil her day. She hadn't realised how excited she would be at the prospect of dressing up in a flouncy gown.

'About bloody time. I was beginning to think you'd left us at the altar,' Cher quipped.

'What's up with you?' Deb asked Sarah, who looked a little pale and drawn.

She shook her head. 'Nothing. I'm fine, just a little tired.'

Deb felt her ribs being nudged by Cher. 'All those late nights, I expect.'

'Late nights, yes. Hot, steamy sex, no. We haven't made love since he moved in. We stay up half the night talking about Chelsea. He rings her every hour on the hour and comes off the phone more depressed than before.'

'Yes, but you've got—'

Sarah held up her hands. 'I know, I know. I can't just expect him to leave his life behind without a backward glance, but he still hasn't unpacked his case. It still lies at the bottom of the bed and he lives out of it. It's become a sort of symbol now, and I won't unpack it. He keeps going back home, I mean, to the house, to get more clothes, which he heaps on top of the suitcase, but sometimes he's gone for hours.'

'Do you ask him?'

'I did the first time, but he gave me such a withering look that I haven't asked him since. I don't want to lose him at this stage through being insensitive to his feelings, but I'm beginning to wonder why he bothered; I mean, I'm glad he did. This David is better than no David, but I don't know what to do for the best.'

'Patience is the only thing you can give him,' Deb said.

'Not my strong point, as you both know,' Sarah said, brightening. 'Anyway, enough about me and my problems. Let's go and try on some gorgeous dresses. I've been looking forward to this all week.'

Deb had chosen her dress a couple of months earlier and this was the final fitting. At the same time, she'd chosen the bridesmaid's dresses for Cher and Sarah, although she hadn't told them that. She wanted their outfits to be a surprise.

She pointed to a gaudy pink creation, its layers of taffeta bustling out from the hanging rail. Sequins decorated the bodice all the way up to the high neck. It was the most garish monstrosity Deb had ever seen. It reminded her of something out of a school play.

'That's what I've decided for you,' Deb said seriously. She hid her smile as they glanced at each other, stricken. She wondered how long it would take them to overcome their respect for the bride's wishes and say what they really felt. 'Something wrong?' she asked, deadpan.

Sensing the smile behind her words, they both shook with relief. 'Thank God,' they said in unison.

The assistant Deb had dealt with approached them with a friendly smile, and Deb introduced Cathy to her two best friends. She noted Cathy's almost imperceptible appraisal of their figures, ensuring that Deb had guessed their sizes correctly. She seemed satisfied, and Deb wasn't offended. It was Cathy's job to make sure that everything fitted. She was thorough and pleasant and Deb had enjoyed dealing with her.

'If you'd like to make yourselves comfortable in the dressing rooms, I'll bring the gowns.'

They made their way to the three dressing rooms, side by side, at the far end of the boutique. Deb watched as Cathy surreptitiously locked the door. Final fittings were carried out in private, which was another reason she liked the subtlety of the small, family establishment.

Deb came out of the changing room first with the others close behind.

'Oh God, you look gorgeous,' Sarah said, raising her lace-gloved hand to her mouth.

'Beautiful,' Cher sighed.

Cathy nodded approvingly. 'The straight line of that dress really suits you.'

Deb nodded, wondering who was the person in the mirror.

The fitted panels of the Thai silk bodice framed her torso perfectly. The square-cut neckline hinted at the cleavage beneath. Inch-wide straps rose from the bodice and travelled over her shoulders. She fingered the delicate embroidery on the front panel of the bodice where it trailed to a gentle V, like a corset, which rested on top of her stomach. The skirt hugged her stomach and hips before falling to the ground in a straight line, emphasising her height. There were no folds, or pleats or layers that fussed around her legs, just a thin lining that caressed her bare legs. The crystal star and silver leaf tiara glistened at her in the mirror. Her feet were encased in plain ivory court shoes with a three-inch heel. Her only jewellery was a silver seed pearl bracelet and matching choker.

Deb smiled tremulously. It was exactly what she'd been hoping for. The dress didn't look like something from a ballroom dance competition, yet she felt like a princess.

'Oh blimey, I think I'm going to cry,' Cher said.

'You don't look that bad,' Sarah joked.

Deb turned to look at her two best friends. Their dresses were similar to hers: in satin with a subtle shade of lavender; though where her shoulders were bare, theirs were covered with a fine lace sheath that rose up over the breastbone and down the back but left their arms free.

Cathy stood back, beaming. 'Well I think you all look absolutely—'

'Debra, what a surprise seeing you here. I was only popping in to get some catalogues for you.'

Deb's heart sank as she turned around to find Margie beaming at her. Cathy's assistant reared up behind, red-faced and apologetic.

'I'm s-sorry but she insisted,' the young girl apologised.

The irritation that crossed Cathy's features was nothing compared to her own, but she waved away the girl's apologies. It wasn't her fault. The poor, waiflike creature was no match for the mother-in-law from hell.

Margie dropped her handbag to the ground and approached Sarah and Cher. 'Oh dear, these aren't really suitable, are they?'

Deb gritted her teeth as her whole body tensed.

Margie pulled at the material around Cher's torso. 'I mean there's not enough er… versatility around the bodice.'

'Margie, how dare you say—'

'Well, I must be honest, Debra. You don't want to be let down by the bridesmaids on your big day. There'll be a lot of people watching.'

Deb saw Cher's face colour; Sarah stepped forward. 'Margie, I think it might be a good idea for you to carry on with your shop—'

'Nonsense, dear. I've just about finished and, judging by what you've got those poor girls dressed in, it looks like I arrived in the nick of time.' She turned around. 'Excuse me, but those over there,' she said, pointing to a bunch of layered tulle dresses that Deb was sure belonged to the Tooth Fairy.

'Do you have those in a size ten and' – she turned to appraise Cher – 'and a size sixteen, to be safe? We don't want anything bulging out at the sides, do we?'

Both Cher and Sarah stared at her accusingly, and Deb felt flames of humiliation lapping at her cheeks.

'Margie, we were doing quite well until you came in. Please leave us to it and I promise I'll pop round later and show you what we decided.' Deb hoped the others realised just how much of a sacrifice that was, but Margie waved away her pleas.

'Of course not, Debra. You need a mother's eye to push you in the right direction. Now, girls, go and take those silly dresses off and try on these.'

Deb watched as Margie all but shoved them back into the changing rooms. She turned to Deb with a look of horror on her face.

'And you can't seriously expect to get married in that. It has no style at all,' she said, attracting the murderous glance of Cathy. Deb looked for a crack in the laminate flooring that was wide enough for her to slip through.

'But I don't want a high neckline or fussy material around my neck. It just makes me look pasty and ill,' she snapped.

'No, dear, that's because of that rubbish food you're always cooking. I've noticed that Mark's beginning to look a little peaky, but enough about that.'

She pointed to a dress with a corset bodice decorated with pearls and beads, and with sleeves that were puffy, as though they'd been inflated. The organza skirt was wide and had more layers than a puff pastry cake.

'Assistant, could you get that one for me?' Margie cried, humiliating Deb further. 'And I'll have the satin gloves, the feather slingbacks, the pearl choker, the three-, no, four-foot veil and the long pearl earrings please.'

She thrust them all towards Deb. 'Now go on, Debra – you'll thank me in the end. You just wait and see. You'll look like you've just walked off the pages of a fairy tale.'

Deb gritted her teeth and started to wonder at what cost she was getting this wedding.

'Hey, you two, where are you?' she whispered as she ducked into the first changing room.

'Next door and not very bloody happy,' Cher said.

'Come in here with your clothes. I've got an idea.'

They bustled in and Deb was relieved to see that neither of them had changed into the dresses that Margie had chosen.

'Fancy a bit of fun?'

'If it's at her expense – yes.'

'Okay, start getting dressed and do it quietly.' Deb popped her head out of the changing room. 'Excuse me,' she cried, catching Cathy's eye, 'could we have a little help in here please?'

'Ouch,' Deb cried as Cher's knee caught her in the back.

'Sorry about this but do you have a back entrance?' Deb asked as Cathy approached.

Cathy smiled and pointed to the end of the row of changing rooms. 'There's a fire exit just there.'

Deb nodded. 'Just one more thing.' She nodded towards Margie who was trying on a lavender hat. 'Do you think you could just distract…?'

'Will ten minutes be enough?'

Deb smiled widely. 'Perfect,' she said as she reached for her jeans.

'Don't answer it,' Deb cried as Mark entered the front door and went to pick up the phone. 'I know who it is and you're not going to be pleased.' The phone had been ringing constantly since Deb had walked in the door an hour earlier.

Mark threw his sports bag behind the sofa and sat beside her. 'What now?'

Deb recounted their escapade of running through the high street to avoid his mother, while trying to finish dressing themselves. To her amazement, Mark threw back his head and roared with laughter.

'Aren't you angry with me?'

He shook his head. 'I think it shows great initiative on your part, and the picture of you three running around half-dressed is just too funny for words.'

'But I gave your mother the slip.'

He frowned as the phone started to ring again. He reached over and switched the ringer off. 'And after what she said to Cher, I think she probably deserved it.'

Deb turned to him. 'I do try, you know. I try to get on with her, but sometimes she just makes it so difficult.'

He nodded. 'Stop worrying. I'm not angry. I love her but I'm not blind to her faults. Won't hurt her to be miffed for a while.'

'But she's your mother.'

Mark touched her cheek gently. 'And you're soon to be my wife.'

'But I want the day to be perfect, for both of us, and if she takes the hump and doesn't turn up again we'll have to...'

'Go ahead and get married without her. Honestly, Deb, stop panicking. It's been your choice to postpone the others, but it's not going to happen this time. We're getting married on the fifteenth of September if I have to drag you like a caveman to the altar.'

She leaned forward and kissed him deeply. He looked at his watch. 'I booked a table for eight at Chinos, if you're interested.'

Deb smiled widely. It was her favourite Italian restaurant.

'But that leaves us at least a couple of hours,' he said, stroking her thigh. 'However will we fill the time?'

Deb burrowed her face against his chest. 'I'm sure we'll find a way.'

Deb found herself stuck in traffic on Monday morning. Having left twenty minutes early to reach an appointment with the head office of a chain of estate agents, a spillage on the outskirts of the city centre kept her sitting in her car for almost half an hour. She was tempted to phone Willow to find out what her next appointments were, but she didn't want to switch on the phone. She'd switched it off first thing after it had beeped three messages at her. She had grimaced, knowing they were from Margie and had switched the phone off before she had the chance to leave another.

She'd been looking forward to this appointment since last Wednesday, when she'd spent the morning cold-calling – a horrible job but sometimes necessary to find new leads. The administration manager had sounded cool but pleasant on the phone, allowing her a fifteen-minute slot to make her case. After making some enquiries, Deb had found out who their current supplier was and knew that she could afford to undercut their prices by a healthy fifteen per cent. Not an amount to be sneezed at when this one woman ordered and controlled the printing and stationery for all thirty-seven branches.

She had spent Sunday afternoon leafing through the local papers and searching online to pick up more lucrative businesses where she might get her foot in the door. The orders for paper clips were all well and good, but she needed something meaty to put her sales figures up. The appointment she'd lost because of Margie's food tasting had seriously reduced her figures. With the leads that she'd jotted down at the weekend, if Willow managed to secure appointments for half of them, she'd be rushed off her feet for the next few weeks, but it would be worth it.

She pulled up in front of the offices with five minutes to spare, then rushed to the reception desk and told the young woman who she was.

The girl frowned a little but pressed the buttons anyway. 'She'll be down in a minute. Please, have a seat.'

Deb sat forward, ignoring the girl's curious glances. Had the client changed her mind? Did she have some stray muesli in her teeth?

Lauren Billingham appeared from a side door. She was a plump lady Deb guessed to be in her early thirties.

'I think there's been some confusion.'

'Have I got the wrong time? It's not a problem; I can come back later when you have more—'

'That's not necessary. Your company already has the order.'

'We have?' Deb asked, surprised. She hadn't even opened her briefcase.

Lauren nodded. 'Yes, not more than ten minutes ago. A Mr Stone apologised for your absence and gave us a presentation undercutting our current rates by at least twelve per cent. If your delivery is half as good as he promised, we will enjoy doing business with you.'

Deb barely heard her last words. That bastard, but when… how…?

She made her excuses and left the building. She punched Willow's direct line into the mobile. 'What the fuck is going on?' she bellowed, trembling in her car.

'I've been leaving you messages since seven o'clock this morning, to see if you were all right. Ricky left a note on my desk that you were ill and he was taking your nine thirty appointment.'

'That bastard has been through the electronic diary on the company intranet. I'll fucking kill him,' Deb screamed, aware that the air inside the car was turning blue.

'Shit, I should have known he was lying,' Willow offered.

'It's not your fault. I'm coming in.'

Deb ended the call and felt like crying. She'd been relying on that order to put her back in the running. At this rate she had no chance of getting that job, and she'd have to start searching the Indeed website for a new one.

She pulled up as Milton was approaching his car. He detoured over to her as she punched the alarm key fob.

'Deb, I've been wanting to thank you for pushing that lead my way.'

'No problem,' she said, edging away. She wanted to get into that office and wring Ricky Stone's neck.

'It was very kind of you. I went to the floor below and managed to set up a meeting with—'

'Very good, Milton. I'm pleased for you but I really have to get inside.'

'But you don't understand—'

'No problem. I'll talk to you later.'

She stormed into the building. 'Where is the little shit?'

'Taken the rest of the day off.'

'Well he can bloody well afford to now, can't he?'

Willow looked down at her paperwork. 'I'm sorry.'

'I'm not shouting at you, but I just can't believe that he could stoop so low. This was supposed to be a competition to see who deserved the position, not to see who could steal the best leads.'

Deb wandered into her office. Willow followed carrying the diary.

'I just don't know what I'm going to do.'

'I have his appointments here,' Willow offered meaningfully, waving to a printed copy of the online diary. For a moment, Deb was sorely tempted but she shook her head. It would serve him right, but she couldn't descend to his level. That would make her as bad as him. She didn't want the job if it meant lying and cheating.

An idea began to form. She nodded towards the computer. 'Let's just have a look.'

Willow fired up the system and started to smile, clearly wanting to exact some kind of revenge on Ricky Stone.

'Clear my entries,' Deb instructed.

'Huh?'

'If Mr Stone wants a game, he can have one.'

Deb made herself a coffee and began making plans in her head.

Willow glanced sideways at her. 'Umm… what are we doing?'

'Add these in,' Deb said before starting to dictate entries for the next couple of weeks. The appointments were strewn all over the country.

'If he wants to steal my appointments, he can bloody well have some fictional ones. Put twos by the ones in Wales and threes by the ones in Scotland. He'll be gagging for those.'

Willow had devised a little system of placing a number by each diary entry for all of the sales people. Anything with a one beside it was of little interest, as it signified a first visit that was likely to turn up little results, but anything with a two or three usually meant a definite order.

Willow started searching company names in the areas Deb was dictating.

'Don't worry about that, just make the names up.'

Willow shook her head. 'No, just in case he checks.'

When the diary was filled up, Deb reached into her briefcase and extracted the list she'd built at the weekend.

'Okay, now I need you to make real appointments for as many of these as you can manage; and when you've finished that, go back and make appointments with old customers who don't order from us anymore; and when you've finished that, line up some appointments in the surrounding areas; and when—'

'But you can't. That's far too many for you to do alone.'

'Let me worry about that, and I don't care what time of day the appointments are. Early morning, late night, weekends – just book them, even if they're only small businesses.'

'But you'll kill yourself,' Willow said, looking at the list.

Deb smiled. 'It's the only chance I have, Willow. At the moment, Ricky is leaving me dead in the water. I can't give up yet. After this morning I need—'

'But it'll take weeks to recoup the value of that order he stole.'

'Don't remind me, but it's time I took a leaf out of Milton's book and got down to some serious plodding to get the business.'

Willow nodded and within minutes Deb heard her on the phone cold-calling the businesses she'd listed.

The mention of Milton reminded her of his excitement in the car park. He'd been wanting to tell her something, but she couldn't remember what it was.

Never mind, she thought – she'd catch up with him later and take him for a coffee.

She picked up the phone to join Willow in the unenviable job of more cold-calling.

CHAPTER TWELVE

Cher woke up with a feeling of inadequacy that refused to leave her after two shots of caffeine. *You're useless, you're hopeless*, the devilish voice chanted over and over. It was a voice that visited almost every Saturday morning when she arose from her bed with the whole weekend stretching either gloriously or boringly ahead, depending on whether she was being delusional or honest.

It was the type of inadequacy that is only to be quieted by the resolve to produce something out of a Nigella Lawson cookbook, which she didn't own – probably making her the only woman of sound body and mind who didn't. Good old Nigella, the sex goddess of cooking, she'd heard someone say. It was at the same time that she heard that Nigella ranked at number eighty-four on the all-time bestseller list. That made her envious. Not that sexy, sultry Nigella could make grown men cry kneading dough, but the fact that someone was able to recite that snippet of information.

It had led her to many a bookshop and produced tingles of anticipation whilst riding home with a fresh, brand-new book that would educate her so that she would have interesting and entertaining snippets to quote.

Romantic visions complete with hazy, furry edges had flitted through her mind of being curled up on a sofa, entranced by a book to the extent that she didn't hear the phone or the doorbell, or the title music to *EastEnders*. She bought books with the intention of devouring them. How wonderful to be able to refer to Anna Karenina as a poor, tortured soul who came to a tragic end, or Madame Bovary, a woman ahead of her time. And she could quote these snippets, but only because she'd heard them. She really had no idea why Anna Karenina's end was tragic, or why Madame Bovary was a harlot; although in the case of the latter, from conversations she'd heard, Cher thought maybe she'd founded Girl Power before the Spices had.

She had purchased a dictionary of beliefs and religions and made it as far as Anthropomorphism before the book fell from her grasp, which she felt was a shame because Antichrist would have come next, and that would definitely have given her some insight into the behaviour of her nephews.

On another occasion, she bought the key philosophical writings of Descartes, and almost got past the contents page before casting it aside and picking up her favourite books by Jo Brand which chronicle her opinion of historical figures of history. Cher had become content to let other people quote the classics and trendy reading material whilst she offered, 'Ooh you ought to read what Jo Brand called Henry the Eighth.'

But on this particular Saturday, she needed to take measures to improve her life.

Her eyes wandered along the bookshelves of pages that had never been turned. Her glance swept over one and held. That was it – *Feng Shui*. The pages had remained crisp and new once she'd decided that she couldn't pronounce it, never mind quote it with authority at parties.

She glanced through the book in her normal thorough way of reading, looking at the bullet points only. Hmm, interesting – 'Put a painting of a bear close to your door to ward off burglars,' it said. She didn't have a picture of a bear but wondered if a painting by numbers of a mean-looking koala would do.

She wasn't convinced that how her home was arranged could improve finances, relationships and luck, but it didn't cost any money and, in the absence of anyone to ring and chat to at six in the morning, it had to be worth a try.

Yes, she had sharp-edged objects that were cutting the chi that flowed into her home, and they were not softened by thriving green plants, unless you counted the sick-looking geranium in the corner.

She began to rearrange the furniture to let chi flow into her home positively. The mirror was taken from the bathroom into the dining area to reflect the food on the table, so that the double image meant that she would never go hungry. Anyone viewing her eleven-stone figure would seriously doubt that anyway. She ensured that the mirrors were not placed so that they could cut off anyone's head, which didn't seem to be a problem, as she wasn't aware of any visiting munchkins in the near future.

She did score a couple of points by having a round dining table, considered good for family harmony, which was wonderful seeing as she lived alone.

She searched the house for crystals that would channel positive energy and ward off ill health. The best she could find was an old wind chime made up of dubious-looking dolphins, which was tangled worse than her tights after a spin cycle. She placed it on the coffee table and resolved to untangle it later.

She hurt her back turning her armchairs towards the doors so that she wasn't vulnerable to chi, though it meant she couldn't see the television that had been placed in the corner to help chi circulate.

A little cacti garden thudded into the bin when she read that they create bad chi, but then she decided she couldn't, in all conscience, blame thorny little plants for all her bad luck and retrieved it guiltily.

The phone rang ominously, disturbing her attempts to place her life in order. No one ever called on Saturday morning, especially at eight thirty.

'Cher, it's Mum, and I, well… we need your help…'

'What's wrong?' Cher's mother never flapped, but she was most definitely flapping. 'Aren't you supposed to be on your way to London?'

'That's why I'm calling. Oh dear, Cher, we should all be on the coach in half an hour, but there's a problem…'

Cher's mind drifted off as she recalled her mother's invitation to join them, but once she'd known that it was her mum, dad, Pat and Marlon she had declined. The kids were going to some sort of day camp while they were gone – possibly Broadmoor, she recalled.

'So because of the fire, the kids can't go, and there isn't enough room on the coach: I've checked,' she finished breathlessly.

Having missed a vital piece of information, Cher was at a loss to understand exactly what she was asking.

'I know it's short notice, but could you take them for the day? They'd love to see you.'

What, what, what? Surely she couldn't be asking her to take care of Satan and Lucifer for the day?

One protest had to be worth a shot surely. 'Oh Mum,' she begged as the fear began to invade her body. 'Can't you find anyone else to do it?'

'I've tried but we only received a phone call ten minutes ago, and the coach is going to be in the high street in twenty-five minutes.'

Oh God, why me? she wondered, looking around at her newly Feng Shui-ed environment that obviously hadn't bloody worked. She knew that damn chair was facing the wrong way.

She sighed dramatically to demonstrate the act of martyrdom that she was making on her behalf. 'All right then but—'

'Oh thanks, love. I knew you wouldn't let me down. Marlon's on his way over. Tell him to meet us at the coach.'

Damn, she thought, throwing the receiver back into the cradle. She hadn't even said who was supplying the rope, hazard tape, Valium and tranquilliser gun. A fleeting thought drove her to hide all matches and lighters from their view. The fact that the camp to which they'd originally been destined had succumbed to fire did not instil confidence into her trembling flesh.

She was in the throes of swallowing a handful of vitamins, knowing that she would need them, when a herd of elephants thundered against the door. She opened it with a smile on her face that felt unnatural and was probably a grimace, but Marlon didn't seem to notice.

'Thanks, sis, I owe you,' he said, smiling. 'Now be good for your auntie Cher and I'll see you tonight,' he shouted to the boys, who had bolted past and were already rifling in her panty drawer.

'Go on, go on. Mum said meet her at the coach.'

He shouted his reply from the bottom flight of stairs as she shut the door, unsure whether it was her imagination that the door closed with ominous tension, like a bad horror movie.

Right, she decided. *I'm in control. I'm the adult. If I start as I mean to go on, there will be no trouble all day. Establish your authority*, she told herself, taking a few deep breaths.

'Hahaha I've got a tusk,' cried Jeremy as he came tearing out of her bedroom with a tampon up his nose.

Oh God, what had she let herself in for?

With the distinct absence of toys, it was blatantly obvious that she wasn't going to be able to amuse them inside for very long. The fact that Philip was running round with a pair of lace knickers on his head, with hair pulled through the leg holes, pretending to be a Klingon, brought this fact home to her.

She checked her watch, sure that her parents would be on their way home by now, and realised that she'd be lucky if the coach had left the area.

'Okay, how about a trip into town?' she asked bravely.

'You can't drive, dummy.'

'We'll go on the bus.'

Their noses wrinkled in distaste.

'It's all right, it won't hurt you. In fact, it'll be an adventure, won't it? Now sit still while I get changed,' she ordered in what sounded like a stern, controlled voice in her head, but actually emerged a pleading whimper.

She scrimmaged amongst the clothes littering her floor and grabbed a pair of well-worn Levi's and T-shirt. The sun was shining its early morning promise through the window.

With her newfound confidence, she bustled them out of the door and towards the bus stop. Their delight in a girl who'd unfortunately got her dress caught in the back of her knickers afforded her great embarrassment as she chastised them, probably not quite as strongly as she should have.

The bus trip passed noisily as they scrambled about on the seat behind, squashing their faces against the window. Cher looked around the bus and accidentally caught the eye of an elderly woman with a chequered shopping trolley. She shook her head as she indicated the boys. Cher rolled her eyes in a way that said, 'I don't know who they're with either but you'd think they'd exercise a little control.' Luckily the woman got off the bus first and never got to see that they were with her.

A tour of the market was first on the agenda, which occupied them more than she'd expected. 'Mum never takes us to markets,' Jeremy informed her with a sneer. If he'd have given her fifteen minutes, she might have been able to come up with a smart reply, but a stall of colourful sweets grabbed his attention just in time.

'Can we have some, Auntie Cher?' begged Philip, who could actually look quite loveable when he was pleading for something. She ruffled his hair, trying to like him, and nodded. He allowed her hand to remain on his head until she'd agreed.

'Okay, that's enough,' she protested when the generously sized bags began to strain at the sides. The shopkeeper weighed them quickly, after seeing Jeremy impersonate a walrus with two sticks of liquorice up his nose.

'Seventeen pounds.'

'Wh-What?' she almost choked. For sweets. She knew before opening her purse that even with her 'rainy day' change she didn't have that much.

'MasterCard,' she offered, feeling utterly foolish.

The shopkeeper huffed before taking it, realising that if she reclaimed the merchandise, she wouldn't get the amount she'd weighed. A good few had been thrown down their sweet little throats.

Nearly twenty quid on sweets. Cher barely spent that amount on underwear, never mind confectionery. She decided magnanimously to forgive their extortion with the sweets and treat them to a burger for dinner. The horror on their faces quickly turned to anticipation as she guided them into McDonald's.

'Don't tell me you've never been here before?' They both shook their heads and moved towards her. A sudden protective urge tore through her as she pulled them closer. It lasted until they neared the counter and spied colourful pictures of burgers and nuggets and milkshakes.

She followed them to a corner seat which afforded them a view of a kiddies' birthday party, sectioned off in a small enclosure with seats that were only inches from the ground. She thanked the lord that she didn't have to get down onto one of those. The party organiser was enthusiastic and friendly and learned the names of the eight children quickly. Why had there been no McDonald's parties when she was a kid? Her party had been a few jam sandwiches and lime jelly shared amongst the other kids in the street. And that was when she turned eighteen.

Her Quarter Pounder insisted on falling apart at the seams every time she picked it up, sending watery mayonnaise sliding down her fingers. She should have been receptive to God's attempt to help her diet as He forced the slippery burger to keep falling back into the Styrofoam box. The fact that she felt God was talking to her through a cheeseburger convinced her that she had too much time to think.

Some fidgeting beneath the table awakened her to the fact that these boys weren't going to stay quiet for much longer. She had a last attempt at trying to bite the burger before it jumped but conceded defeat when it landed in a heap on the shiny, rectangular table. A few smirks from the boys had her thinking that maybe a piece of gherkin had strayed to her forehead. She excused herself politely, warning them to stay still while she visited the ladies.

She arrived back at the table just in time. The little gits were eyeing up little Tommy's presents.

An idea occurred to her. 'Hey, kids, how about we go and buy a football and take it to the park?'

Philip's eyes instantly lit up and then sobered as he awaited confirmation from his brother. He nodded his assent, as though doing her some great favour. Her only purpose was to get them out of a built-up, residential area. At the park they could run and burn off a little of that energy that Cher couldn't help being envious of.

'I want that,' Jeremy demanded of the ten-gear mountain bike in the sports shop.

'In your dreams,' she muttered, walking towards the footballs.

'I'll make you sorry.'

'Go ahead,' she said bravely as the colour gathered in his face. She stared on in wonder as tears miraculously appeared and began to course over his cheeks.

He took a deep breath and cried at the top of his voice, 'The lady at Childline said if you keep thumping me—'

'Get over here, you little bastard,' she cried, realising she hadn't done herself any favours in the eyes of the fifty people who had turned to stare. He smiled cunningly through the tears that still ran free. She had to admit that that was a gift. 'Now listen here, I'm gonna take you to the police station myself in a minute and have you charged with mental cruelty and terrorism. If you know what's good for you, you'll stop that crying and set a good example for your brother, or you'll be locked up in a police cell until your parents come back and collect you.'

The sobs ceased immediately, forcing her to wonder once again if she'd been too harsh. Maybe she was the one in the wrong. What was the use of telling him that he couldn't have something if she didn't explain why? How was he supposed to understand that?

She reached for her purse. 'Look, I can't buy it for you because I don't have enough money,' she explained, feeling quite pleased with her own logic. 'You see, Jeremy, if I haven't got the money, I can't buy it, can I?'

'Well put it on your credit card, dummy.'

She snapped her purse shut and walked away. So much for trying a logical explanation. She walked towards the basket of footballs, waiting for some sort of jeering about social services and cigarette burns, but none came.

They followed her out of the store and remained silent until they reached the park. She plonked herself down onto warm grass, secure in the knowledge that she was losing her mind, and that all would become blank and hazy as soon as she travelled to a world where nothing mattered except the next dose of mood-enhancing drugs.

She was in the process of deciding which child to name Chucky when a shadow blocked the sunlight.

'Looking a little frazzled there, Cher.'

'Dan, what are you— I mean…' She didn't care what he was doing or why. It was just good to see a face that wasn't pouting petulantly or baring teeth.

'He brought me,' Dan explained, pointing to a little boy who was throwing a cricket ball into the air with one hand and trying to hit it on descent with the other. He missed every time.

'Yep, just about ready for his trial with the England team.'

She chuckled in spite of her black mood. He did seem to be having fun, even though his tiny forehead was set in concentration.

'Your son?' she asked.

'Yep, that's Jamie,' he said proudly.

'I've been kidnapped by those two terrorists over there, who should be cutting my ear off and posting it for ransom any time now.'

'Rough day?' he asked, sitting down.

She rolled her eyes, too exhausted to explain.

Silence fell between them as Cher realised that she had no right to be enjoying his company after the way she'd treated him at work.

'Listen, about your first day when I snapped at—'

He waved away her apologies. 'Forget it. I admire your loyalty, which I think I've already mentioned, but seriously,

Cher, I haven't jumped into anyone's shoes and your opinion does matter,' he said with an appealing smile. 'After all, we do have to work together.'

She nodded, thankful for his graciousness and the fact that he wasn't going to have her sacked. It wasn't exactly the most challenging job in the world, but it paid the rent.

She glanced sideways at him and wondered how he acquired that cool, relaxed air while the sweat was running out of her like a geyser. His jeans were faded, with grass stains on the knees that matched Jamie's. He didn't keep his arms clamped together in case there were round circles of sweat peeping out from underneath his striped rugby shirt. She crossed her arms over her chest, just in case.

'I was just about to get us an ice cream – want one?'

She nodded with a smile. The burger had put paid to her allotted calories for the day.

He pushed himself up to his feet. 'I'll get your kids one as well, shall I?'

She laughed and shook her head, denying any genetic responsibility for them whatsoever. She would have denied any blood tie at all if she'd thought she could get away with it.

'Nephews,' she offered.

Realisation dawned on his face. 'I wondered why you'd never mentioned them.'

That would be because I can't stand them, she thought but kept her mouth shut.

'Would you keep an eye on Jamie, just in case he's in any danger of hitting that ball sometime soon?'

She was strangely relieved, as he strolled away, that the atmosphere was okay, yet she wasn't sure why. Maybe it was because he was now her boss instead of 'good old Dan', worker's foreman. He seemed to have grown larger since his promotion, she thought, tearing her eyes away as he walked towards her with hands full of ice cream cones. She glanced over at the boys who were tackling each other roughly for the ball. Dan detoured towards the boys, who accepted the Cornettos without knowing him from Adam, and then to Jamie, who walked with him and plonked himself down a few feet away.

'Come here often?' Dan asked with a smile as he sat beside her. His arm brushed hers as he sat.

'If that's your best pick-up line, I'd fire your scriptwriter,' she replied, and instantly coloured. 'I'm sorry I—'

'For what?'

'Well it's not really appropriate to be saying things like that to you now, is it?'

He grinned. 'I'll tell you what, I won't report it as sexual harassment if you don't.'

She smiled and nodded, trying to will the colour out of her cheeks.

He shook his head. 'Don't close up on me, Cher, please. Half the reason I took this job was that I thought we'd get on okay, and maybe have a laugh now and again.'

This time the smile was genuine. It was nice to have been considered as a pleasant person to work with. In fact, it was nice to be considered at all.

'We do need to talk though.'

She knew what was coming. Here was the rebuke for the way she'd spoken to him when he'd first taken the job.

'Umm… I don't know how you feel about overtime, but I hope you'd like the extra money.'

She'd never been offered overtime. She'd asked in the past if Mr Williams needed her to put in extra hours, and have the time off in lieu, but he'd always refused.

'But I'm salaried. I don't get overtime.'

'Actually, you're not. You're classed as one of the engineers,' he said apologetically.

A glob of ice cream fell onto her jeans and remained there. 'I'm what?'

'You're hourly paid, like the lads.'

She absently licked the ice cream, annoyed. Why had no one ever thought to share this information with her? She'd always felt like a peasant amongst the 'ladies' and now she understood why.

'Why has no one ever wondered why I don't walk around with a screwdriver and an air-conditioning unit?'

Dan laughed. 'If you'd ever been downstairs and seen the size of an aircon unit, you'd realise how ridiculous that was.'

He saw her bewildered expression. 'Listen, don't be pissed off about it. Use it to get extra money.'

'How?' she asked, becoming interested.

Dan ran his hand through his hair. 'Well the thing is, I know how fond you were of Mr Williams, but the truth is he's dropped us in it. Everything's gone – disappeared.'

'Huh?' she asked intelligently. She had no idea what 'everything' was.

'Paperwork, contracts, schedules, manuals, warranties – everything.'

She nodded, not knowing what to say. She wasn't sure exactly what was expected of her, but Mr Williams had found it necessary to do all those things himself.

'Indispensable,' Dan offered, as though reading her mind. 'I reckon he must have thought we wouldn't be able to manage without him.'

'Can we?' she wondered, glancing over at Jeremy who was bouncing the ball off his younger brother's head.

Dan shrugged. 'We don't have a choice. This is where the management gets to feel very indignant and stubborn, claiming that "we'll manage without him", and what they really mean,' he said, indicating them both, 'is that *we* will manage without him.' He paused to shake his head at the mess Jamie was making. The child looked like he was foaming at the mouth. 'I'm afraid it's going to mean quite a lot of time spent in the office, working together.'

That wouldn't be too bad, she decided, as long as Michael Hunter got to find out what a loyal and dedicated employee she was. He'd realise just how much of her valuable social time she was prepared to sacrifice for the good of the company at time and a half.

She opened her mouth to ask what sort of work she'd be doing and felt it being forcibly slammed shut as a leather baseball hit her on the back of the head, sending the rest of her ice cream slithering down her T-shirt and uncomfortably into her bra.

Dan tried not to laugh as he looked around for the culprits. Cher didn't need to. They were the ones with the horns and forked tails.

'Get over here you little' – she stopped as she spied Jamie looking in her direction – 'monsters,' she finished lamely.

They swayed towards her, holding their stomachs, eyes bright with laughter.

'Who's he?' Jeremy asked rudely, nodding towards Dan.

'The man you accepted ice cream from,' she snapped, still smarting from the blow.

Jeremy eyed Dan suspiciously and then looked towards Jamie. 'Is he with you?'

Dan nodded, trying not to smile at Jeremy's attempt at an intimidating stare.

'Saw him trying to hit that cricket ball. He's crap.'

'Jeremy,' she snapped as Philip began to chuckle.

Dan nodded. 'Well it might be a good idea if a boy as smart as you could try and teach him then.'

No, no, her mind screamed as she glanced at Jamie, who was popping the last bit of Cornetto into his mouth. *Don't do it*, she pleaded with her eyes. *Don't let that sweet little boy become infected by them*. It would take them less than an hour to teach him how to hot-wire cars and build incendiary devices.

Jeremy nodded, accepting the challenge. He motioned for Jamie to follow and take his cricket bat with him.

'I'm not sure that was such a good idea,' she said fearfully.

'They'll be fine; they're just kids.'

Even so they both turned to face them. Cher was pleasantly surprised to hear a joyous laugh come from Jamie's mouth as Jeremy hit the cricket ball high into the air.

A sudden feeling of sadness washed over her as she watched Jamie laughing with delight at Jeremy's antics.

'Does he miss her?' she asked before she could stop the words tumbling out of her mouth.

Dan needed no explanation of the question. Dan talked little of his wife, but Cher knew she had tragically died of breast cancer.

Dan shook his head. 'He was just eighteen months old when Rachel died, so I'm not sure how much he remembers. He did point to a photo of the two of them together and said "Mummy" a couple of years ago. I tell him how wonderful she was and how much she loved him, but he often looks at me blankly, as though he can't put the two things together and he doesn't know who I'm talking about.'

A lump of emotion formed in her throat as she watched the little boy laughing with her nephews.

'It's okay – we do all right,' he said, following her gaze. 'He's close to Rachel's parents, and stays overnight with them every other weekend, but for the most part, we spend our time smoking, drinking and watching inappropriate YouTube videos.'

Cher laughed, loosening her constricted throat as her eldest nephew started hitting the ball further and further away.

Being a panic merchant, she shouted for Jeremy to stop being silly. He saw her chastisement as a challenge to infuriate her further and misaimed the next shot, narrowly missing a family enjoying a picnic.

'That's it,' she barked, raising herself from the grass.

Dan put his hand on her arm and eased her back down. 'Let me try.'

She agreed, enjoying the feel of his hand on her arm. It was rough in places, but his touch was soft.

He kneeled on the floor and called them around him as though it were a huddle in the middle of a basketball game. Whatever he was saying had their attention. With what could he be threatening them? she wondered. Was it a night in the London Dungeon surrounded by ghosts and monsters, which would suit Jeremy down to the ground? Was it a visit to Worm-wood Scrubs to show them their future home?

Dan returned to sit beside her. She turned to smile triumphantly at him as the ball once again flew towards Jeremy. He raised the cricket bat, aimed it at the ball and tapped it lightly towards Jamie, who missed it but thoroughly enjoyed running after it.

'I'm not sure sport is where his expertise lies,' Dan observed lightly.

'What the hell did you do?' she fumed. All day the little thugs had been murder. Nothing had worked. She'd tried to be firm, she'd tried to be fair and she'd tried to be reasonable for hours, and this man had the nerve to exert control in a matter of minutes.

'Nothing.'

'Hey, I watched from here. You didn't have a chance to feed them drugs or perform full-frontal lobotomies, so tell me what you did.'

'It's my secret. If I tell you, I'll have to kill you.'

She considered for a moment. 'It's worth it, just tell me,' she demanded, aggravated. 'I was almost at the point where binding and gagging were the only options left to me.'

'Did you give them a reason?'

'A reason for what?'

He eased himself back using his hands to support him. 'Do you spend much time with them?'

'Not if I can help it,' she replied honestly.

She saw what he was driving at. She wouldn't see them again other than at her parents' house, where she would run from room to room or hide in the linen cupboard to avoid them.

'So why would they behave for you? It's not like you're going to take them out next week either,' she asked sulkily, feeling the weight of her own failure.

'Nope, not next Saturday,' he said cagily.

'What do you mean?'

He forced his expression into a sombre pose. 'I promised them we'd go and see the new *Star Wars* film in about an hour.'

'You didn't?'

He shrugged. 'Why not? We're going anyway. I think I mentioned it, so why don't you come along?'

The offer was tempting, if only for the fact that they would be in a dark movie theatre and they would be forced to be quiet for a while. Although *Star Wars* wouldn't have been her first choice, it might give her the opportunity for a nap.

'So, basically, your great achievement was nothing more than bribery and corruption?'

'Absolutely.'

They sat and chatted easily in the fading sunshine, about work more than anything, although most of the time she was thinking about how wonderful it would be to tell her friends of something she had done at the weekend. Her normal response was 'Oh quiet, you know', as though she'd taken the opportunity of some quality time to relax from the hard labours of the week and attain some inner calm. The only inner calm she managed at the weekend was found at the bottom of an Asti bottle.

Dan motioned for the boys to follow to his car, to dump the sports equipment. Just as the boot was being closed, her ears were assaulted by the ringing of a mobile phone. Her head turned towards Dan. He shrugged and shook his head.

'It's me,' cried Jeremy, producing a phone from his jacket pocket that she could see was a much newer model than her own.

From the excited conversation she guessed it was Marlon. 'Yeah, yeah, we're going to the pictures with Cher and her new boyfriend…'

She ripped the phone out of his hand, mortified. 'He's not my boyfriend,' she cried down the receiver as passers-by turned to look. 'He's my boss,' she shouted, and then realised that she probably hadn't done herself any favours with that statement. Marlon said it was a shame he wasn't her boyfriend, as he would have liked to bestow the good news on their mother, who would have asked if Christmas had come early. She thanked him for his generosity of spirit, assured him everything was fine and she'd look forward to seeing him later.

Once inside the darkness of the theatre, the tension of the day eased out of her and a light-heartedness had taken its place. So much that she started throwing popcorn at the two heads in front of her.

'Oh, Auntie Cher, grow up,' Jeremy snapped.

Duly chastised, she ate her popcorn in silence.

The boys turned mute as the opening credits rolled. Dan's leg fell absently against hers. She could feel the taut muscle of his thigh beneath the denim. Heat flared in her cheeks and she concentrated harder on the popcorn, until she felt Dan's leg fidgeting against hers.

'Christ, I'm bored rigid,' he whispered.

'Me too.'

'I've been to plumbing conferences that were more interesting than this.'

She laughed loudly, provoking stern looks from three small faces, which she felt was extremely ironic after what she'd coped with during the day.

Dan leaned slightly in his chair, offering her a sip of his watery cola. She tried to catch the straw in her mouth, but he moved the tumbler backward and forward, making her giggle.

'Sshhh…' Philip cried from in front.

The boys cheered uproariously as the credits rolled up, and she tried to instil a bit of life into a back end that was so numb it felt like it had been chopped off.

Jamie fell asleep in the back of the car as Dan drove them home. The others weren't far behind, once they'd finished arguing about who was now to be known as Finn.

After making sure that Jamie was okay, Dan helped her get the two lolling bodies upstairs. Before he left, he thanked her for a pleasant time, which normally only happened after she'd slept with someone.

She cursed as her foot met with the umbrella stand. Panic flooded her mind, thinking she'd been burgled, but it was just the way the furniture was laid out from the Feng Shui caper that she felt must have happened days ago.

Before the kettle boiled for hot chocolate, a soft tapping at the door signalled the return of Marlon.

He enquired about their behaviour, to which she lied, and then handed her a small package, which was a miniature beef-eater in a glass case, resplendent in red and black finery. She was just about to thank him for his thoughtfulness when he smiled facetiously. 'I thought someone had better bring you a man.'

He smiled at the boys on the sofa. Philip was comatose and Jeremy was barely conscious. Marlon scooped up the younger boy and helped Jeremy stagger to the door.

'Thanks again, sis.'

'Cool day, Auntie Cher, cool day,' Jeremy mumbled through exhausted lips.

She leaned forward impetuously and kissed them both.

When they were gone, she undressed quickly and fell asleep surrounded by a romantic haze, and the realisation that the day could only have been better if Dan had been Michael Hunter.

CHAPTER THIRTEEN

The following Monday morning, for the first time in ages, Cher was on time. She entered the office to find the contents of filing cabinets strewn all over the floor, a jigsaw of computer discs covering her desk, and Dan looking as stressed as a spider at an arachnophobia convention.

They spent the morning on the floor, trying to trace the documents that supported what the department did. Dan thought it was worth a day trying to find them, but after that they would need to start from the beginning. The 'we' terminology caught her attention. It felt good to be part of a 'we'.

There had been one moment of acute embarrassment the previous week when Dan shook his head disbelievingly and observed, 'You really don't know very much, do you?' She lowered her head apologetically. He smiled reassuringly and said that was no fault of hers. The rest of the week had been spent slaving over paperwork that would point them in the right direction, and, as much as working from six in the morning until nine at night was physically and mentally exhausting, she enjoyed being a necessary part of the process.

On Wednesday night, as she'd been trying to seek his opinion on Michael Hunter, Dan had seemed detached and distant.

'Just tell me if I'm getting on your nerves,' she offered tartly. She'd thought their growing friendship meant she could seek his advice.

'No, you're not. I just think you're wasting your time, that's all.'

'Wh… but… I… er thanks a lot, mate. I mean, I know I've got more rings than the Michelin Man, but that doesn't make me a bad person.'

He laughed loudly. 'I didn't mean that. I just meant that I don't think you're right for each other.'

She cocked her head to the side. 'Look, ham and cheese are completely different but they both taste good on a bap with Branston pickle.'

'Maybe…'

'You think he's too good for me, is that it?' she challenged. She wanted to know why he thought she was reaching so far above her station. It wasn't that she particularly disagreed with him, but the fact that he thought so bothered her.

'No, actually, it's not that at all,' he snapped. 'Have you finished that report yet?'

She tapped loudly on the keyboard to show her irritation, which did nothing except produce three lines of gobbledygook. She wanted to let it rest but couldn't. At eight o'clock in the evening, she didn't feel the same sense of professionalism as she did during normal hours. It had been kicked off with the shoes that lay beneath the desk as she padded around the office, barefoot, while Dan sorted paperwork on the floor.

Dan sighed and returned his attention to the Contracts folder. 'I think you just need to find out what you want, Cher,' he murmured.

Of course she did. And that was something she could decide over one cappuccino and cheese toastie. Didn't he understand that she'd spent the last ten years trying to work that one out?

'I mean, do you want to have kids?'

She'd never really made up her mind completely on that score. Some days she did and some days she didn't, so until she could rent them on a temporary lease, she felt it probably wasn't a good idea to rush into anything.

'Because I'm not convinced,' Dan continued, 'that Michael Hunter wants the same things as you.'

'Humph,' she said intelligently, just managing to stop herself saying that that was okay because she wanted whatever he wanted, realising that it made her sound pathetic.

'But if someone had told you not to go after Rachel, would you have listened?' The words almost burned in her throat for no apparent reason.

A shadow passed over his face but his smile chased it away. 'She actually cornered me behind the bike shed and offered to buy me a Mars Bar from the school cafeteria. How could I refuse?'

'Did you let her?'

'Of course.'

'You tight-fisted…'

'Hey, I thought you women liked the modern man,' he said, holding his hands up in defence.

Cher's hand was raised, poised to throw her pencil at him, as Michael Hunter sauntered into the office.

'Glad to see you're having a good time at the company's expense,' he said, frowning.

His hands were in his trouser pockets, which pulled the fabric of his trousers tighter across his high, sporty bottom. He wore no jacket, and his light blue shirt was open at the neck.

'What do you expect at this time of night?' Dan snapped without looking up from the floor.

Michael's lips tightened slightly, but he let the comment pass. 'Just thought I'd see how you were getting on in your new position.'

'And of course you knew we'd still be here at this hour with the mess that this department is in.'

'You shouldn't see things as a problem, Daniel. You should see them as challenges to be met and conquered.'

Dan snorted in reply.

Michael perched on the edge of Cher's desk. 'Any coffee, sweetheart?'

Cher opened her mouth to answer.

'It's all gone,' Dan snapped, nodding towards the empty percolator.

'It's okay,' Cher offered. 'I'll make a fresh pot.' She'd do anything for him to call her sweetheart again.

Cher grabbed the empty pot and went to the kitchen next door. As she turned the water off, she heard voices.

'Do you really think you should speak to her that way?' Dan asked in a ground-out whisper. 'She's a person with a name, not your sweetheart.'

'She likes it. It makes her feel special.'

'It's inappropriate and gives her the impression…'

'Oh, Daniel, lighten up, for goodness' sake. It's harmless and why should it bother you?'

Cher listened closely, unable to understand the exchange between the two men. What was Dan's problem?

'Oh, I see – touched a raw nerve, have I?'

'Don't be ridiculous,' Dan spat.

'Sorry, Daniel, I had no idea that you felt so strongly about…'

Cher missed the last few words as Michael's voice lowered to a whisper.

'But I'll be sure to bear it in mind,' he said with a smile as Cher re-entered.

He'd repositioned himself on the sofa and had one arm draped across the back. His right foot rested nonchalantly on his left knee.

'You're an absolute darling, Cher. We must see about getting you transferred upstairs where your assets would be better appreciated.'

Dan's head snapped up and he gave Michael a withering glance.

Michael smirked. 'Yes, I'm sure we could find you a nice little office, not too far from mine. After all, you were invaluable during my little stint down here.'

Cher smiled and said nothing. She sensed that something was going on between the two men, but she didn't know what and thought it was best to keep her mouth shut, even though she wanted to whoop at the thought of working more closely with him. Her heart swelled; she'd been right after all. Michael did care for her and wanted her close by.

'What do you say, Daniel – you could manage without her, couldn't you?'

Cher got the impression that he was deliberately provoking Dan now, though she couldn't understand the animosity that emanated from Dan.

'I would think that's Cher's decision, not mine,' he grunted.

'And I think we both know what she would choose, don't we?' he said, rising to his feet. 'Thanks for making the coffee, sweetheart, but I can't stay.'

'See you soon?' Cher ventured bravely.

He gave her a dazzling smile.

'Of that you can be sure.' He walked towards the door, trampling all over Dan's sorted piles of paperwork on the floor. 'Keep up the good work,' he said to Dan as he closed the door.

Cher recalled their earlier conversation. 'Do you think Michael Hunter is a modern man?' she asked, remembering the way he'd let her carry those boxes.

'Damn that man to bloody hell,' Dan cursed, throwing an empty folder across the room.

'I'm trying my best,' she apologised, feeling the full weight of their predicament resting on her shoulders. Maybe if she'd paid more attention, Mr Williams wouldn't have been allowed to leave them in this mess.

He turned, confused. 'What... oh, Harry you mean? Yes, of course.'

'But we're making some progress, aren't we?'

He nodded. 'Do you feel like getting out of here for an hour? This office is starting to feel like a monkey enclosure.'

She agreed, frowning at his preoccupation.

'What is it, Dan?' she asked as they walked out into the falling darkness. The suit he was forced to wear still didn't fit him psychologically. Most days, the tie had been discarded by lunchtime, and the top two buttons of his shirt unlocked to expose a couple of sandy-coloured hairs trying to escape.

He thrust his hands deep into his pockets. 'I'm just feeling a bit pissed off that we're in such a mess. I feel like I've been set up as the fall guy for everything that's not there, ready for when the auditors come in.'

'So take your own advice.'

He turned his head questioningly.

'Remember what you said to me in the park. Don't be pissed off. Use it. It's a chance for you to show those idiots what you can do.'

'To be honest though, Cher, I don't really know what I'm doing. I'm an engineer, for God's sake.'

'And I've been nothing more than a typist for the last eight years, but I'm having a jolly good try.'

He made no reply as they turned into the high street. It was deserted except for a couple coming out of the chip shop. The smell got the better of her. She hadn't eaten since breakfast. 'Fancy sharing?' she asked. He shrugged and waited outside.

They sat on a bench in front of an Oxfam shop.

'Did you want to be an engineer forever?' she asked, thrusting the cone towards him.

He shook his head. 'I just didn't think I'd be forced into it,' he admitted. 'I like the challenge of doing something new. I even like the slight increase in salary, but I can't get rid of this feeling that I've been set up. Two weeks since I took this job and we've been trying to salvage something out of this mess, and we're no closer than we were then.'

She could see his fear. If auditors came in now, they'd be slaughtered and probably both lose their jobs.

'Then it's up to us to make sure we shock them, isn't it? After all, we do have the element of surprise on our side. No one will be expecting us to succeed.'

'Why do you always do that, Cher? Why do you always put yourself down?'

She shrugged and rummaged in the cone for the last chip. She knew why she did it: if you insulted yourself first, there was nothing anyone else could say to hurt you. She'd learned it at school when the other kids realised how wacky her parents were. Insults and jibes had been an almost hourly occurrence, and that was the way she'd chosen to fight it.

She balled up the chip cone and threw it in the bin, which reeked of rotten fruit and dog pee. 'Come on, Daniel Rickman, I've had enough of this moping. I'm taking you back to the office, pouring you a coffee and then we're going to attack that paperwork like demons on speed.'

'Coffee and chips. Christ, Cher, you know how to show a bloke a good time.' He laughed.

That was better. Long hours, hard work, disbelief and anger at their predicament she could deal with. Seeing him lose hope was not acceptable.

'So when we get back to the office, we'll list the most important things to have in place by the time the auditors come in. We'll concentrate on health and safety policies, risk assessments and—'

'Slow down.'

She hadn't realised that her legs had been speeding up at the same rate as her mouth. Dan leaned forward to open the door for her.

'Okay, on one condition: tomorrow night you'll let me repay the favour of dinner.' He blushed slightly. 'I mean, tonight was a hard act to follow, but do we have a deal?'

Lost for words for the first time she could remember, she merely nodded and ushered him inside.

The act of telephoning her mother she prepared for with the precision of a military coup. The coffee was the correct temperature; the television was turned down so she could hear the appropriate cheerful whoops. It was news that warranted celebration.

She answered on the second ring and launched into a monologue about Fred's fiasco at the doctor's with his ingrown toenail. Cher grimaced at the phone. It was a sight that had been paraded before her on her last visit, and not one that she would forget easily.

She felt like a fish as her mouth opened repeatedly at the mere promise of an approaching pause.

'Mum, listen,' Cher managed to interrupt as she launched into the problems with next door's cat crapping in the borders. 'I won't be able to make it tonight.' She paused for dramatic effect. 'I've got a date.'

The silence echoed through the handset. 'Mum, are you there?' she asked, with visions of her mother prostrate on the ground, gasping for air.

'Really, Cher,' she said frostily. 'If you don't want to come, you only have to say.'

'No, Mum, honestly, I really have got a date,' she insisted, wondering why her mum had more trouble believing that than the 'my bike has a headache' story.

'Well, if you really say so.'

'Sorry, Mum, I'll have to go. The hamster's climbing out of the cage.'

'But you haven't got a—' she heard as she ended the call and then stared at her phone. What had possessed her to say hamster? Now she'd either have to get one or make up some excuse about its untimely demise. She was just relieved to be off the phone. How could her own mother be so disbelieving that she had a date, with an actual man?

She unloaded the contents of her trip to Superdrug: conditioning shampoo with added moisturiser; face cleanser with added moisturiser; shower gel with built-in moisturiser; Veet leg cream with added moisturiser; and some deodorised foot spray – without moisturiser – due to it being so hot. The last thing she wanted was to cream and pamper herself and have her feet smell like the sole of a pig farmer's welly.

The two hours between getting home and arriving at the restaurant she had planned to the last minute, even so far as doing a practice run. Although, she had to admit to feeling a little foolish sitting on the side of the tub pretending to shave her legs. She had even tried out her new hair straighteners, but after clamping the jaw-like contraption around her curls for longer than necessary, her hair was so straight it was pointing at her shoulder.

So far, so good, she thought, making a pot of coffee to keep her alert and focused. She was only five minutes off schedule. She showered, enjoying the red-hot needles pounding her skin. She stepped out of the shower and prepared to cream legs that really weren't too bad. She caught a red flash in the mirror and froze. The water had been hot and she looked like a walking radish. Shit, she cursed, wondering if that top layer of skin would grow back before seven thirty. Cool down, cool down, she instructed her scalded skin urgently, wondering why she hadn't felt the pain that surely should have had her wrapped in gauze.

She rubbed atrocious green cream all over her legs, trying to get into the mood for romance, which was almost impossible to do: Dan had only been polite in asking her out.

She scraped the goo off her legs, trying to look like the woman on TV, but she didn't have wobbly green stripes, like minty toothpaste, running down her legs. After close inspection, she deemed them complete and moved onto the hair.

The wound-up towel revealed a mass of curls that fell across her face in what she would have liked to call a sexy, gypsy fashion but actually made her look like a rain-drenched poodle.

Her next task was to rub a little fake tan over the sticks of white chocolate that were protruding from her dressing gown. It was a balmy night and bare legs were necessary. The instruction leaflet seemed to be far too long and complicated, so she discarded it. How hard could it be? She rubbed the cream smoothly halfway up her thighs. That was a safe distance, as there'd be no action in that area, thank you very much.

A tingle of delight shot through her as she approached the little black dress that she'd been dying to wear since picking it up in a half-price sale. An array of spaghetti straps, like a spider's web, caressed her smooth shoulders before leading down to a square-cut bodice. The dress hugged her down to the hips before folding into generous waves of material that caressed her calves as she sashayed in front of the mirror. But those damn straps were tighter than they'd been last night. She moved one to the side, revealing a thin red line that travelled down and over her breastbone. Shit, that was all she needed. If the straps moved just a fraction, he'd be able to play a game of noughts and crosses on her. Great, she was not only his date, she could also double as a board game.

She frantically searched her wardrobe for an alternative, but nothing suited the picture in her head: a vision of her looking seductively sexy in a 'little black dress' with cascades of black curls tumbling over her shoulders. There was no such thing as cascade with her hair, and the curls weren't tumbling – they were falling to their deaths over her branded shoulder. No, the black dress would have to do.

Her watch told her that her schedule wasn't going to plan. She cursed loudly and thanked her lucky stars that going out with Dan was just a practice, and she was beginning to realise just how out of practice she was. She promised herself that once this night was over, she would spend one night a week preparing for a date, so that when the time came for a real one, she'd at least be able to get ready without the supervision of a responsible adult.

The timer on the cooker sounded to tell her that she was supposed to be booking a taxi. She grabbed her black stilettos that had only graced her feet once, but her foot wouldn't go in. Of course, she'd bought those shoes in the winter when she'd been wearing tights, and now her feet were swollen because it was warmer. She scrambled in her closet to find anything else, but after rifling through a pair of hippy sandals, work shoes, trainers and snow boots, she realised that the shoes were going to have to fit, even if it meant losing a couple of toes.

*

She made no attempt to strike up conversation with the taxi driver, who weaved in and out of the traffic on the dual carriageway, for fear that light conversation might cost her her life.

The taxi came to a thudding halt, almost giving her whiplash. As she leaned forward to hand him the money, she felt something tickle the inside of her breast. She stole a quick glance to see that it was snowing from her armpit.

She climbed out of the taxi, right into the only puddle in the entire Black Country. The harassed driver pulled away abruptly, sending a few more spots of liquid onto her 'golden brown' legs. She turned her head, wondering at the sudden sewer smell, and almost cried when she realised that the acrid stench she was looking around for was coming from her feet and the drain overflow into which she'd stepped. The spots that had been deposited onto her lower legs had left marks like tiny bullet holes on the skin. Great, the bottle had said waterproof, but it hadn't claimed any protection against murky, turgid drain water.

Dan was seated as she entered the restaurant. He glanced at his watch apprehensively before looking up. She gave him a dazzling smile to avert his attention from the full-frontal view of her spotted legs, which looked like she'd been sunbathing under a colander.

He stood self-consciously as the waiter withdrew a chair for her. She'd always found that a tricky practice. Did he push as she sat or did she sit as he pushed? Either way, split-second timing was imperative.

They leaned towards each other not knowing whether they should kiss, hug, rub noses or shake hands. They both laughed before Dan instructed the waiter to give them a few minutes.

'It's lovely,' she murmured, glancing around. The tables were small and intimate with a low floral arrangement of yellow roses and baby's breath.

Her eyes ran along the scrumptious selection of dishes, but she was determined not to appear greedy. She could always have a plate of oven chips when she got home.

'Ready?' Dan asked as the waiter approached.

'I'll have the flower power salad to start, and the fresh tuna salad for main course please.'

Dan glanced sideways before ordering the calamari followed by Caribbean chicken.

Her mouth watered at the thought of it, but she merely smiled.

'What the hell is flower power?' Dan asked as the waiter retreated.

'A selection of edible flowers with a low-fat dressing.'

Dan pushed the roses towards her. 'Why not just have that?'

She chuckled, pushing it back. 'It's okay for you. You don't have to live your life as though Joe Wicks is watching.'

'Hmm… I think he may be a little busy this evening, so you might be safe to eat something that's not a salad, which is surely gonna stump you when it comes to dessert.'

'Did Mr Hunter come down to the office after I'd left?' Cher asked. Dan had sent her off home early after the hours they'd put in the night before. She'd been mildly anxious that he'd come seeking her assistance on some major project while she'd been gone.

Dan took a sip of water before answering.

'No, Cher, he didn't appear and that's fine with me.'

'You really don't like him, do you?' she asked, seeing the hint of thunder that passed over his face.

'It's not that I dislike him intensely, I just disagree with some of his opinions and policies, that's all.'

'Like what?' she challenged as the waiter approached.

'I don't want to spend the entire evening talking about Michael bloody Hunter,' he snapped. 'And I think it would probably end in an argument if we did.' He lowered his voice as the waiter reached the table.

She took a moment to gaze at Dan's mound of squid rings before glancing at her plate of leaves. Rich, tantalising smells of garlic and lemon emanated from his steaming dish, whereas hers looked as though she'd been to the garden centre.

Dan saw the expression on her face and shook his head.

The waiter offered Chablis or Muscadet. Dan deferred to her. She deferred back, aware that she wouldn't be able to pronounce either with the finesse of the waiter. Dan chose the Muscadet.

She forced an expression of enjoyment onto her face as she speared a leaf that looked suspiciously like the ones in her mum's borders that next door's cat kept pissing on. She pushed it to the side of the plate.

'Food okay?' Dan asked.

She nodded with a piece of curly lettuce protruding from her mouth.

Dan laughed. 'Liar. Here, try this,' he offered, guiding a perfect circle of calamari towards her. She closed her eyes and savoured the taste.

Dan moved the flower arrangement to the side and positioned his plate in the middle of the table, handing her a fork. She protested weakly, but he insisted. There was something frighteningly intimate about sharing a plate of food, much to the disdain of nearby diners.

Her leg slipped off the other under the table – damn moisturiser.

'Ouch,' Dan cried as he leaned down and rubbed his shin. She decided to share her 'getting ready' experience with him. After all, it wasn't a real date.

'Oh well,' he said, laughing as she finished her story. 'A nice bath later and you'll be okay.'

She stared in horror. 'Oh God, you sound just like my mum.'

'Thanks!'

'No, it's just that she thinks a good bath cures all evils – teenage thugs, looters, pillagers, serial killers – just give them all a nice long soak.'

'My dad feels the same about national service.' He lowered his voice to a deep rumble. '"We never had these problems when I was a lad. We had respect."' He rolled his eyes, indicating that he'd heard those words many times. 'I wouldn't mind but he didn't even do it. Asthma sufferer.'

'What are they like – your parents?' Damn her need to hear about other people's families, in the hope that somewhere there were some like hers.

'Well, my dad has worked for the same car line for thirty years. He's a "with chips" sort of bloke who spends every spare minute in his garden shed pottering but never has anything to actually show for it.'

Hmm, that sounded pretty normal. Maybe his mother had been imprisoned for killing the local vicar or something.

'My mother's one of those that answers simple questions with: "You know who I mean, Daniel, he was sitting on the same table as Aunt Alice with the prosthetic breast, in between Cousin Humphrey and his tarty wife, opposite Justin – who has to be gay with those tight trousers and that earring."'

He paused for breath as she used a napkin to wipe the tears from her eyes. His whole demeanour and mannerisms had altered to accommodate his impersonation, which had caused a few people to turn and stare. Dan ignored them. 'Oh, and my sister specialised in setting free all the local battery hens she could find before leaving for a kibbutz in Israel.' He shook his head. 'She's a little strange, I suppose, but we always got on okay as kids.'

Cher felt herself brightening at his admission. 'Do you keep in touch?'

'Occasional postcards but I have no return address. She's been home twice in nine years. Mum and Dad don't seem able to communicate with her anymore.'

'Do you see yourself ending up like them?' she asked, to see if he had the same fear as she had: she dreaded finding herself cooking the Sunday lunch dressed as Alice in Wonderland.

Dan shook his head. 'I don't want a garden shed,' he said meaningfully. 'Do you see yourself ending up like your parents?' he asked as she took a mouthful of wine.

Her only choice was to spit it back out or allow it to continue its journey the wrong way, which seemed like the best option, but brought on a choking fit.

'Hell no,' she spluttered.

'It's all right,' Dan explained to the curious onlookers. 'It's not the food. I just told her that I don't want us to be swingers anymore.'

Their shocked expressions did nothing to aid her as the coughing turned to laughter.

Dan turned calmly back to face her. 'Are they that bad?'

She pulled herself together and reiterated some of the events of her childhood, like when her parents turned up to the junior school nativity play dressed as Mary and Joseph, and how she hadn't told them about the production of *Star Wars* the following year. God only knew she didn't want them turning up dressed as Han Solo and Princess Leia, which was not a sight she hadn't seen before.

She paused, enjoying Dan's amusement. 'It must have been fun though,' he observed with a light in his eyes and a look that said it explained so much.

'Oh yeah, it was great at times. It just pissed me off when my mother named my imaginary friend just because she'd only had one shot at the "name the female child" game. I didn't even want an imaginary friend but she insisted.'

Dan roared with laughter. 'I'd like to meet them.'

'Yeah, you and most of the psychiatrists in the country,' she said fondly. But he was right: her early years had been fun, if a little wacky. Her parents were happy and they still loved each other, so she couldn't complain.

'Of course, you're my new imaginary friend. Because they'll never believe that you exist. I don't go on dates, you see. I emit some sort of anti-men repellent.'

A slight frown cooled his features and quickly vanished, but not before she saw it. Oh dear, maybe she shouldn't have referred to it as a date. It was nothing more than a 'thank you' for all the late nights and extra working.

She felt herself redden at her goofiness, but Dan had the good grace to change the subject. The waiter approached bearing their main courses. She had almost forgotten that they were here to eat, and when she saw even more lettuce leaves on the plate coming her way, she almost wished they weren't. Dan caught her look and laughed.

'I'm sorry but do you think you could change that dish for the same as mine please?' Dan asked pleasantly.

'Of course, sir,' the waiter said without altering expression. He did a sharp turn and walked away without having set the plates down.

'If you're not going to touch your meal, it might as well be something I can finish.'

She accepted defeat. 'Yours did look delicious.'

'I've never really had a chance to ask what you like to do. We only ever seem to talk about contracts and spreadsheets.'

Oh God, she thought, *be interesting, think of something I do*. 'I like to read,' she said, hoping he'd leave it there, visualising her spending the weekend immersed in Deepak Chopra and Freud instead of Sidney Sheldon and John Grisham.

'What?' he asked. Damn him to hell. She would have to be honest. For some reason that she couldn't fathom, she felt he'd know if she lied to him.

'What do you do when you're not cracking the whip at me?' she asked in return, more to get him away from realising just how empty her life was.

He thought for a second. 'I usually relax by having a potter on the wheel. Excuse the pun.'

She stared blankly.

'Pottery. I like to dabble in clay.'

A vision of Patrick Swayze and Demi Moore swam romantically before her eyes. Dan continued. 'I'm really not very good but it unwinds me. When I first started, my efforts looked more like sunken soufflés in a varying array of shapes and sizes. I wrapped them up as Christmas presents, just to see which of my relations would manage to remain polite in the face of such atrocities.'

'What did they say?' she asked, chuckling. That was definitely something she'd have done.

'Well everyone was polite and thanked me profusely. My auntie Maude even commented that it was the first piece of modern art she'd ever had the good fortune to own. I enjoyed myself immensely until my father roared, "Danny my lad, stick with your day job and don't bring any more of this crap in this house. Your mother hoards enough."'

She listened as he spoke of the first kilns used in the sixth millennium BC and temperatures that were beyond her comprehension. He talked of learning the texture and the personality of the clay, and the gut instinct that a piece is going to work. She leaned forward as she imagined those hands caressing and shaping lifeless clay and getting dirty with water dripping all over his fingers.

She pulled herself back in the chair. What the hell was she thinking? This was Dan – good old dependable Dan. He wasn't a sex god, although there was nothing wrong with his looks or physique, but he was Dan. She didn't have feelings like this about Dan. That was why she found it so easy to laugh and joke with him, even sharing her misadventures. She'd never have told those things to someone she found attractive or was interested in. Hell no.

She steered the conversation back to work, where she could place him back into the box she'd labelled and taped. In that persona she knew who he was, and they were just two colleagues enjoying a nice meal and friendly conversation after having spent many long hours together. She had to get the picture of those large hands manipulating grey mud out of her head, because those thoughts would do her no good at all.

CHAPTER FOURTEEN

'For goodness' sake, give her a call then,' Sarah snapped, survey-ing a wrinkled-looking David in scruffy tracksuit bottoms and sweatshirt. So far only two work shirts had made it into the wardrobe.

'I used to take her swimming on a Saturday morning. She'd get out of the pool, wet and excited, and we'd always go for hot chocolate before going home to Bi—'

'She's not bloody dead. Ring her and take her swimming. There's nothing to stop you.'

'Do you think I should?' David asked wanly.

Sarah nodded and took her coffee into her office. She took a minute to calm herself and wondered where the old David had gone. She tried to remember that night at the cinema when they had almost fed off each other, but it seemed like a distant memory. They'd made love a few times since he'd moved in, but it was automatic. It was like he was trying to satisfy her to keep her quiet. There was none of the spontaneity that she'd imagined. In her dreams, she'd pictured him making love to her on the lounge floor because he couldn't wait to get her to the bedroom. She'd pictured him stepping into the shower early in the morning to satisfy their need for each other before going to work. She'd anticipated meals left to go cold while they made love, sensuous baths together by candlelight while they soaped and caressed each other's bodies, but so far the few times had been in bed, late at night with the lights turned off and in the missionary position.

Sarah wondered where the assured, confident man that she loved had gone. Was he still in the suitcase waiting to be unpacked? Since the night he'd turned up on her doorstep, he seemed unable to make a decision for himself. His confidence had been left outside.

She heard his low voice from the lounge. She was almost relieved that he was talking to Bianca. She reached for a notebook; he would be on the phone for some time. The average phone call took about half an hour, so no sooner was he off the phone than it was time for him to call again.

Sarah had realised that Bianca was more a part of her life now than she'd ever been. While she had been the mistress, Bianca had been the woman to whom he was married, tied, but who didn't understand him. Now she was a paragon of virtue. 'But Bianca vacuums every day,' he'd said yesterday when Sarah had reassured him that there was no need. The two of them made very little mess. 'Bianca changes the sheets every Saturday morning,' he'd said an hour ago.

'Well Sarah changes them every Sunday morning, and that's only if she feels like it,' she'd retorted.

Sarah pushed her notebook aside and took out her journal. She had four different books on the boil. One for recording random thoughts, one for short stories, one for a novel that had been churning around her head, and a journal where she expressed her deepest emotions and kept locked in the drawer where the 'baby project' folder had been. That had been shredded a couple of weeks ago.

It occurred to her that she was doing more writing now than she ever had, and at the point where she had finally got what she wanted.

She reread the journal entry from the night before, shocked at its honesty. These were feelings that she would never have voiced to anyone. They were too raw and honest and much too secret. They were feelings in progress, emotions that may be just passing and therefore better not seen by anyone else. Doubts that she couldn't voice. It was the one place she could open herself up to what was true inside without fear of blame or repercussions.

She wrote the date and underlined it.

'Sarah, Sarah, you'll never guess what.'

Sarah jumped, mildly irritated that he'd barged into her personal space. She hid her feelings. He looked more animated than she'd seen him in weeks.

'What?' she asked, instinctively covering the journal as he came closer. He didn't notice.

'I'm taking Chelsea swimming. Bianca is going to the salon for a bit of a makeover and needs some time to herself.'

Sarah laughed with him. She felt almost as relieved as he did. 'That's wonderful. Oh sweetheart, I'm so pleased for you.'

He pulled her to her feet and began dancing her around the room.

'And that's not all. Bianca said she can stay overnight. She's off out with some of her friends and won't be back until late. Isn't it wonderful?'

Sarah nodded, surprised. It was a lot to take in.

'She wasn't too happy about you being here, but I talked her round in the end.'

Sarah forced herself to bite back the words that it was her bloody home. 'Th-That's nice, darling.'

He stopped dancing and let his hands fall to the sides. Sarah felt ridiculous standing in the middle of the room.

'I wonder where she's going that'll keep her out that late,' he mused, staring out of the window.

'Does it really matter, David?'

'No, I suppose not.' He grabbed her around the waist again. 'Oh, it'll be lovely to have her here. We can watch videos, read books, play games and eat…'

Sarah became still. 'David, have you forgotten that we're going to my sister's tonight?'

'We can do that any time. Tonight is just for Chel—'

'No,' Sarah exploded. 'We have not left this house for weeks, and I am not going to let my mother down. Chelsea is more than welcome to come with us, but I am not missing my sister's party.' David opened his mouth to argue, but her look silenced him. She wasn't particularly relishing the prospect of Stacey showing off her new pool and big house, but it was their first opportunity to present themselves as a couple. It was important to her.

He nodded and kissed her more passionately than he had in weeks. 'Okay, sweetheart. I'll go and take Chelsea swimming and then I'll bring her back here. You'll love her and she'll love you, so don't worry.'

'Okay,' Sarah said, although she hadn't been worried at all.

'We'll be gone for about two hours. Is that long enough?'

'For what?' Sarah asked, placing the journal back into the bottom drawer.

'To get this room ready for her, of course.'

Sarah looked around. The bed was nestled up in the corner; she only needed to change the sheets. 'Of course.'

He kissed her lightly on the forehead. 'I'll see you later, sweetie, and don't worry, you'll be fine.'

Sarah locked the bottom drawer and lit a cigarette. She blew the smoke out of the window so David wouldn't smell it. He hated nicotine, and she rarely smoked anyway, but since he'd moved in she'd felt the need to smoke more. She found it ironic that all the things she'd had the freedom to do before had now taken on a greater importance.

She looked around the room. What exactly did David expect her to do with it? She didn't have a design team waiting around the corner to do a quick makeover with some purple paint and a sheet of MDF. And it was only for one night, after all.

She puffed on the cigarette and then ground it out on the wall beneath the windowsill. She was determined to make the effort and ensure the room was pleasant for his daughter. She changed the sheets and swapped the tartan quilt for a small daisy pattern. She had no idea what a typical five-year-old would be into, but as she wouldn't have it in her closet, the daisies would have to do.

She fetched one of the pillows from their bed and placed it at the head of the bed and scrunched up her surplus clothes in the old wardrobe, to make room for anything that Chelsea might bring with her. She vacuumed and polished the room and lit some scented lavender candles. She looked around the room, which seemed a little tidier and fresher, but pretty much the same as before.

Sarah tried to ignore the fact that she would have nowhere to retreat to this evening. David was a much earlier sleeper than she was. He chose to go to bed around eleven, whereas she kept going until the early hours. Recently those hours had been spent in her office, writing in her journal, making notes in her books or typing ideas straight onto the laptop, or some nights just reading by the light from her desk lamp in the peace of the early morning hours.

Sarah checked her watch: she had about an hour until he returned with Chelsea. She switched on the computer and began to put the finishing touches to a story she'd been writing to send off to a magazine. She wasn't going to make the same mistake as before. This time she would tell no one, and then she wouldn't have to tell anyone when it came back rejected; but the tingling in her stomach had started once she'd decided to send it off.

The idea for the story had come to her when Cher had mentioned something about the local supermarket staying open all night on Saturdays. Deb had joked that it was probably more of a pick-up joint than a place to get your weekly groceries, which had set Sarah's mind whirring with ideas. Her heroine, who desperately needed pasta at midnight, had to overcome obstacles as to whether or not to choose a basket or trolley and the fear of appearing homely if she spent too long around the bakery section. Sarah had laughed loudly during her attempts to show the subliminal messages of late-night shopping if you were trying to snare a man and had thoroughly enjoyed writing the story.

She read through it one more time, deleted a few unnecessary words and deemed the story ready to be sent off. It was a story that held no deep and meaningful moral, though it was quite entertaining in its honesty, and she was pleased with the result. It was her first completed work and she was proud of it. She played a drumroll in her head as she pressed the send button. Instantly the anxiety surged into her stomach. What if the seven times she'd checked it hadn't been enough? What if she'd missed just one spelling mistake or grammatical error? Would an editor reject it because of minor mistakes? No, they'd reject it because it was crap, she assured herself, but there was still a tingle mixed with the trepidation. She'd finally submitted something.

The doorbell sounded, surprising Sarah. She wasn't expecting anyone. She heard childish giggling from outside and sighed. David had not yet used the key she'd given him almost three weeks earlier.

She took a few deep breaths and opened the door, smiling brightly. The child's smile vanished and a look of petulance settled, as though it lived there permanently.

David appraised her and frowned slightly. 'Chelsea, this is Sarah, a friend of Daddy's.'

Sarah held her hand out to shake the girl's hand. Chelsea placed her overnight case onto Sarah's outstretched hand before barging past.

David smiled proudly. 'She's excited and inquisitive about where Daddy is staying.'

Again, Sarah noticed the absence of the word 'home'.

'You didn't change. I thought you might have combed your hair.'

'Umm... er... sorry... I just got caught up in something.' Sarah hadn't known she was on parade, but she kept her thoughts to herself. He looked once more like the man she'd fallen in love with.

David followed his daughter into the lounge. She stood by the television, her short, stubby fingers tracing a line on the screen.

'Look, I can put my name on the screen.'

Sarah knew she hadn't polished for a day or two, but it wasn't that bad.

'Do you want a drink?' Sarah asked pleasantly. This was David's child and she had to make the effort. None of this was Chelsea's fault.

'Daddy, I want lemonade,' Chelsea said without looking at Sarah.

'Is that in the top cupboard, Sarah?' he asked, infuriating Sarah further. He still walked around as though he was living in a hotel. His manners were impeccable, often asking 'Is it okay to make a sandwich?', but Sarah wished he'd just do it.

'We only have blackcurrant or orange juice. Which one would you like?'

'Want lemonade, Daddy.'

'I'll fetch some later, sweetie, okay?'

'She can fetch it.'

'That's Sarah, darling. You have better manners than that,' David said, ruffling her hair fondly.

She smiled upward at her father but cut her eyes in a dramatic manner towards Sarah, which she almost burst out laughing at. She really was a pretty child, with curly blonde hair and big brown eyes in a natural, outdoor complexion and, for some reason, she reminded Sarah of Angelica from the *Rugrats* cartoon she'd watched as a child.

'Let's have a look at your room, shall we, and you can put your night clothes away.'

Chelsea followed her dad back out of the lounge and towards the room next to theirs. He pulled the door shut before opening the door to the study.

His eyes narrowed as he looked inside. 'Oh, you didn't do much to it, did you?'

Sarah opened her hands. 'What exactly were you expecting?'

She'd tidied her desk and straightened up the bookshelves that dominated two walls. She'd picked up the strewn magazines and placed them in her desk drawer. The easy chair she used sometimes for reading had been cleared of the weekly ironing, which had been thrown back in the airing cupboard. In her opinion the room was quite welcoming. She certainly wanted to hide in there and shut the door.

'Go and hang your things up, sweetie, and put your bear onto your pillow. We'll be in the lounge when you've finished.'

'You could have made a bit more effort with her room, Sarah,' he said once the lounge door was closed.

'I don't know what you thought I could do in two hours.'

He shook his head and spoke in hushed tones. 'I don't know either, but you could have used your imagination a little more to make it into a proper bedroom for her. It's a strange place to her and made all the stranger by the fact that it's still an office more than it is a bedroom.'

'I don't have anything to put in there,' she exclaimed.

'Never mind. We'll go out during the week and buy some things for her.' He touched her lightly on the cheek. 'I know it's hard, love, but it's Chelsea's bedroom now. We have to make it comfortable for her, so she knows it's always here ready and waiting for whenever she wants to visit. It's going to be hard on her and we need to create a stable environment. I know it's all up in the air at the moment, but once Bianca and I agree a schedule, I'm hoping it will be every weekend and maybe one night in the week. After all, with you not starting work until nine, you could easily get her to school on time.'

Sarah opened her mouth to ask him to stop the rollercoaster. They hadn't even talked about visitation schedules or school runs, and now was not the time to start.

The door to the lounge burst open. 'But, Daddy, there's only one bed in there. Where are you going to sleep?'

Sarah looked towards him with a wry smile. At last he was going to have to make a declaration on the state of their relationship: the 'friend' reference when they'd first been introduced had not gone unnoticed.

'Daddy sleeps on the sofa, of course, sweetie.'

Sarah grabbed her handbag and headed for the door, trying to stem the tears pricking at her eyes. She understood that it was a lot for Chelsea to take in, but his denial of their relationship after all these years cut her deeply.

'I'll go and get the lemonade while you get Chelsea settled.'

*

She drove around the corner and stopped the car, unable to drive any further. The stinging tears turned to raging sobs that came from deep inside her stomach.

Her own home felt alien to her. There was a strange man whom she didn't recognise and a petulant child who had taken root. She had hoped to feel a part of his relationship with Chelsea, but she felt more excluded than when he'd been with his wife.

She dried her tears and tried to stop the involuntary shaking of her body. A part of her knew she was being unreasonable. How could she expect David to be open and honest about their relationship so soon after the break-up of his marriage? Chelsea was five years old and her dad had simply disappeared. Her whole routine had changed. For the past few weeks he hadn't been there when she'd gone to sleep or there when she'd woken up in the morning. For some reason that she couldn't explain that fact affected her more now she'd seen the child in the flesh. Until ten minutes ago Chelsea had been an abstract factor in her life; a name. Now she was a five-year-old girl who had no idea why her life had suddenly changed.

Sarah slipped the gearstick into first. She would try to be more understanding of them both. It was hard for David – she knew that. He probably needed a little more time to adjust to a new situation. She should be pleased that he was spending time with his daughter, and if it took a little more effort than she'd first anticipated to bond with Chelsea, then it was up to her to do it.

She wandered around the supermarket and bought lemonade, chocolate, sweets and crisps. There, that was what part-time fathers were supposed to do when they had their child for a limited period: spoil them rotten.

On the way to the checkout, Sarah spied a pretty doll called Ashley, dressed in a vivid purple ballgown. There were accessories inside: handbags and shoes. Sarah grabbed it for good measure and waited in the checkout line. The two women in front talked animatedly.

'But how can he not know what's going on behind his back, what with her being pregnant and all?'

'Ooh, I know and with those two sons to look after on his own, and his mother in that institution.'

Sarah began to listen more closely as the cashier joined in the conversation.

'And he never even knew his own father, did he?'

'No, cos the bloke he thought was his father was his great-uncle…'

Sarah wondered how they could all know so much about this poor devil's private life.

'I can't wait until tonight. It's an hour special.'

Sarah almost laughed, realising that they were discussing a television soap opera. Their concern had been so real.

Her hand itched for paper to record everything she saw and heard, realising that everyone had a story to tell. She paid for her groceries, trying to memorise everything she saw for when she got home, but more observations assaulted her senses, which seemed to have been awakened from a deep sleep. She noticed how the sun reflected off the plate-glass windows. She felt the sun-softened tarmac of the car park mould itself against the imprint of her sandals. She smelled the car fumes, aggravated by the heat. She could hear a child screaming for another ice cream, and she tasted a hunger to record every second of it.

*

She opened her front door with a bright smile and a calm manner. It was going to be a pleasant afternoon if it bloody well killed her.

She almost balked at the state of the lounge. She'd only been gone for twenty minutes, but now colouring books and felt tips without the tops on littered the room. The cream throw, which had been nestled over the sofa, was crumpled on the floor with what looked like half a jam sandwich stuck to it. David and Chelsea sat on the sofa watching cartoons.

She smiled serenely. It was nothing that couldn't be put right later. She must remember that this was a temporary situation. She tried to ignore the voice that said 'until next weekend'.

'Look what I've bought,' she said brightly, showing them the contents of the carrier bag.

Chelsea looked less than impressed and turned her attention back to the television. 'She doesn't eat chocolate, Sarah. All those E-numbers and preservatives. Did you get any fresh fruit?'

Sarah shook her head, deflated. 'Sorry, you never said.'

David came in behind her and closed the door to the lounge. His hands circled her waist. 'I'll pop out later and get some other stuff, but thanks for trying, darling.'

'I am, you know,' she whispered as he turned her to face him, and for a moment their eyes locked and she felt the same magic. For a brief second there was only them.

He nodded and opened his mouth to say something, but Chelsea called from the lounge that *Bugs Bunny* was coming on.

David looked at her with a half-smile and a slight shrug.

'Go on,' she said. 'I'll fix us some lunch. Does Chelsea like tuna?'

'Sounds great,' he said, loosening his grip.

Sarah turned on the radio and let the music take her away from her surroundings. She took longer to prepare tuna sandwiches than was necessary but could put it off no longer.

'Lunch is ready,' she called from the kitchen and knocked the door open to find them both sitting and waiting at the wicker table that only had two chairs.

'I think we might need a bigger table,' David said as she placed their lunch before them.

Sarah nodded. There was no way she'd get rid of that table. Deb and Cher had bought it for her when she'd first moved in. It was an elongated oval with a chair at each end and fitted into her living room nicely without being obtrusive, nestled beneath the window.

Sarah took her place on the sofa and bit into her sandwich.

'Ugggh, vinegar,' Chelsea exclaimed, pushing the plate away.

'Don't tell me, she doesn't like it,' Sarah said to David.

He shook his head and rose from the table.

'I'll just nip to the shop. I'll be back in a minute,' he said, ruffling Chelsea's head.

Chelsea appeared to share her own sudden panic. 'But, Daddy, I don't want—'

'It's okay, sweetheart. Daddy won't be long. It'll give you a chance to get to know Sarah.'

As the door closed behind him, Sarah fetched the doll from the carrier bag in the kitchen and handed it to Chelsea, who ripped it from the packet. Her eyes appraised the cheap doll, looking for any features that she didn't have on other dolls at home, and found it sorely wanting.

'Look, we can change her shoes and match them with her handbag,' Sarah said, trying to drum up some interest. She fingered the doll's silky blonde hair. 'My mum used to say that I had hair like a doll when I was a little girl.'

For the first time the child looked directly at her with an expression of interest. Determined to hold the moment, Sarah offered her another glass of lemonade. Chelsea nodded slowly, still watching her. Sarah took the opportunity to make herself a cup of tea, to calm her frayed nerves, and heard a low chuckle from the lounge. Her spirits rose – maybe she was getting somewhere.

'Here we are,' she said brightly, placing the lemonade on the table. Chelsea held up the doll with a bright smile. Sarah was horrified. Every single hair on the doll's head had been cut off.

'Lovely,' she muttered, feeling her insides tighten. 'Shall we watch the cartoons until Daddy gets back?' Sarah asked. She really had no idea how to communicate with this child and wished David would hurry back. She was sure it was just a matter of time and they both had to be patient with each other. She couldn't force Chelsea into liking her, so maybe it was best if she just backed off and gave her some space.

Sarah sat on one sofa staring at the screen as various animated characters fired guns or threw stones or hung in mid-air, before falling and leaving an indentation in the ground. Chelsea watched with fascination, but Sarah couldn't see where one cartoon ended and the next began. Her eyes kept wandering around the room, her hands itching to tidy up the mess. She wasn't the most houseproud person in the world, but she did hate clutter.

David returned just as Sarah was contemplating calling his mobile. For more than half an hour not one word had passed between her and Chelsea, and the atmosphere without David was heavy.

'Here we go, this should make you feel better,' David said. Sarah noticed that his eyes were bright and his cheeks slightly flushed. He removed posters of cartoon characters she'd never heard of from the bag, and Chelsea danced with glee. He also extracted five stuffed bears of varying shapes and sizes and a pack of Blu Tack.

Sarah told them to go ahead when David looked at her questioningly and took the opportunity to have a nice long soak, which was disturbed by Chelsea desperately needing to use the toilet. She then retired to the bedroom and took two hours to get ready to go to her sister's, unaware of what David and Chelsea were up to. She reminded David that it was time to get ready and ignored the brief look of frustration that shaped his eyebrows. She knew that given the choice he would prefer to spend the evening in the flat with Chelsea, but the idea of sitting around watching them play together for the rest of the evening was provoking feelings inside Sarah that she didn't want to acknowledge.

By the time Sarah pulled up in front of her sister's house, Chelsea seemed to be in good spirits and Sarah saw that she could be quite a pleasant child, as long as Sarah wasn't communicating with her directly.

Roger answered the door and pulled Sarah into a bear hug immediately.

'Good to see you, love. It's been too long.'

Sarah nodded. It had been almost six months since she'd seen him but he'd barely changed. He was still a huge bulk of a man, with a full head of hair that was greying more by the day. His face was kind and wrinkled around the eyes, and he looked older than his forty-seven years but in a pleasant, comforting way.

She introduced David and Chelsea, who followed her father's example and thrust her hand out to be shaken. Sarah smiled at the comical gesture.

Roger guided them through the house to the indoor pool. In truth, Sarah hated the house. It was full of gold and gilded edges that had screamed opulence and wealth some time back in the eighties but now looked outdated and crass.

She spied her sister leaning against the bar, holding a flute. She was dressed in black cropped trousers that hugged her calves and emphasised her height and slimness. She wore high-heeled sandals decorated with gemstones and a strapless, figure-hugging halterneck top that tied around her bare back. Her hair was swept back, and huge hoop earrings swayed as she moved her head.

'Sarah, darling,' she exclaimed, putting down her glass. 'And David, how nice to see you again.' She lifted his hand and held on to it for a long few seconds. She leaned down towards Chelsea. 'And who is this gorgeous young lady who, I suspect, is going to be the next supermodel?' she asked in a voice so false it was dripping with treacle. Sarah cringed inwardly, but Chelsea was beaming at her.

'Oh, you're absolutely adorable.' She leaned down even further. 'Come and meet the old people,' she whispered conspiratorially, taking Chelsea's hand. Sarah was amazed that the child offered it readily. A slow smile spread over David's face and he visibly relaxed.

Sarah introduced David to her parents with bated breath. Her mother smiled nervously while watching her father, who shook his hand cordially but offered no greeting, just a brief nod. Her father believed that marriage was for life and any tough bits you just worked through until it came good again.

David sat beside her mother, who struck up a conversation with him about Chelsea. Her father looked quite formidable in his navy suit. He had retired almost two years ago, yet Sarah had never seen him in anything less than a shirt and tie. He saw no reason why someone should give up on their appearance just because they no longer had to go to work.

Roger offered drinks, and Sarah readily accepted a brandy and Coke. David was driving back, so she could quite happily enjoy a few drinks. She was hoping they would quiet the unwanted voices in her head.

'Where's Stacey?' Sarah asked as Roger came to stand beside her. He pointed outside.

Sarah found it strange that a section of the garden was dedicated to children's entertainment, like swings, a sandpit and a five-foot-high slide, when they didn't have children.

Stacey and Chelsea reappeared in the doorway. 'Who wants a swim?' Stacey asked.

'Me, me, me, me,' cried Chelsea excitedly.

'I think I might just have something that was specially delivered for you today,' Stacey offered. Chelsea looked up at her adoringly, and Sarah fought down the stab of jealousy.

Stacey turned her way. 'Did you bring anything, Sarah? Because I'm not sure I have your size.'

'I'm fine,' Sarah said, lifting her glass. She was quite content to sit by the pool, nursing her drink, and watch the patterns of the water dance on the ceiling.

'Roger?'

He too lifted his glass. 'I'm with Sarah.'

'Of course you are, but do you have anything that will fit David?'

David protested mildly, but Chelsea pleaded with him and he eventually caved. Her father became responsible for inflating the pool toys, and her mother cheerfully looked on.

Stacey's squeals of delight could be heard from the changing room next to the steam room, as could David's low rumble of laughter. Sarah felt her cheeks redden. Roger offered her another drink with a sympathetic smile.

'Doesn't she look wonderful?' Stacey asked, leading Chelsea by the hand. She wore a yellow-coloured costume covered with purple dolphins. Chelsea clearly loved it.

Sarah took a long gulp from her fresh drink and wished that Stacey would hurry up and get into the pool. Her white two-piece bikini was welded against her bronzed skin, which offered no white bits that Sarah could see. Her long, lean legs were a shapely golden brown and her stomach toned just short of a six-pack. Stacey pushed David in and then lowered herself gracefully into the pool. They played around and splashed each other, with Chelsea squealing excitedly with a rubber ring around her midriff.

Sarah downed the rest of her drink.

'You okay?' Roger asked as her father took himself for a walk around the garden.

Sarah nodded miserably. 'That child has not spoken one word to me all day, yet here she is playing and splashing with someone who can barely stand to be around children. Sorry, Roger. I didn't...'

'I know what you meant but to Stacey it's like having a living, breathing doll. It's fun to dress her and play with her and make her squeal, but even the hint of a frown or tears from Chelsea and Stacey would be reaching for the Valium.'

Sarah chuckled, feeling the heat of the brandy circulate her body and aim for her brain cells.

He sighed. 'There's very little I don't know about your sister,' he murmured.

Sarah glanced sideways at him. She wondered if he really did know everything.

The doorbell chimed through the house. 'That'll be Amelia from the house opposite. Excuse me a minute.'

Sarah had seen the houses opposite and they were even grander than this one. She wondered why Amelia had been relegated to the 'B List' party.

Sarah did a double take as she entered with Roger: they made a striking couple as they entered the pool house together. Amelia was dressed in cream slacks with low-heeled sandals. She wore a summer top with a cashmere cardigan draped over her shoulders, with the sleeves tied in a knot. Although in her mid-fifties, her face showed the memory of great beauty that had folded into a pleasant, welcoming face.

Amelia shook her hand warmly. 'I've heard so much about you from Roger.'

Sarah warmed to the handsome woman immediately.

'And this is David,' said Roger. Sarah was unaware that David had materialised beside her. 'Sarah's partner, and his daughter, Chelsea.'

Amelia gave a small wave to Stacey whose demeanour had definitely tensed. She still played with Chelsea in the pool, but one eye was on Amelia.

Sarah sat back and hugged her drink. This was becoming very interesting, she thought as Roger guided Amelia to her parents. Amelia's greeting was genuine and warm, in spite of the difference in their social status. *This is one classy lady*, Sarah realised, watching how Amelia's hand rested on her mother's arm as they talked, and instantly saw her sister's discomfort. Amelia exuded class and confidence. Something Stacey hankered for and would never have. She wanted the effortless grace that surrounded Amelia as she laughed engagingly with Roger and her parents.

Amelia followed Roger out to the barbecue, which was surrounded by colourful lights on a portion of raised decking, and caught up with her father wandering around the garden. Her mother was carrying dishes of salad and pasta out to where Roger was turning the meat, and David and Stacey continued to play in the pool with Chelsea. Sarah fixed herself another drink and realised that everyone was with the wrong person: with every combination that developed in her head, she ended up alone.

Sarah watched the shapes dance on the ceiling of the pool house until her head began to swim. She closed her eyes, letting the effects of the alcohol wash over her. She couldn't recall if she'd eaten anything but seemed to think that tuna had been a part of her day. She didn't care. Although she could hear chattering and laughter, her brain was closing down and she was happy to let it.

She rose from her position and wobbled towards the bar, stumbling over her mother's handbag.

'You okay?' she heard David call from the pool.

She nodded in what she hoped was his direction and couldn't seem to stop. She poured more brandy and less Coke and drank it straight off, feeling the effects rush to her head. Her legs became weak and no longer wished to support her body. She leaned against the bar, listening to David, her David, merrily throwing his daughter around the pool and dunking her sister under the water. It was so good to hear him laugh. It had been so long. Suddenly Sarah wanted to be a part of it. David should be laughing with her not bloody Stacey. So what if she hadn't brought her bathing costume? Her body wasn't like Stacey's but it was presentable: she could swim in her underwear; she'd dry off later. Sarah began to remove her clothing: she wanted to frolic in the water with David. She wanted to play around with Chelsea so the child would like her. She didn't want to sit on her own on the edge of the pool anymore.

She kicked off her shoes and pulled her cotton dress over her head. No one would mind her swimming in her bra and panties. Her dress landed somewhere in the water, attracting the attention of David and the others. Chelsea gave a small squeal, and David looked horrified. A small smile played on Stacey's lips. What was wrong with them? Had they never seen lacy underwear before?

She looked down. 'Oh bugger,' she mumbled as she remembered that she hadn't bothered to put any on.

CHAPTER FIFTEEN

Deb surveyed her appearance critically. The light blue jeans and vest top that had felt comfortable ten minutes earlier now provoked great debate. The jeans fitted her long legs well without being tight, and she prided herself on still being able to go without a bra at twenty-seven. Her short red hair had fallen feather-like around her face. A fringe touched lightly on her eyebrows, softening her strong cheekbones. The dark circles beneath her eyes showed through the concealer that she'd shovelled on. She would have loved to spend the day lazing around in bed. For the last couple of weeks she'd taken any appointment she could get. Most mornings she was on the road by six thirty, and not one night had she returned home before eight. Long-distance appointments were set for the beginning or end of the day, so that she was travelling either there or back on her own time. Her weekends had been spent typing up presentations, quotations and analysing discounts to offer the best possible prices.

Her decision to visit her father had come from the realisation that she didn't have long left to ask him. In her heart she knew what his decision would be, but for her own peace of mind she had to ask him the question.

'Of course he'll give you away,' Mark had reassured her. 'He's only got one daughter so it's the only chance he's going to get.'

She had smiled, aware that he was only saying it for her benefit. He'd known her father long enough.

'I'll have something nice waiting for when you get back,' he'd promised, and it was only the thought of their night ahead that would get her through the visit with her father. That was their normal Sunday routine. He always cooked a romantic meal while she soaked in a scented bath, and she loved him for the night off. They would turn the TV off and either listen to music or just talk, languishing over a bottle of wine.

That was one of the things she loved about him: they could still talk for hours and not get bored. He never *pretended* to listen to her – he always did. Once when he'd been staring heavenward without even grunting for a full five minutes, she'd become convinced he was thinking about the football results.

'And then the pigs went flying out of the window,' she interjected in a normal voice.

'And were they headed north or south?' he'd answered without a missed beat. It had convinced her that he really was listening.

How the hell had she managed to land such a total bastard? she wondered as she pulled up outside the terraced house that had been her childhood home. It had remained the same for over twenty years. The front door still bore the burns that Carl had inflicted with a box of firecrackers. A trace of lime paint clung to the glass that hadn't been covered properly from a paint job fifteen years earlier.

She saw the house through adult eyes. The whole street had an air of greyness about it, even in summer.

The entry to the side of the house was narrow and dark. There was little point knocking on the front door. He couldn't hear it, and even if he could, he wouldn't answer it. He only answered the door if he was expecting someone.

She let herself through the rickety gate with two slats missing and tapped lightly on the glass-panelled door that had stringy cobwebs in the corner.

'Come in,' he grumbled from the lounge, although the word lounge didn't really fit: it was a small, dark room in the middle of the house with any brightness hindered by the old, rickety furnishings and newspapers that littered the chairs. Deb hadn't noticed it before but it was like walking into an episode of *Hoarders*.

'What brings you here?' he asked grumpily.

'Just passing,' Deb said, feeling as though she needed to apologise.

She moved a fishing magazine that was dated 'Spring 1974' and sat down. Her foot rested against a plate with remnants of gravy dried around the edges. She moved to pick it up.

'Leave it,' he growled. 'Edna will be over for it in a bit.'

Couldn't he even wash the bloody plate? Deb seethed inwardly. The woman over the road had been kind enough to cook his Sunday dinner for the last twelve years, and not once had he bothered to soak the plate for her. In fact, he'd rarely moved out of the armchair since a back injury, which had never been traced, had lost him his job at the foundry.

'How've you been?' she asked as she always did.

'Fair to crap,' he answered, switching television channels. 'There's tea in the pot.' He indicated towards the kitchen.

Deb refused the offer with a shake of the head. She hadn't eaten or drunk anything in this house since the day she'd left.

'Dad,' she said softly. 'You know why I've come, don't you?'

He shook his head. 'You must want something.'

Deb's teeth clenched. She had never asked him for anything. She remembered when she'd needed her first bra, and in spite of what her friends had said at the time, it had not been a competition. Her small breasts had become sore through lack of support and her poor attempts at hiding them from her father, postponing the day when he would realise she was a girl. She'd saved her lunch money because she knew that she would have to make that journey alone and in secret. If she'd asked her father or her brothers' advice, they would have laughed mercilessly.

The woman on the market stall had palmed her off with a 32A cup that had been tight and uncomfortable, with bones and underwires piercing her young flesh. To make a joke out of it, she had smiled bravely and bragged about being the first whilst wishing that she could slice her breasts off.

The day she got her period she'd stuffed her pants with toilet tissue and ran to the nearest chemist. A female assistant had taken her around the back, away from the crowds awaiting prescriptions. Seeing the tearstains on her cheeks and sensing her fear, the woman had explained to her exactly what had happened. Deb had listened, finding the whole thing disgusting. The kindly woman kitted her out with a box of Always sanitary towels that stretched halfway up her back and sent her packing with a reminder that she would need money next time. Deb took her kindness and her sanitary towels and never went in there again.

'So what do you want now?' her father muttered without looking at her.

Deb looked at the old gas fire that had filthy black soot attached to two of the grills. It would take such little effort to clean it up. It told her so much.

'Dad, I'm getting married in two weeks' time. You know I want you to give me away—'

'Would have been so much better in a registry office, but that old cow had to go meddling and now there's all this pomp and ceremony for a piece of bloody paper.'

It was the response she'd expected but she ploughed on anyway. 'I know, Dad, but will you?'

He knocked the remote control against the arm of the chair to get a bit more life out of the batteries. 'You know how I feel about things like that, and my back has been acting up real bad this last couple of days.'

Deb knew it was an excuse. His back got worse every time he was called upon to leave the chair.

Deb accepted defeat gracefully. There really had never been another answer. She wouldn't beg. 'But you'll still be coming if I get someone to collect you, won't you?'

He frowned and shook his head. 'It's me back, see. I'm just not up to it.'

Deb studied him as he made a vile noise that she remembered well. The phlegm from sixty cigarettes a day gathered in his throat. He reached for a stained handkerchief before chewing silently on a sliver of meat that had dislodged from between his two front teeth. She didn't fight the waves of revulsion for this man from whom she had tried desperately to get attention and love. And for what? Even now, when he had no one else, he couldn't find it inside himself to get close to her.

'Dad, I'm going now. I have to be somewhere.'

She stood in the doorway looking at the greasy grey hair that arced over his ears. She would have liked to believe that there were hidden depths and complexities to her father that had prevented him from comforting her as she'd cried for a mother that she didn't have. Maybe that she herself had represented to him the searing pain of the loss of his wife but, truthfully, she believed that his reasons weren't as deep and complex as that, and it truly was because her crying had grated on his nerves.

'It wasn't easy, you know,' her father muttered without turning around.

'Goodbye, Dad,' she whispered and left the house without the faintest idea of when she would return.

How dare he claim it wasn't easy for him? She didn't want to listen to tales of woe about his inconvenience, and if that made her a bad person, tough. Not once in her life could she remember him giving her any piece of advice that had led her to the person she was today. Not once in twenty-seven years had he offered her a helping hand or attempted to guide her, and now he claimed it wasn't easy. He had treated her brothers like workmates or drinking buddies. He had always tried to be their friend but, realistically, he had never tried to guide them either.

She sat in the car looking at Carl's mobile number. He'd had the good sense to move to Norwich when he was in his mid-twenties. Maybe she should give him a call. He was her brother after all. She pressed the number but pressed end before it even connected. Had he ever questioned their father? Had he received the same response as her, or maybe he just remembered more about their mother. It wasn't information he had ever volunteered but, then again, she'd never asked.

It wasn't easy, you know, her father had said. Nothing was easy. Few people's lives were easy, but they didn't just shrivel up and die because of it. For all her faults Margie had been placed in a similar situation, yet she had managed well enough and produced a son who was loving, charitable and strong. Deb admitted grudgingly that what she sometimes labelled smothering was nothing more than a fierce sense of pride.

She put the phone down, pushing away this sudden need to surround herself with family. She pulled away from the kerb to head towards her next visit, wondering again why she was submitting herself to such torture.

It was the first time in ten years that she had voluntarily visited the woman. Last night, as she'd been falling asleep, the image of a pleasant Sunday afternoon visit with Margie had seemed plausible.

The haziness of forthcoming sleep had brought with it a blurry vision with tinted edges of polite conversation and restrained insults. She'd pictured the two of them sitting on wrought-iron patio furniture in wide-brimmed hats, delicately sipping tea and discussing the weather whilst maintaining an eighteenth-century politeness, with the biggest conflict being who would have the last fairy cake. 'Oh no, *you* have it.'

'No, I insist, please.'

And then a good-natured smile as the cake remained on the plate.

Deb laughed at the image of them being 'oh so cordial' to each other and wondered where her conviction of the previous night had gone: back in la-la land, where Jack climbed his beanstalk and Humpty Dumpty was put back together again by private doctors who charged him a fortune.

'Debra, what a surprise?' Margie gushed, opening the door.

So far, so good, Deb thought, smiling pleasantly. *That's it, just keep your mouth shut. If you stay quiet, you won't be able to spoil the effect.*

'I didn't know you knew anyone else in this area.'

Here we go, Deb thought. *That means: 'You've rarely just visited before so what brings you here now?'* Deb ignored the half insult and remained stoic in her conviction that this could work.

'I thought we could finalise the seating arrangements.'

'It's a little late for that, Debra, with the wedding so close. I thought you were looking forward to putting together all our relatives that haven't spoken for decades and watching the fireworks.'

Deb clenched her teeth as the picture of mutual respect and effortless cordiality smashed into a million pieces and fell from the viewfinder.

'We only have to let the hotel know. It's not something that needed months of preparation.'

'Good job, really, isn't it?'

Deb felt the weight of defeat bearing down on her already. She continued into the lounge and once again found herself startled by the ducks. No one had any idea why Margie had developed a liking for the bright yellow ornaments that sat on the sideboard. They held up the lampshades and even flew across the wall. Deb tried not to look at them too closely. Rather than seeing anything remotely endearing, she found them a sinister-looking bunch.

'I like your new sofa,' Deb complimented, trying desperately to appear friendly.

'Oh, it doesn't really feel new anymore. I had it a couple of months ago.'

Deb forced a smile onto her face. She refused to be baited by the woman's digs, which were so well aimed she'd have been useful looking for the tombs of the hidden pharaohs.

She studied the woman for a moment, wondering how Mark had managed to put up with her for so long. Couldn't he smell the nastiness bubbling beneath the surface, even though it was hidden well? Casual navy trousers and loose cotton shirt did not scream evil in all its forms, and the short, tidy hairstyle did look rather stylish. Deb's thoughts were drawn to her own father who sat welded to an armchair, clad in worn corduroys and a food-stained shirt, watching his stomach grow.

'Shall I make us a cup of tea?' Deb offered, purely to get out of the room.

'That would be lovely, dear. The cups are in the cupboard above the sink,' she called as an afterthought. Deb bit hard on her lower lip, realising that she would have been forced to ask, because she didn't know where the cups lived.

She stood and watched the kettle boil, focusing on her objectives: maintain a pleasant demeanour; involve her in the last few preparations; find a middle ground on which to converse; mollify any objections she might have; and, above all, leave her in a cheerful mood to ensure attendance at forthcoming nuptials.

'Here we are,' Deb said, placing the tray onto the coffee table.

'Oh no, Debra, you should have used the best cups. I save them especially for visitors.'

Deb lifted her cup with the hand that wanted to reach across and slap Margie's smug face. It would be almost possible to get along with her if she listened to her first sentence only and totally disregarded the rest. The first sentence was always pleasant and inoffensive: it was the rejoinder that had claws.

Deb placed her cup onto a coaster decorated with a bathing duck. 'I've brought the seating plan and all the confirmed guests. There are about twenty-five who can't come and another four who haven't yet replied.'

'Well you only wanted a small affair anyway,' Margie sniffed.

'One hundred and twenty-five is hardly small, and seating them appropriately is going to take some doing.'

'I'm sure you'll manage, dear. You've insisted on doing everything else yourself.'

Deb felt the guilt swoop down and rest heavily on top of the displeasure. She'd be lucky if she could raise herself from a sitting position at this rate. She swallowed her retort and only wished that Margie's observation was correct. This was going to be harder than she'd anticipated; still, she had to try harder for Mark's sake. She had to make sure that there was absolutely no reason for Margie to ruin this wedding as she had the other two. Swallowing her pride had to be worth it.

'Please, Margie, I need your help.'

She glanced over the table plan. 'Well you'll have to make sure that the older guests are close to the front. Auntie Mavis will never hear the speeches from over there.'

'Okay, that's fine,' Deb said, placing a small 'm' for Mavis on one of the tables nearest the front.

'And then you can space all Mark's cousins around these four tables with some of your relatives.'

Deb had thought about that and in her experience it didn't work. 'To be honest, Margie, I think people feel a little uncomfortable eating if they're placed with people they don't know.'

'Have it your own way.' She prodded the rectangular top table. 'Well there's not enough room there for everyone, is there?'

Deb nodded.

Margie began counting on her fingers. 'Me, Mark, you, the best man, the bridesmaids and your father.'

'I'm not having Sarah and Cher on the top table. I assume they'll both be bringing someone, and whoever it is won't know anyone else in the room. They prefer it that way.' She paused. 'And my father isn't coming.'

'What…? Your own father… not coming to the wedding. You're not serious?'

Deb felt the heat flood into her cheeks. She felt embarrassed enough without Margie making an issue of it.

'It's okay, I understand. It's not a problem.'

'Don't be ridiculous. Your father can't possibly miss this day.'

Deb wanted to get off the subject. 'Really, Margie, I don't mind. He has his reasons.' Deb was infuriated that she was defending actions that she didn't understand, purely because of the accusatory expression on Margie's face.

'But the photos will be off balance. The speeches will be over too soon. No, Debra, it's not good enough.'

'And what do you propose I do about it?' Deb asked in an icy tone. Her back began to stiffen.

'Well you'll have to make him, that's all. I've never heard anything like it.'

'Leave it, Margie – I've said I don't mind,' Deb replied, folding up the seating plan and stuffing it into her bag.

'Honestly, it's the single most important day of your life and he can't be bothered to get off his—'

'Margie, leave it. I mean it.'

'Well it would be different if there was something genuinely wrong with the man, but all he does is sit at home, watching the television.'

Deb rose and put her jacket over her arm. The bait was being dangled and she was in serious danger of biting the worm's head off. If she wanted to get married at all, she needed to leave the house immediately.

'It's no use running away from the problem. And it is a problem. I don't know how you can let him get away with it. I've always said that you're a very strange family. I mean, there's nothing wrong with him: he's a downright malingerer.'

Deb stopped walking. Wedding or not, her pride came first and the pride of her family. No one was going to speak about her father in such a manner. She was sick of being held to ransom for the sake of one day. For months she had taken everything that Margie had to offer, but the time had come to say *no more*.

'Okay, you acidic trout, do your worst. Come on, out with it, every last insult you can manage. I want them all, come on,' Deb goaded, moving towards her.

Margie backed away.

'Come on, do it. You're not content to insult me at every opportunity, you even do it to my friends and now my family.'

'I have never insulted you in my life.'

'Oh yes you have,' Deb cried, half expecting a return cry of 'oh no I haven't', so sure was she that they were acting out a pantomime.

'When?' Margie asked, closing the front door after checking that there was no one about.

'You're always dictating how I should behave, and I've just about had enough of it. You think your son is too good for me? Well, tough shit, because he chose me and there isn't a bloody thing you can do about it. You've ruined two weddings for us already and I'll be damned if you're going to ruin this one. I have bent over backward to have you involved, just to keep the peace for Mark's sake, but no more, because it doesn't matter how hard I try, there's always a snippet of evil hiding dying to burst out of those pursed lips and—'

'I only say what I think. I would have thought you would appreciate that, being the sort of person you are.'

Deb was outraged. 'And what sort of person is that?'

'Well you are rather overbearing, aren't you? I thought straight talk was your sort.'

Deb blanched. *Me overbearing*, her mind screamed as she stood before the epitome of overbearing.

'I can't listen to this anymore. You're losing your mind if you think I'm overbearing, and all you've ever done is advise me, you spiteful old woman.'

She held her chin out stubbornly. 'You can't blame me for wanting the best for my only son. You'll understand if you ever have children of your own, although I doubt you'll be able to take the time off work to—'

'At least I'll know when to let my child go and stop suffocating and choking him with the apron strings.'

'Is that what you call a caring mother then? Because parental involvement is not something you'd know much about, is it?' Margie spat.

Deb fell silent. That was low. She saw the horror flash through Margie's eyes as they faced each other silently, like pieces on a chess board. The anger drained away, leaving a low, dull ache somewhere in her stomach. She pushed down the ball of emotion that had gathered into her throat and appraised Margie for a moment before walking past her without another word.

She pulled away from the kerb but parked the car in the next street and took deep breaths, fighting the tears down. No way would Margie ever make her cry. She stubbornly refused, focusing her emotion into breathing exercises, but the tears spilled over onto her cheeks. The fact that her father had flatly refused to walk her down the aisle had hurt her deeply, but his refusal to attend her wedding at all was something that she would never forgive him for. His refusal to be a part of the most important day of her life had wounded her enough without it being used as a deadly weapon in Margie's hands.

She wiped the tears away. She'd come with such good intentions. She'd wanted to be able to go home to Mark with the news that they had finally found a common ground, one where they weren't trying to get at each other: she'd tried. She'd wanted this time before her wedding to be enjoyed, savoured, heavy with excitement and anticipation without bad feelings and negative energy. She'd wanted to walk down that aisle in peace without tension or anger.

She put the gearstick into first, realising she'd be lucky if Mark wanted to share a hamburger with her never mind the rest of his life.

'Shit,' Deb cursed, pounding the keyboard.

'No better than you thought?' Willow asked, placing Deb's last eleven weekly reports on the desk. It was seven fifteen and an hour before her first appointment. She'd calculated her figures yesterday and had hoped that there were a couple of orders that she'd overlooked: there weren't.

'I might as well just kiss goodbye to the job,' Deb said, feeling the tension gather in her throat.

She leafed through the previous reports. 'Respectable but hardly dynamic.'

'No one could have worked harder, Deb. You've made a lot of new contacts who have placed try-out orders with us but—'

'I know, but nothing to poke a stick at.'

Deb pushed herself away from the desk. No matter how many times she recalculated, the figures looked the same. She'd shown a steady increase week on week and she knew she couldn't have worked any harder, but this was the last week of figures to go to Ms Stringer: these would seal her fate.

'If you could just have got that one order…'

'I know,' Deb agreed. If she'd landed that one order on the day that Margie had arranged the caterers, she would have been way ahead in the first week. But Deb didn't want to hate Margie for anything else. She had more than enough reasons.

The minute she'd walked back in the door, she'd told Mark about the huge argument she'd had with his mother. She had held back one or two comments his mother had made, and she was glad she had when she'd been forced to almost restrain him physically from going to see her.

Deb had begged him to leave it alone, and he'd gone to the other extreme: claiming that he wouldn't be making any kind of contact with her until she offered Deb a full, genuine apology.

She understood that he was acting in defence of her and she was grateful for his support, but she had worked so hard to ensure he would have his mother there when he got married and yet she'd fallen at the final hurdle. She couldn't help feeling that she'd let him down somehow.

'If only Pricky hadn't stolen that one order,' Willow said, bringing her back to the present.

Deb's head rested in her hands. Willow had shown her Ricky's figures and, in spite of the work she'd put in, the hours on the motorway, the early mornings and late nights, she wasn't even close.

'Oh well,' Willow said, sighing. 'At least we had a bit of fun. We fooled him for a couple of days.'

'It taught him a lesson,' Deb agreed. For two days he'd been ringing in to Willow constantly to ask for directions, before finally realising what was going on. Even so, his figures had hardly suffered for it. Ricky had a major advantage over her: the buyers of stationery were invariably female and Ricky had the gift of turning an order for biros and staples into a sizeable order for machinery and furniture with a dazzling smile and a few choice words.

'Come on, it might not be that bad,' Willow offered, pouring coffee. The emptiness of the words echoed around the room.

'It's not just that, Will. I'm getting married in a week. I'm walking down the aisle on my own, my father's not even coming to the wedding and Margie is gonna be a no-show. This is the whole reason why I wanted to get married in a registry office.'

As the words came out, Deb was horrified to realise they were true: in a registry office she wouldn't have to suffer the humiliation. All along she'd convinced herself that she just preferred a low-key affair because she hated being on parade, but like most other women she wanted her future husband to watch her glide serenely towards him, see his expression of love and pride as she approached. She wanted her father to look down on her in wonder as he passed his little girl to her future husband with a look that said 'cherish her or die'. She wanted to feel the pride of her family beam down on her as she vowed to love and cherish Mark for the rest of her life. She wanted all the people she'd ever cared about to witness her commitment and love on the most important day of her life. She wanted to feel like a princess as she gazed lovingly into Mark's eyes. Dammit, she wanted the fairy tale. She wanted the whole world to hear her words of love for Mark.

The tears gathered in her throat. 'Oh, Will, it's all gone so wrong. How on earth can I walk down that aisle on my own? He won't even be there and, on top of all that, I've got to find another job after putting years into this one.'

'But you could always stay. No one is forcing you to—'

'Come on, can you imagine how much pride I would have to swallow to work for him? I don't have enough saliva, and I'm not prepared to lose that much of myself. I'll have to go. I don't see that there's any other choice. If I stay—'

'Deb, thank goodness I caught you,' Milton huffed into the room. He fell into the vacant chair the other side of her desk. His tie was askew and small beads of perspiration were in danger of running down towards his eyes.

'Are you okay?' Deb asked, glancing towards Willow.

He nodded and took a couple of deep breaths. 'I-I've been trying to tell you. That appointment you sent me to, I got the order. It was a biggie.'

Deb smiled. He'd needed it to keep his job and, regardless of the consequences, she didn't regret throwing it his way.

'I know, Milton, you did a good job to secure—'

'You don't understand,' he growled, anxious to get the words out. 'I did a little cold-calling around the building, and the three floors below are occupied by one of those no win, no fee solicitors. They're setting up branches all over the country. Big business it is now.'

'But what does that have to do with me?'

He rolled his eyes, which Deb found quite amusing. 'Because I've been to see them twice now and they're about ready to order.'

'And?' Deb asked, feeling the butterflies in her stomach.

'Your appointment is in twenty minutes with a Mrs—'

His last words were cut off as Deb launched herself around the desk and kissed him on the cheek.

He blushed and wiped his forehead with his tie. 'Oh dear, I don't—'

'Hang on though. You've secured the order,' Deb said, standing back. This wasn't fair.

He smiled shyly after Deb's emotional demonstration. 'Pretty much like you had a few months ago.'

Deb felt a rush of emotion for the good-natured, bumbling man who hadn't had an easy life and, for years, had battled to keep his job against people younger and fitter. Her one act of kindness was being repaid by a man who'd helped her when she'd first joined the company, who was under constant pressure to prove himself able to do his job in an ever-changing environment. His old-fashioned legwork had served him well for years and, over the last few weeks, had served her well too. She'd learned lessons from him in those early weeks that had not been easily forgotten. Each day, he plodded around getting the door slammed in his face in the hope of landing any order that might prove that he was still an asset to the company. She often felt sad for him, going home to an empty, wifeless, childless house.

Deb wanted to hug him again, but suddenly she had a better idea. Her wide smile turned into a broad grin.

'Milton, I could do with one more very small favour.'

'Anything. What can I do?'

Deb knew he thought they were still talking about the race towards the job of sales manager, but that was no longer on her mind. If this order came to fruition, she was in with as much chance as she was ever going to get. That decision was now beyond her control. Now she was thinking of something else, something much closer to her heart, and the honour she hoped he would take in her request.

'Have you got any plans for this coming Saturday?'

Ms Stringer had been sitting waiting for them when they arrived, and they took the same places that they had three months ago. She sat with a file on the table and tapped it, but didn't bother to open it. Deb looked for some sort of sign as to who had got the job. She scrutinised Ms Stringer's smile. Was it cooler or warmer? Which way was her body language pointing? Were there any further hoops to jump through or burning coals to walk, or was it now a foregone conclusion?

Ms Stringer lay both hands on top of the folder. 'I'd like to start by congratulating you both on a very productive three months.' She smiled, first at Ricky and then at Deb. 'Much more than we'd hoped.'

Deb noted that Ricky, unlike last time, was staying very quiet. At their previous meeting, he'd taken any opportunity to dive into the conversation and personalise it by using sexual politics to suck up to her. Deb guessed that he saw no point now, as the decision was made and he either had the job or he didn't.

'I'm not going to draw this out any longer than it needs to be.' She opened the folder and took out two pieces of paper. Deb guessed them to be summaries of each performance. She held her breath, praying that she wasn't going to walk down the aisle unemployed.

Ms Stringer took a moment to study the papers, which slightly infuriated Deb. She wouldn't have called the meeting unless she knew the outcome already.

'There were a number of criteria on which you were being judged: some you were aware of and some you weren't. The most important of these was, of course, sales figures.' Deb noticed Ricky try to see what was on the paper. Ms Stringer closed the file.

'The highest figures recorded were by Ricky with a margin of six per cent…'

Deb stopped listening as the blood rushed to her ears. Ricky's smile and wink at her across the table sickened her. Her mind started to think of the opportunities once she escaped this office. There were countless job websites, recruitment agencies; she'd even clean the council toilets before she'd call him boss.

'Debra, please pay attention. I'm not finished yet,' Ms Stringer said, smiling at her for the first time in eight years.

Deb nodded. Now would come the details of his position, his title, his responsibilities, the new company structure that she wouldn't be around to see.

'The other criteria that we thought important when we developed this contest were things like the type of order, effort and commitment and new customers, and although Ricky has done very well in the sales figures, he hasn't really expanded the business.' She turned towards Ricky. 'You've achieved a great deal with the large electronic orders for valuable sums of money, but that's not all that we sell. We also need orders for all of our other products, so where you have succeeded in gaining the highest sales figures, those orders are focused only on large items of equipment and, as I'm sure you both know, if we don't continue to move our more cumbersome basic office products, we no longer get them with the same discount, which means that our profit comes down.'

Deb began to listen more intently. She had thought that the decision would be made on the back of sales figures alone; after all, everyone wanted to see the bottom line increase.

'The effort and commitment by you both has been remarkable. I've checked your mileage receipts and, again, I have to say that, judging by hers, Debra has travelled the entire length of the country, whereas yours, Ricky, have pretty much stayed the same.'

Deb saw the panic creep into his eyes. The decision was not as clear-cut as he'd first thought either.

'But surely it's not cost-effective to be spending so many hours on the road if you're not achieving the sales figures.'

Ms Stringer smiled at him: not like the flattered female she had three months ago, but like she was explaining how the TV works to a small child. 'It depends on whose time you do those miles. I think anyone prepared to get up each morning to be on the road for seven and not return home until twelve hours later is demonstrating a suitable level of effort and commitment, don't you?' she asked pointedly.

'But I was committed too,' he said, sounding like a petulant child.

Ms Stringer nodded. 'As I've already stated, you both did exceptional jobs, but I don't seem to recall your Friday afternoon squash game suffering for it.'

Ricky opened his mouth to say more but decided against it. Deb could feel her knees knocking together under the table. She'd had no idea that her petrol receipts would be scrutinised in such detail.

'The final criterion was new customers and, again, Ricky, you didn't do as well as you might have done. You achieved two new customers in three months, whereas Debra managed a grand total of thirty-three.'

'But the value of those sales wasn't equal to the value of mine,' he argued, trying desperately to make the sales figures count for everything.

'Ricky, you're being rather short-sighted, which is something that seems to have let you down a little. Those new customers may not have placed orders to equal the value of yours, but through Debra we have thirty-three new clients who will undoubtedly order with us again and, hopefully, their orders will get bigger as they begin to trust us. You have to widen the net to catch fresher fish.'

'But six per cent…'

'Shows that all you did was persuade our existing customers to buy more.'

Deb couldn't help enjoying the exchange between the two of them and crossed her fingers in her lap.

'So, in conclusion, we had to weigh the higher sales figures against the demonstration of suitability for the job. The job of sales manager is not only about the dynamics of achieving the sales figures: it's also about encouraging other people to do it and, in doing so, there must be an understanding of the bigger picture and the direction that the company is taking.' Ms Stringer paused and Deb couldn't move her eyes from her face. 'And so I would like to offer Debra my congratulations on her new position.'

Ms Stringer stood and walked around to where Deb sat in stunned silence. Ricky paled, his eyes darting around the room as though trying to discover a missing angle that he could argue. Ms Stringer stood before her with her hand outstretched. 'Again, congratulations, and I'm sure we're going to work well together.'

The handshake was firm and the smile was warm. She turned on her heel and left the room.

Deb wanted to jump to her feet and hug someone, but the only person in close proximity was an almost-comatose Ricky Stone.

Deb rose and approached him, offering her hand in the same gesture that Ms Stringer had to her.

'No hard feelings?'

He shook her hand limply and hurried out of the office.

CHAPTER SIXTEEN

'Don't bother to switch the computer on,' Dan said as Cher sloped into her seat.

'Huh?'

'You won't be staying,' he said, sliding some contract folders into the cabinet.

'But what have I…?'

'You're going upstairs for a couple of days. Letitia is on a training course and Mr Hunter needs your help.'

Cher jumped out of her chair. Thank goodness she'd bothered to make a little effort with herself this morning, as she tended to do nowadays. 'So… er… umm… did he ask for me?'

Dan nodded without turning around. 'You'd better go.'

Cher hesitated. They'd been planning on working through the outdated operating manuals together this morning.

'But…'

'Go on, Cher. It's what you've wanted, and you don't want to keep him waiting.'

Cher headed to the lift, not feeling the level of excitement she'd expected to feel. She'd been looking forward to getting stuck into those manuals with Dan, but Michael Hunter had asked for her and she'd thought he never wanted to trust her with even making him coffee again, after her last efforts. She'd ring Deb and Sarah immediately, after seeing to any urgent business Michael had, just to rub their noses in it. She'd known that he wanted to see her again and her best friends had refused to believe her.

She arrived in the executive suite, slightly breathless. Wendy, the receptionist, sniffed slightly as Cher breezed past. 'Can you fill your name in the book like other visitors?' she said snidely.

Cher smiled sweetly. 'Not today, I'm working for Michael Hunter.'

Cher knocked lightly on his door. He smiled and came towards her. His desk was the size of a football pitch, and a minibar dominated the far corner.

'Cher, thanks for helping me out at such short notice. Letty's away for a couple of days.' He smiled disarmingly. 'And you know I need someone to organise me. I'm just hopeless without a little female assistance.'

Cher coloured. 'No problem, Mr Hunter. Where shall I start?'

'Please, call me Michael, and your desk is just out there. There's a little filing in the tray on Letty's desk to keep you going for a while, and the percolator needs to be filled. Letty always cleans it on a Monday morning.'

She nodded and left the room. Her desk was right outside his office within a small office of its own. The cabinets were made of mahogany, and the telephone looked like a miniature switchboard with lights flashing and dancing all over the place. The chair was comfortable with full lumbar support and adjustable arms. *Christ, how the other half lives*, she thought, glancing at the filing tray. The pile rose out of it by a couple of inches. Based on how much work Michael had produced downstairs, Letty must not have filed for months, she thought, glancing at the bottom sheets to find that she was right.

She cleaned the percolator and filled it before attacking the mountain of filing, which kept her busy until lunchtime. Once

Michael's sandwiches had been collected from the deli, she meandered into the canteen, which was a few tables shoved together in a kitchen area, with a few easy chairs. She retrieved her sandwiches from a fridge that groaned under the weight of SlimFast cans and sat in the corner away from a group of women delving disinterestedly into various shapes and sizes of Tupperware. The collective aroma of tuna wafted towards her. She glanced sideways as various magazine pages were flicked. She heard occasional comments about Kim Kardashian's bottom or which reality stars had broken up recently. They made no effort to speak to her, though they never did anyway; their glances seemed even more frosty than normal. They were probably jealous because Michael had requested her specifically.

She ignored them and bit hungrily into her ham sandwich.

'Hiya,' said Vicky, the security administrator.

Cher looked around to see who she was talking to.

Vicky sat beside her and started munching on a chicken roll. 'Is he keeping you busy?' she asked, opening a can of diet cola.

Cher nodded, unable to speak without spraying the girl with a shower of breadcrumbs. 'Quite a bit of filing to do,' she managed.

'Hmm… there would be. Poor old Letitia didn't exactly get any warning of what was going on,' Vicky said.

Alarm bells began to ring in Cher's head. 'But isn't she on a training course?'

Vicky started to laugh and turned to the others. 'Hey girls, do you reckon Letty's enjoying her training course?'

The page flicking stopped abruptly. A couple of the girls snorted or cut their eyes in Cher's direction and started to leave the room.

'But I was told—'

'Well you were told lies. Letty was given the boot on Friday afternoon.'

'Really?' Cher asked with interest. Maybe this position could become permanent. Oh God, if only.

'Yes, right out of the blue. Just told her to leave.'

Cher put the rest of her sandwiches back into her handbag, feeling a little queasy. In this day and age you couldn't just tell someone to leave. There was an eight-page section in the employee handbook detailing the process. 'But surely she must have done something wrong, like seriously wrong,' Cher offered. Only the most egregious acts justified instant dismissal.

'Think what you like but no one has had any reason to complain about Letty's performance before this. He gave her ten minutes to pack up her personal belongings and then had a security officer march her off the premises. She was in tears.'

Well that explained the lack of personal effects around the workstation, Cher thought as her head began to spin. What had Letty done to deserve such treatment? Something didn't feel right. Letty had been employed by the previous managing company for four years, so she had to have been doing something right. What did this mean for her? Was she on trial for the permanent position of assistant to Michael Hunter? Had she been summoned to fill the role based on her few weeks of experience with him downstairs?

'He's like that though. Everyone knows it. He has his little toys, and if they don't want to play the same game as him, he tires of them. Letty did everything for him, but the moment he felt that her loyalty had come into question, he binned her. I mean, you can't blame the poor girl for wanting something to challenge her a little bit. It's not as though anything he produces stretches the intelligence, as I'm sure you—'

'Sorry, I must get back. I told Michael I wouldn't be long,' she said imperiously. She didn't need to be listening to idle gossip behind his back. Despite her misgivings, she trusted that he wouldn't treat anyone unfairly, and if she wanted to know anything about Letty she'd just ask him.

She returned to her desk to find that Michael had left to attend a management meeting. She leafed through the diary and found the whole afternoon blocked out. With the filing tray empty and no sign of anything for her to sink her teeth into, she made another pot of coffee and sat back down. The desk drawers were empty, except for a couple of files which she placed back into the cabinet. She delved into some of the suspension files, to see if there was anything that needed tidying up or re-filing, but they were all in perfect order. Cher brightened when one of the personnel girls came into the office. She smiled brightly, hoping to engage the young girl in some sort of conversation.

'Can you make sure Mr Hunter gets this?' she said solemnly, placing a memo on the barren desk. Cher nodded and wondered whether she should do the job of putting the solitary piece of paper onto Michael's desk immediately or save it for later.

At four o'clock she rang down to Dan's phone. He sounded pre-occupied when he answered. Cher could imagine him at his desk with the door open into her alcove, his floor littered with folders and piles of paper.

'Hiya, just wondered if the Coolex tender had come in yet, because we said if it hadn't come in by this lunchtime, we were going to offer the contract to someone else and—'

'It's in.'

'Oh, is it competitive?'

'I'm just doing the figures.'

'Umm… I couldn't remember if I'd told you that the printers rang about the health and safety policy. It's been delayed by two weeks because of a technical—'

'You told me.'

'I wasn't sure if—'

'Well you almost got whiplash this morning, so I'm not surprised but it's okay, I'm managing quite well without you.'

Cher felt her face fall. She didn't want him to manage without her, but she got the impression that he was just saying that to make her feel better about being summoned upstairs. She could imagine the paperwork that was piling up on her desk.

'Maybe I could collect some work to bring—'

'Cher, why did you call?' he asked shortly.

She was shocked at his tone. It was almost like he was talking to a stranger. It was cool and distant and nothing like the Dan that she knew.

'I just wanted to check that—'

'What? That I knew exactly where you were. Don't worry, I know.' He paused. 'I just hope that you're finally where you always wanted to be,' he said quietly and replaced the receiver.

Cher stared at the phone. What was wrong with him? It wasn't her fault she'd been chosen to assist Michael, and if he thought she was going to refuse then he must be out of his bloody mind. Yes, she was where she wanted to be. It had taken her long enough, and so what if there wasn't much to do? Once she learned the job, Michael would be able to hand anything to her and she'd be as busy and as happy as she'd been downstairs.

Cher was still smarting from her conversation with Dan when Michael bustled back into the office. He looked slightly ruffled.

'Everything okay?' she asked automatically.

He nodded without smiling. 'I need you to type a couple of things up before you go,' he said, closing the door behind him.

Half an hour later he reappeared, looking much brighter than before, smug almost. 'I'm sure you can understand that the nature of these memos is of the highest confidentiality. I need to be sure that I can trust you. Do you understand?'

'Of course,' she answered, noting his gravely serious expression before he handed her the paperwork.

'I knew I could count on you,' he said, placing the pages face down on her desk. He smiled brightly and went back into his office, leaving the door open.

There were five separate pieces of paper, all numbered and dated. The first one was dated six months earlier and was in the form of a file note to the personnel department. Cher frowned as she read the 'Confirmation of Informal Reprimand' from him to Letty about her poor time-keeping. The second sheet was dated two weeks later and similar to the above but concerned the number of days taken as sickness.

The third was dated a month later and was a confirmation of verbal warning and went into more detail of her poor performance, with double-booked appointments, botched travel arrangements and shoddy paperwork. At the bottom of the page was a review date of her performance.

The fourth sheet was a written warning detailing Michael's efforts to discover the root of Letty's recent decline, but with no reply forthcoming, the fifth was an explanation memo for the file detailing his reasons for letting her go.

Cher sat back as they rolled off the printer. It was a watertight catalogue of events that showed Michael had followed the disciplinary procedure to the letter. According to his records, he had given Letty every chance to redeem herself and improve her performance. He had even asked what could be done to assist her. Did she need better equipment? An assistant? But her performance had remained unsatisfactory.

The young girl from personnel reappeared at the doorway. 'Has Mr Hunter seen that memo?' she asked as Cher slid the handwritten pages into the drawer.

Michael heard her through the open door. 'Yes, and I couldn't believe what I read. Who the hell does she think she is?'

The young girl coloured. 'I need the paperwork that proves what you say or she might well have a case.'

Michael stood behind Cher and placed a hand on her left shoulder. Cher shuddered. 'It will be with you shortly. Cher is just finding it on the system.'

The girl nodded nervously and left the room.

'Are they done?' he asked.

Cher nodded and handed him the printed sheets as the uneasy feeling grew in her stomach.

He smiled approvingly. 'Perfect. Where are the handwritten ones?'

'Shredded of course,' Cher answered, glancing at her top drawer.

He squeezed her shoulder again. 'Well done, Cher. I knew I could rely on you.'

'But the dates are—'

He waved away her words. 'Pay no attention to the dates. That's merely my poor paperwork skills. The events happened and I was just a little slow in documenting them. Now you can see why I need someone as efficient as you to organise me.' He smiled disarmingly as he followed the girl from personnel. He turned at the door. 'Don't go home yet; I'd like a quick word.'

Cher waited until he was out of sight and took the crumpled pieces of paper from her top drawer and placed them in her handbag. She'd get rid of them later. Nellie the cleaner was pretty nosey, and Michael wouldn't want her seeing confidential items.

She took a moment to convince herself that everything was above board and that Michael had acted professionally and ethically. After the way Letty had performed, no wonder Michael had been forced to get rid of her. How could he continue to work with someone that he couldn't trust to make the simplest of arrangements for him? A man in his position needed to only give a hint of an instruction and be sure that his wishes were being carried out. He didn't have the time to check people's work.

'Good, another problem solved,' he said, closing the door behind him. 'Now I think we've both earned the right to a little drink after work. What do you say?'

'Okay,' Cher said, unable to think of anything else to say. Just wait until she got home and rang Deb and Sarah. They would be mortified that they'd doubted her word. She'd known that Michael was going to ask her out.

'Would you like a few moments to refresh?' he asked.

Cher nodded and took her handbag to the bathroom. The rest of the executive suite was deserted. She touched up her make-up and combed her hair, wishing she could just pop out for a full makeover instead.

They walked across the car park in silence and reached his car, just as Dan reached his parked two spaces below.

'Aaah, Daniel, early night, is it?' he asked, coming to stand beside Cher.

'Just trying to get away on time for once,' he snapped without looking her way.

Cher felt Michael's arm snake around her shoulders. 'We're just going for a drink. We'd love you to join us but we have things to discuss. You know how it is.'

Cher felt her cheeks colour as a muscle jumped in Dan's jawbone. His gaze was fixed on Michael's arm. His eyes moved up and Cher thought she saw a slight disappointment in them, but he smiled. 'Well I hope you have a nice night.'

'We will,' Michael said, just as Dan closed the driver's door.

Cher glanced through the window at him as he put his car into gear. She wanted to say something, apologise for Michael's rudeness or just smile, but his face was set and he didn't look her way. She watched as his car left the car park ahead of them and felt a mild nausea rise in her throat. She tried to pull herself together. She'd waited for this for months and now she was going to let it be spoiled because Michael had been rude to Dan. This was her night and she wasn't going to let anything ruin it. She mentally checked herself in an effort to banish the image of his stony expression, but the way he'd looked at her made her want to cry.

Michael drove to a wine bar on the other side of town and not one that Cher had entered before. The frontage was unassuming, giving no clue as to the opulence inside.

'Have a seat there,' Michael instructed, lowering himself into the plush red velvet chair opposite. A waiter appeared instantly.

'Your usual, Mr Hunter?'

Michael nodded.

Cher ordered a dry white wine and glanced around. No one stood as they did in the bars that she frequented. There was no music just a low hum of voices. The waiter placed the drinks on the tortoiseshell table that separated them. Cher looked around and felt her M&S trouser suit clashing with the abundance of Armani. She was glad they were sitting by the door. The walls were a deep velvet texture that matched the chairs, and the place exuded an expensive air and held more suits than Savile Row.

'So how is our Daniel these days? He appears to be struggling.'

'He's doing well, getting his head around the procedures of the company and trying to put everything in place, ready for the audit.'

'And how do you get along with him?'

'Fine,' Cher answered, wondering why he was asking about her relationship with Dan.

He tipped his head sideways slightly, as though he was playing a game. 'Only I got the impression the other evening that there seems to be a little something developing between the two of—'

'Oh God no,' she blurted out. 'I mean, don't get me wrong, we get on well, we work together extremely well, but we're just friends,' she said, reddening.

He nodded with a satisfied smile. 'Good. As you know, loyalty is very important to me and I'd like to think that I have yours.'

'Of course,' Cher said.

He removed his jacket and loosened his tie. Cher swallowed. In some ways he was much too good-looking to be a man. His features were almost feminine: soft and beautiful and untouched, with a clean-cut preppie youthfulness.

'Because I have to be honest that I'm a little concerned about Daniel. I'm not sure he's handling the job too well. I know we shouldn't expect too much with his background and everything, but I wasn't too sure that he could manage it in the first place. You see, some people are never meant to expand their horizons. They're happy and content where they are and anything a little more challenging is frightening for them. They're plodders and they have no motivation to—'

'But Dan's not like that. Admittedly, he found it a little difficult to begin with, but he's settled into the job very well and he understands what's needed from him.'

Michael relaxed back and his legs fell open, so he was almost pointing his crotch towards her. Cher had trouble looking anywhere else.

'I think a lot of it stems from education. Within the state school system, I think under-achieving is actually encouraged, whereas in a public school, you're more focused on being the best that you can. Take me for example. I was educated at St Christopher's, an all-boys school, from the age of nine and was only ever encouraged to aspire to the higher positions of management or banker or even politician. Everything we did was for a purpose. Debates were designed to weed out the best prospective lawyers; physical education was used for discovering the most talented athletes. Everything had the purpose for us to aspire to be the best. The words "bus driver" were not part of our vocabulary.' He chuckled lightly. 'To be completely honest, I didn't know what a bus was. I spent years reaching higher and here I am, managing a shopping and entertainment complex worth more than half a billion pounds.' He shrugged and took a sip of his drink. 'Intelligence is not something that's limited to the upper classes, I'm not saying that for one moment, but I think the ability to use it and focus it on higher expectations is.'

'But it's not that easy for people not born into a wealthy background to aspire to certain levels of employment.' Cher coloured slightly; the wine was circulating her system on half a ham sandwich.

Michael chuckled. 'Oh, Cher, you never let me down, but let me ask you a question: had you been born into a wealthy family, do you really think that you would now be a mere secretary?'

Cher forgave him the word *mere*. She understood what he meant. 'Maybe…'

'If I were to meet your parents, do you think I would be able to guess where your career aspirations came from?'

It depends what they were dressed as, Cher thought, but stopped herself from saying it, just in time to realise that Dan would have laughed at that.

'But there are only certain opportunities open to certain people,' she maintained.

Michael shook his head. 'The opportunities are there for everyone. You just have to want it badly enough.'

Cher was getting into the debate, fuelled by mild irritation, although his words about meeting her parents had registered.

'So tell me how I could have got into Oxford or Cambridge?' she asked.

'Hard work, saving money from part-time jobs—'

Cher's raucous laugh interrupted him. 'Do you have any idea how much money I would have had to save to get into Oxford?'

'But it's possible,' he challenged.

'Maybe by the time I was ninety.'

'But still possible.'

'What does this have to do with Dan anyway?' she asked.

He shook his head. 'I just don't think he's capable of what we want. When the auditors come in, he needs to be able to answer or field any question that comes his way, and I'm not confident that he can do that. A position might become available back in his old workforce, but I can't say for definite that—'

'You're not considering putting him out of work?' Cher asked, aghast. There was Jamie to think of.

'It's not as simple as that. We have to look at the damage that could be done when the auditors—'

'But he's done everything he possibly can. He was lumbered with the position that he didn't want, and now that he's cracking it and making it work, you can't pull the rug from underneath him again. It's just not fair.'

Michael frowned. 'The decision has not yet been made, but I did want your thoughts on the matter and your assurance that your loyalty is focused in the right direction.'

Cher heard the warning in his voice. 'Of course.'

He downed the remainder of his drink and glanced at his watch. 'Oh well, got to go. Will you be okay getting home from here?' he asked, sliding his jacket back on.

'Umm… yes… I'll be fine,' she answered, surprised at the speed of their after-work drink.

She called a taxi and stood outside. Being in there without Michael made her feel uncomfortable, and she couldn't help the feeling that this was a reward, like a doggie biscuit, for keeping quiet about the Letitia situation, as though she was a circus animal to be rewarded for doing an entertaining trick. His words about Dan stayed on her mind, but how could she warn him? If she even hinted at what Michael had said, Dan's pride would force him to walk out. Cher knew he wouldn't tolerate being treated in such a manner.

Cher stood waiting for the taxi in the warm sunlight and felt that she hadn't yet seen the real Michael. So far she'd seen the intelligent, educated man who was at ease with himself and had an assured confidence that carried him through most situations, yet she felt there had to be more to him than that. Cher wondered how long he spent around real people.

An idea occurred to her: he'd mentioned meeting her parents and that was exactly what she intended for him to do.

CHAPTER SEVENTEEN

By the time Cher got home, hours earlier than usual, she was desperate for someone to talk to. She called Deb and Sarah, to see if they fancied trying the new seafood restaurant that had just opened on the canal front. She felt sure that prawns was something Sarah could eat, providing their bill of rights hadn't been violated.

When she realised how excited she was to tell her friends about her after-work drink with Michael, she conceded just how sad she was, although she'd decided not to mention anything about Dan. She didn't want them making something out of a relationship that just didn't exist. And her friendship with Dan was something she wanted to keep to herself. It was just hers.

She walked the short distance to the canal front and, complete with brandy and Coke, sat outside the restaurant, surveying the trendy wine bars that were littered along the side of the water. Office blocks rose up behind the silhouette of the new development that attracted hordes of teenagers at the weekend.

Within a week of the complex opening, she, Sarah and Deb had treated themselves to a night of showing off their dancing skills, thinking that the place would be frequented by people their own age. Their rude awakening came when four girls who appeared to be prepubescent offered them their table.

She allowed herself to be hypnotised by the bright lights dancing on the barely moving canal and found herself wondering what Dan was doing and why he'd left work on time for the first time in weeks.

'Earth to Cher. Come in,' said Sarah as she removed a pashmina from her shoulders. 'Fantasising about Michael Hunter?'

Cher was surprised to find that she wasn't but nodded anyway.

'Hiya,' Deb greeted, throwing herself with her usual finesse into the silver metal chair that looked like it had been stolen from the set of a science-fiction movie.

Cher wasn't surprised to see that she was still wearing a navy trouser suit. Dark shadows beneath her eyes, coupled with her high cheekbones, made her look tired.

'You okay?'

'I've really done it this time,' she said, shaking her head. 'My attempt at offering Margie the olive branch resulted in me poking her eye out with it.'

Cher sat forward, riveted. In all the years Deb had been with Mark, she had never once retaliated, which was most unlike her, but around Margie her mute button became activated.

'What happened?'

'I felt so sure that I would be able to ignore anything the evil little witch threw at me and I almost succeeded, right until the very last minute. After all the digs and nasty remarks had gone unchallenged, I was crossing the finishing line and I just snapped and gave her what for.'

'Hang on,' Cher ordered as the waiter tentatively approached their table. Normally she would have shooed him away for a while, but the delicious aroma of steamed salmon and saffron was killing her.

'I'm not hungry,' said Deb, pounding her cigarette into the tin ashtray. She immediately lit another.

Cher ordered the salad of scallops, and Sarah pointed to a dish on the next table. She was informed that it was red mullet with pesto sauce. Once the food was ordered, Cher was able to concentrate on Deb's big news.

'Carry on,' Sarah prompted.

'Well, one remark too many led to an all-out boxing match, which resulted in me calling her a trifling old bag and she calling me a hardened cow.'

'Christ.'

'Bloody hell,' Sarah said.

'Surely you must be relieved though? After all these years of harnessing that slippery eel you call a tongue, you must be pleased that you've finally had your say?'

Deb shook her head. 'That's the thing. I drove away from her house with my heart in my mouth, terrified about what Mark would say when I told him what had happened. But he only wanted to go over and have a go at her for what she called me.'

'Go Mark,' Sarah and Cher cheered, causing expressions of disdain from nearby diners.

'I stopped him,' Deb said sheepishly.

'Why, why, why?'

Deb shrugged. 'That's what I can't understand. I was frightened to death that my actions would drive a wedge between us, and when it didn't, the sick feeling wouldn't go away. I wanted him to be on my side. I would have been hurt if he wasn't. I wanted him to go racing around there to defend my honour, but when he showed he was on my side, there was nothing I wanted less.'

Sarah and Cher looked at each other, dumbfounded. This was what Deb had been after for years.

'It's all a bit of an anticlimax,' she admitted.

'How exactly did you think it would be?'

Deb shrugged again. 'I dunno. I thought that everything would be so much better without her, and it is, in a way, but I'm sure Mark must be unhappy with the situation.'

'Just don't ask him to take sides.'

'I'm not. I suggested he go and see her last night. Strangely, the last thing I want is for him to lose contact with his mother. I know how hard it is not to have one in your life.'

'I'm not exactly flavour of the month with mine,' Sarah said, shuddering. 'She was not too amused when I stripped naked at my sister's "new pool party" in front of everyone because I'd forgotten that I wasn't wearing any underwear.'

Deb laughed. 'You dopey tart. Just enlighten me as to how you could forget.'

'The brandy ate my memory, and it was the fact that David was in the pool splashing with Chelsea and Stacey, Roger was showing my father the optics at the bar, my mother was discussing lobelia plants with a woman from across the road and I was the odd one out. I vaguely recall wanting to join in but didn't have a costume, so decided that my undies would do.'

'But they were in your bedroom where you'd left them,' Deb said, not even trying to contain her amusement.

'I can't really remember much after the collective shriek of horror, and now David is barely speaking to me.' Sarah shrugged. 'Honestly, anyone would think I'd scarred the child for life.'

'Well it must have been traumatic for her. She is young, after all,' Deb said, trying to keep a straight face.

'Don't even get me started. I tried everything I could to get on with her, but she doesn't want to know. When she visits, she insists that she isn't left alone with me, and David becomes a totally different person when she's there. It's quite nauseating in a way,' Sarah said.

'You've not quite got that maternal instinct thing right yet, have you?'

'I honestly can't find much to like about the child and, believe me, I've tried. She's spoiled and mean-spirited and in my house far too often. I mean, when she comes the place turns into Chelsea's entertainment area. No place is safe. The other night she was dyeing some of her doll's clothes in the bath: they were hanging to dry in our bedroom; the living room had been made into a camp with old sheets and the dining chairs; and the kitchen was trying to recover from them making a strawberry cheesecake.'

'But David must be loosening up now that he gets to see his daughter quite regularly. He must be happier surely?'

'He works late the nights he doesn't see Chelsea, then eats something before going back to his laptop and then he goes to bed. I see less of him now than I did before.'

Cher tried to stop her foot from tapping. When was she going to get a chance to tell them what she'd been up to?

The waiter materialised with two plates, one balancing on the inside of his outstretched arm.

Cher's mouth watered at the creamy truffle vinaigrette that draped the scallops and new potatoes. Sarah's looked equally delicious, though Cher had a slight problem with eating anything that colourful. It was like depleting the sea life beneath the barrier reef.

Cher speared a scallop and offered it to Deb. She shook her head. Cher shrugged. The sharp movement sent creamy white sauce slithering down her black shirt.

She dabbed at it awkwardly, trying not to turn a drama into a dry-cleaning nightmare.

'Had a little accident there, Cher?'

She turned instantly towards a voice that she recognised. The smile froze on her face. Dan smiled down at her, then turned to the woman on his arm.

'Lucy, this is Cher – a colleague from work.'

Cher undertook a swift inventory of his companion. Her blonde hair seemed to be of Swedish origin and was brushed feather-like onto a pleasant face, its only flaw being a very square jaw, which actually became more attractive the more you looked at her.

She felt Deb's heel against her shin. 'Oh s-sorry. Deb and Sarah. My friends,' she spluttered, becoming more aware of her cream sauce stain, unruly hair, friendly features and size-fourteen figure next to this woman. It didn't help that she towered above Cher, thereby provoking all her inadequacies to sit up and beg for food. Well they wouldn't go hungry now, she thought as Lucy opened her mouth and smiled. It was warm and genuine.

'Nice to meet you,' she breathed.

'Would you like to join us?' Sarah asked, obviously thinking Cher had left her manners at home.

Dan shook his head. 'We'd love to but we have a reservation,' he said, pointing to a small Italian restaurant. Cher had never been in but she knew that it was a cavernous, dimly lit environment.

'Well I'll see you tomorrow then,' Dan said, smiling down at her. She tried to smile back.

Lucy put her arm through his as they walked away.

'Put the fork down, Cher, before you kill someone with it,' Deb advised, removing the stabbing implement from her hand. Her tight, white knuckles relinquished their hold.

'Who's he?' Sarah asked, still watching them.

'He's my boss,' she mumbled disinterestedly.

'He's gorgeous. I've no idea what Michael Hunter looks like, but I can't imagine why you've been fantasising about him when that man seems to be lacking in no area that I can see,' Sarah joked, turning her head sideways, appraising him as he walked.

'He's my boss,' she repeated, seeing him through Sarah's eyes. Out of the restrictive sombre suit, he did look relaxed and assured. Light grey jeans hugged and fitted him perfectly, hinting at the taut muscle of thighs that had fallen absently against hers at the cinema. The short sleeves of his polo shirt strained slightly at the top of his arms.

'Well he certainly is—'

'Sarah, leave it,' she snapped for no reason that she could fathom. She took a gulp of brandy which enabled her to glance at them one more time before they entered the restaurant. Dan stood back and held the door open for his companion to enter. He seemed to pause before following her inside.

'Why are you throwing your teddy in the corner?' Deb asked suspiciously.

'I just don't know why you're going on about him, that's all.'

Deb and Sarah exchanged knowing glances.

'It's nothing like that,' she protested hotly.

She snatched her fork back from Deb and speared a lettuce leaf. It jumped across the plate but it didn't matter: the scallops had suddenly lost their charm, and so had the evening out.

'Ooh, Cher's expression is giving me the urge to write a love story.' Sarah gazed up at the blue sky with a smattering of white congregating clouds. 'A tale of unrequited love.'

'You'd be better off trying to write yourself out of your own predicament,' Deb snapped. 'Honestly, Sarah, there's no pleasing you. Now you have what you always wanted, you don't seem to bloody want it.'

'And you're a good one to talk. You've finally got Margie off your back and you're not shouting from the rooftops.'

This was the moment that Cher should have stepped in with some distant memory of them making necklaces out of paper clips at Sunday school, but she couldn't be bothered. She just wanted to go home.

She sat and listened to their bickering with one eye on the Italian restaurant. She could imagine Dan and Lucy in that romantic setting, a candle flame dancing between them. She found herself wondering if their conversation would be as easy as the night that Dan had taken her out. Would he be throwing back his head with laughter?

Her mouth opened to tell them about her drink with Michael Hunter, but she realised that there was nothing to tell.

'For God's sake, does he have any idea how you feel?'

'Huh?' Cher asked. The last she'd heard they'd been bickering between themselves with no involvement from her, so why had their attention turned her way?

'Stan, Dan or whatever his name is. Does he have a clue?' Deb asked.

'I don't fancy him. We're just colleagues,' Cher snapped. This night out hadn't been such a good idea. She should have gone home and fantasised about Michael.

'Is that why you've not taken your eyes off that place?' Sarah asked.

'I'm just curious about Lucy. He's never mentioned her.'

'Should he have done?' Deb asked quizzically.

'Well we have spent a lot of time together. We have talked.' Sarah and Deb exchanged looks.

'Stop being stupid. He's my boss, that's all.'

'Oh well, I'd better be getting back. David will be returning from his squash game and I'm going to try, yet again, to inject a little romance into our dreary existence. Either that or go into my office and write about all the hot sex that I'm not getting.'

'Yep, I'm under strict instructions: Mark has something special planned but he wouldn't tell me what it was,' said Deb rising. 'Coming?'

Cher hesitated. 'No, I think I'll just have another drink.'

She waited for the others to turn the corner before ordering another drink and placing herself at a different table in the shadows, but one which still afforded her a view of the Italian restaurant. It was a nice evening and she had nothing better to do. She felt a little like a voyeur, but she wanted to see Dan again with Lucy. She wanted to see if he had a softness in his eyes the way he did when he looked at her. She wanted to see if Lucy held his attention every time she opened her mouth. She wanted to see if Dan touched her lightly on the waist as they came out of the restaurant – but why, she had no idea.

Two brandies later, the cool breeze from the water brought goose pimples on her skin. She shivered in the darkened shadows until almost eleven thirty, when she finally gave up and went home.

CHAPTER EIGHTEEN

Cher rode into work the following morning determined to put the picture of Dan and Lucy out of her head. She parked next to Michael's BMW and entered through the executive suite reception.

'I'm here to assist Michael,' she said imperiously.

'But he's interview—'

Cher didn't listen and breezed past.

'Cher, what are you doing here?' Michael asked as his forehead furrowed.

'I've umm… come to er… help…'

Michael checked his watch. 'Oh well, now you're here, you might as well make a pot of coffee.'

Cher reached for the carafe, getting the distinct impression that she hadn't been expected.

Michael returned to his office and closed the door. Cher set the pot to perc and sat at her empty desk. Her feet knocked against each other beneath the table. She had promised herself that she would ask him today. It was time for her to go after what she wanted. The image of Dan and Lucy had spurred her on. It was now or never.

'Michael, can I have a word?' she asked tentatively.

He nodded distractedly.

She took a deep breath and held her hands behind her back to stop them from trembling. She felt like a schoolgirl asking the teacher for more time to do her homework.

'It's just that my er… ummm… parents are having a little party… well not party really, more of a family gathering, really…'

Michael grunted without looking up from a magazine.

Cher felt herself blushing but surged forward. If she didn't, she would hate herself for not sticking to her convictions, and the picture of Dan with Lucy spurred her on.

'Well I was just wondering, I mean, it's probably short notice and you've probably got loads of things to do, but well…'

'Spit it out, Cher.'

'Well I was sort of wondering if you'd like to come,' she blurted out.

Cher's heart leaped as his face creased into a smile. He was going to say yes. Her heart started to beat rapidly.

He closed the magazine, his lips twitching. 'Let me get this right. You're asking *me* to come to your parents' house for a party?'

'Y… y… yes.'

Michael's head was thrown back with the force of his laughter. Cher hopped from one foot to the other, wondering what was so funny.

'Oh, please tell me you're being serious.'

Cher nodded, feeling a leaden weight settle in her stomach.

He stopped laughing, but his eyes held the amusement of a hilariously funny joke that he kept remembering. 'And why would you think that I'd care to go with you?'

Cher felt the heat flush into her face. In all truth she hadn't expected him to say yes: she had expected him to claim the pressure of work or prior commitments, but not humour.

'Please don't answer that,' he said, chuckling but trying to compose himself. 'Is Ma cooking a good ole pot of stew and dumplings for the brood?' he asked, losing control of his laughter.

Cher felt her throat constrict with pressure. She was rooted to the spot.

'Really, Cher, you never cease to amaze me,' he said, dabbing his eyes with his handkerchief. 'The very idea of me visiting your parents, and why the hell would I want to?' His eyes bored into hers, genuinely perplexed and waiting for a reply.

'I j-just thought… after…'

'Oh, I see, because we had a brief drink together after work, you thought that was the beginning of something special between us. God, Cher, you're so funny.' His eyes turned serious and his expression became grave. 'I asked you to assist me temporarily because I had some delicate paperwork that needed to be treated with care, and I knew that you with your dewy-eyed devotion would not question for one second what I was doing. I took you for a drink to thank you, but that is the end of that, and your services are no longer required.'

His voice had turned cold as though Cher had insulted him, instead of the other way around.

'I'm interviewing for my new assistant today, and if you'd like to stick around, you're more than welcome.' His mouth had a cruel edge to it. 'You might even like to apply, although I don't think you've really got the attributes that I'd be looking for in a—'

Cher turned and ran out of the office. She blindly grabbed her jacket and helmet and was vaguely relieved that the reception area was empty.

She reached her bike and sobbed aloud, letting the tears wash over her cheeks. She tried to choke them back so that she'd be able to get on her bike and get away from the place as quickly as she could and never come back.

She visualised Michael sitting at his desk having a good old laugh at her expense. She kicked her rear wheel. How the hell had she been stupid enough to think that Michael Hunter could ever be interested in her, and why had she never seen the brutally cruel side to him before? It was like a veil had slipped away from in front of his face. She saw the ruthless, cold side of him that made him a good businessman and a heartless bastard.

She fiddled with her key, trying to get it into the ignition. She didn't care where she went, just as long as she got away from here. He was probably already telling everyone now how she'd made a complete idiot of herself. The story would circulate by jungle drums, grapevine and carrier pigeon for months.

'Cher, are you okay?' She heard Dan's voice beside her as he got out of his car.

She nodded and kept her back to him. She didn't want anyone to see her in such a state.

'Your friends seem nice. I looked for you after... Cher... what's wrong?' he asked, turning her to face him. 'Shit, what's happened?'

'Nothing, it's okay. I just don't feel well. I'm going home,' she said, pulling her arm out of his grasp.

'You're not going anywhere in this state.' He pulled her across the car park towards the facilities entrance in silence.

He pushed her into her seat. 'Now tell me what's wrong.'

Cher felt the tears burn again. She took deep breaths to force them back down, but they spilled over and ran down her cheeks. 'Nothing, it's... my... own... fault,' she said between sobs.

Dan kneeled before her and took her hand in his. 'What's your fault?' he asked softly. 'What's happened?'

Cher could bear his searching expression no longer. The words tumbled out as she recounted what Michael had said. Dan's expression hardened.

'Fucking bastard. He needs teaching a goddamn lesson. He can't get away with treating people like that.' He slammed his other fist against the side of the desk. 'Who the fuck does he think he is to speak to you like that?'

'It's my own fault. I shouldn't have asked him. I was being stupid to think that—'

'To think that he'd be honoured to be asked to meet your family. Why the hell shouldn't you ask him? He's not fucking God, Cher. He's an ordinary, mortal man. No, scrub that, he's a total wanker and I've a good mind to—'

'No,' Cher cried. 'Don't do anything. You'll lose your job and I don't want that on my conscience. You have a child.' She smiled tremulously. 'But thanks anyway.'

He squeezed her hand. 'Come on, Cher, don't let that bastard destroy you. He's not worth it. No one is. You deserve better than him.'

Cher started to get up. 'I just want to go.'

Dan pushed her back down. 'You're not going anywhere. You are not going to give that bastard the satisfaction of driving you out of a job that you love.'

'But how can I stay after the things he said to me?' She winced, remembering his horrible words. But at least the tears had stopped.

'Don't give him that satisfaction. If you run away, you'll regret it later. You'll always shudder when you think of what happened and, eventually, you'll hate yourself for running away, and I'll bet you've never run away from anything in your life.'

Cher smiled wanly. Once when she was about eight, a girl had said some particularly horrible things about her parents in front of half the class and she'd walked away. All day she'd felt like a failure for not defending herself and for allowing the girl to think she'd won. That night an anger had built in her stomach for being so weak, and the following day she'd placed two good-sized beetles into the girl's Barbie sandwich box.

'But how can I face anyone?' she asked. The humiliation was just too much to bear. By lunchtime everyone would know.

'The same way you've faced them for all these years. Bring it back to what actually happened. You asked him out and he said no. There are better ways he could have said it,' Dan said, trying to place a comforting smile on his hardened features. 'But at the end of the day that's all that happened, as far as you're concerned. You've held your head high up there all this time, safe in the knowledge that you're a more intelligent, caring person than all of them put together. But is it worth losing your job?'

A few months ago Cher would have said yes, but since working with Dan she'd learned a lot. They'd learned a lot together and as a result the department was coming together. For the last few months she'd gone home physically and mentally drained from her workload. It wasn't something she wanted to give up.

'I suppose you're right,' she admitted, squirming at the thought of having to go upstairs again.

Cher realised that Dan was still holding her hand when he squeezed it reassuringly. 'See, you're stronger than that, Cher. You're not a quitter. That's one of the things I respect you for, and how the hell would I manage without you?' He loosed her hand and sat on the edge of the desk.

'You seemed to be okay yesterday when I called you.'

'Just having a bad day. Seriously though, we make a helluva team.'

Cher smiled and nodded, beginning to feel a little better. Once the humiliation subsided there wasn't as much damage as she'd expected. There was fierce anger in her stomach that he thought he could get away with treating people that way, but the rest of her seemed unharmed.

She removed her jacket and dabbed at her eyes for the last time. 'Oh well, my mum will have to wait a little while longer to see me arrive with an actual living, breathing member of the male species.'

Dan tipped his head. 'How about two?'

'Huh?'

'I think Jamie and me could do with a good old home-made stew,' he said, nudging her with a smile.

Cher blushed. Trust Dan to take pity on her after what she'd told him. 'Thanks, Dan, but I don't need you to feel sorry for—'

'Oh shut up for a change. I'd love to come, and Jamie already knows the boys and would love to see them again.'

Cher thought about it. It would be nice for the boys to see Jamie again. They had all ended up the best of buddies after the *Star Wars* male-bonding experience, but she didn't need Dan's pity. That would just make everything worse.

He tipped her head upward to look into his eyes. They were bright and mischievous. 'After the things you've told me, I really would love to meet your parents.'

Cher giggled, remembering their frank discussion over dinner. 'Okay, but don't say I didn't warn you.'

The only thing that spoiled Cher's growing excitement at the forthcoming tea with her parents was that she had learned it was to be a barbecue. Her father's idea of a barbecue was dragging a rusty wire mesh out of the shed and laying it across two stacks of house bricks. He would also insist on donning a white chef's hat that poked up through the clouds, obstructing any low-flying aircraft. The plastic apron declaring 'I'm Every Woman' in a fetching shade of magenta did nothing to improve his manly image.

The barbecue fare would be crucified sausages and cremated burgers forced into finger rolls because her mum would have forgotten to get the round baps. There would be a warm bowl of salad that had been taken out of the fridge too early. This culinary feast she had come to expect, and so had her cast-iron stomach, but she feared for the safety of lesser mortals.

She rode home and changed into jeans, T-shirt and trainers in anticipation of the delights she would receive from the little horrors out in the garden. She tied her hair back, feeling the irritation of having it around her face all day, and added a flash of lipstick.

Dan's car pulled up outside, and Jamie waved enthusiastically from the back seat. She ruffled his hair as she got into the car and passed him a Milky Way. Dan opened his mouth but she silenced him. '"It's the sweet you can eat between meals without ruining your appetite,"' she quoted as she turned and winked at Jamie, who already had the paper off.

'So, how you doing, Finn?'

'Poe, now,' he mumbled. 'Went again, like Poe now. Johnny's mum likes popcorn.'

'Johnny's mum?' she enquired, turning towards Dan.

'Lucy – you met her the other night. She doesn't go out very much, so we occasionally—'

'You don't need to explain,' Cher snapped. It was nothing to do with her but it brought back to her that tonight, despite his kindness, was nothing more than a mercy mission.

'Johnny's mum ate two Mars Bars and got chocolate all around her mouth. Daddy helped her wipe it off and they—'

'That's enough,' Dan snapped uncharacteristically. His voice softened. 'I'm sure Cher doesn't want to hear about that.'

He was right. She didn't. She sat back and glanced out of the window, trying to understand why it bothered her. Dan was her boss and, to some extent, her friend, and him going to the cinema with another woman had nothing to do with her. A stab of jealousy coursed through her to which she had absolutely no right. She stole a sideways glance at him. She wanted to strike up a pleasant conversation, but she felt an anger inside that prevented her making any small talk like normal, yet he'd done nothing wrong. Her directions were the only words that passed between them. Great, what a fun evening this was going to be, she thought.

This didn't have to take very long, she decided. A couple of burgers, a cold drink and they could be out of there just as quickly. He could deposit her home, she would see him at work tomorrow and they'd forget that any of this had ever happened.

He pulled up outside her parents' house and she saw that Marlon and *Patreesha* were already there. Dan already had the background on her family, so she didn't need to update him any further. He followed her silently up the entryway to the back of the house, with Jamie behind him carrying a small box.

The family was already assembled in the garden, with her dad at the barbecue, which seemed to be emitting far too much smoke in the direction of next door's washing. Her mother was placing salad bowls onto a small table, and Marlon was playing rugby with the boys. Her mum spotted them and approached immediately.

'Hello, love,' she cried, hugging Cher.

'Hi, Mum. This is Dan, he's…' Her words trailed off. How the hell did she introduce him? He wasn't her boyfriend, and she wasn't sure that introducing him as her boss would do her any great favours either. Her mother waited expectantly for her to finish the introduction so that she could take his hand. She looked blankly from her to Dan and back again.

'Friend and colleague of your daughter,' he said with an engaging smile as he took her hand warmly. She shot him a grateful look as Jamie barged between them holding out his small package.

'I'm Jamie and this is for your hosp… hos… tal…' He looked up towards Dan, who was smiling proudly.

Her mum chuckled warmly and bent down to receive the present. 'Thank you very much, Jamie,' she said as she bent and kissed the top of his head.

Jamie's attention had already been diverted to the high-jinx on the lawn.

'Rugby, cool.'

Cher watched in amazement as he entered the game easily, after receiving some good-natured thumps from the boys. Marlon glanced up and waved in their direction, rolling his eyes and sweating profusely. Why wasn't it that easy for adults to mix? Cher wondered. Jamie and the boys had met only once but appeared to be like cousins.

Cher guided Dan to where her father stood over charcoal that was glowing slightly more than him.

The introduction went smoothly as her dad took his hand and said, 'Good to meet you, lad,' as he did with anyone whose name he was in danger of forgetting later.

She guided Dan indoors to the lounge where *Patreesha* sat perched on the sofa, as usual. 'You must be Pat,' Dan enthused, moving forward to shake her hand. If he noticed the quick down-turn of her mouth, he didn't show it, but Cher almost laughed.

'Oh doesn't this look nice?' her mum asked from the man-telpiece that ran above the gas fire. The present was a delicate, intricately shaped glass perfume bottle, no bigger than her thumb. Cher peered closer and nodded. It really was lovely.

Jeremy burst into the living room, knocking Cher half out of the way to scream some sort of injustice at his mother about the game outside. Pat smiled indulgently and told him to kick his brother back, which Cher thought was just about the worst case of parenting she'd ever seen. Satisfied that he now had permission to go and beat his younger brother senseless, he tore back out of the room.

Cher's mum picked the perfume bottle up and placed it back within the protective confines of the box. 'I think I'll place that properly a little later,' she said with a sideways glance that Pat didn't catch.

'You're a researcher on the local news, Cher tells me,' Dan said pleasantly.

Pat's feathers fluffed as she smiled sweetly at him. She looked even thinner than usual, with a V-neck T-shirt exposing a long neck that reminded Cher of a metal binding comb.

'I was watching a piece the other day about closing the old steel factory that's been in operation since 1860, only it hasn't. That was when it was built, but they didn't start production until 1874, I think it was.'

The smile froze on Pat's face. 'Oh… umm… er… that wasn't mine; it was…'

'I'm sure it doesn't matter. I wouldn't imagine too many people caught the mistake.'

Pat nodded but the colour had drained from her face as though she'd been personally attacked. Cher guided Dan back out to the garden before she burst out laughing.

'What?' Dan asked innocently. 'I only told the truth.'

She punched him playfully as they sat on a bench that her dad had liberated from the local park two decades earlier. How it had travelled the three miles had remained a family secret to that day.

Dan sat comfortably in the shade from an outside toilet that had been turned into a pigeon enclosure. The contented cooing reached them through the vents installed by her dad. He began to laugh at Marlon's Jonah Lomu impression.

Her dad paused from his culinary efforts long enough to place cans of beer in their hands. Cher sipped gratefully on the lager while Dan held his can on his knee.

'Umm… er… Cher…'

'Oh, sorry, I'll just get you a glass.' Not everyone drank straight from the can, she realised.

'No, it's not that. It's umm…'

He looked a little uncomfortable.

'Look, if you don't want it, just say so,' she snapped, wondering what was wrong with her dad's beer. So what if it was the supermarket's own brand? It tasted all right to her.

'It's not that.' He looked from Jamie to the can and back again. 'I just don't touch it when I'm driving.'

Duly chastised, she took the can from him and placed it next to hers.

'Okey-dokey,' Cher's dad shouted. 'Who needs their bellies filled?' The kids ran towards him, screaming joyfully. Marlon took the opportunity to introduce himself to Dan. They immediately started talking sports and found a common interest in cricket, while Cher fetched food for them all, unable to break up their male-bonding session.

'He's all right him, Cher, not bad at all,' her dad grumbled as she reached for sausages. High praise from her dad indeed. He leaned closer. 'I didn't think when I passed him that can,' he admitted. Impetuously, Cher leaned across and kissed him on the cheek for no reason whatsoever. In his younger days he'd sported a full head of tar-black hair and a bushy beard. Now his beard was tinged with wiry grey hairs, showing his age around his mouth like an old Labrador.

'It's not like that though, Dad. We're just friends,' she explained. She didn't want him to get the wrong idea. She followed his gaze to where Dan sat talking animatedly with

Marlon. He said something that made Marlon laugh heartily, before glancing in her direction with a slow smile and a quick wink that surprised her by making her go weak at the knees. His easy manner, sitting there chatting with her brother, as the kids gathered around to listen to their conversation, was having a very strange effect on her nerves. How was it that he fitted into her family so easily and painlessly?

Her dad, having watched the exchange, nodded. 'If you say so, love.'

She took her place beside Dan and passed him a plate: again, that smile. She listened intently while they discussed scores, batting averages and tests and decided to give them the benefit of her opinion.

'How can you watch a game where it takes the bowler twenty minutes to walk backward and forward rubbing the ball against his crotch before throwing it to the batsman, who taps it literally inches away and it all starts again? I mean, how can you contain the utter excitement as you watch?'

Dan and Marlon exchanged glances, burst out laughing and completely ignored her. She shrugged and turned her attention to the food, chomping away in the early evening sunshine. She wasn't the least bit surprised when Dan approached the barbecue in search of more. Her father turned to say something serious to him. He listened intently before nodding, placing more food onto his plate and returning to sit beside her. He placed one of the burgers he'd fetched directly onto her plate.

'Are you trying to fatten me up for Christmas lunch?'

He turned and whispered against her hair: 'There's no personality in a stick, Cher.'

His words warmed her more than the sun, but not as much as the way his knee fell absently against hers. She let it stay there, feeling a trail of flames course through her that was fanned when his arm snaked around the back of the bench. She leaned back to see if he would move it once he realised what he'd done. Instead, his thumb and forefinger began to caress her bare shoulder.

It didn't matter that it was purely acting for the benefit of her family. This would give them hours of conversation after they'd left. She didn't care that it was merely another scene in the whole performance of her having a boyfriend. It felt good and it didn't hurt to enter into the charade for a short time. It didn't matter that tomorrow they would be work colleagues once more, although that thought did sadden her a little.

Dan turned towards her. 'You okay?' he asked softly as his fingers gently squeezed her sensitive flesh. She turned to smile back when a thump sounded on the concrete, followed immediately by a loud cry.

Jamie lifted himself up from the path and ambled towards them. Dan raised his arm from behind her back as Jamie threw himself directly at her. Instinct curled her arms around his sobbing body as Dan leaned towards them both.

'It's okay, sweetheart,' she soothed, trying to gauge the damage. She immediately looked for the whereabouts of her lovely nephews, but they were nowhere to be seen.

'It was just an accident, Cher,' Dan murmured, reading her thoughts.

She cuddled Jamie protectively as he forced himself further into the circle of her arms while Dan started to inspect him.

'Just a grazed knee,' he said, smiling as he ruffled the child's hair.

'Come on, I'll take you upstairs and find a nice big plaster to put on it, so you can show all your friends at school tomorrow, eh?'

The sobbing ceased immediately at the prospect of a war wound as she took him by the hand.

'Thanks, sweet... umm... Cher...' Dan didn't finish the sentence. He must have realised that there was no one around to hear him, so the endearment would have been wasted, she thought, even though it sounded good to her ears.

She made a big deal of Jamie's courage in being able to walk up the stairs with such a wound on his knee, assuring him that she would have been in tears, if it had been her.

He struggled bravely not to cry when she dabbed on Savlon to clean the graze. He cheered slightly when she let him choose the biggest waterproof plaster in the box, which they put on together.

He leaned across and touched her hair. 'Prettier than Johnny's mum,' he offered quietly in a lost little voice. She kissed his forehead and pulled him to her, seeing the innocent pain in his eyes. How hard was it for him to see kids with their mums, yet not understand why he didn't have one? She wondered if he would ever remember anything about her. It would be so sad if he didn't. She made no effort to move the child's small body away from her. Strangely, it felt right.

'Your daddy loves you very much,' she whispered against his hair. He burrowed against her and she tightened her hold, wondering why tears were gathering in her throat and why she didn't want to let this child go.

A slight movement drew her attention to the door, to Dan, who stood watching with a strange look on his face. 'Is he okay?' he asked gruffly.

Cher nodded and pulled herself away. 'I bet he's just about ready for another burger, eh, Jamie?' she said, hearing the strangled way the words came out. 'You take him down. I'll be there in a minute.' Dan nodded and took his son's hand. Cher needed a few minutes to collect herself and force the unbidden emotion back where it belonged, and to erase the imprint of the child's small body against hers.

Her mum was busying herself serving up home-made fruit salad. 'Lovely chap, that bloke of yours,' she observed as she speared a wayward plum.

'For the last time, he's not my bloke, Mum. He's just a friend.' It really hadn't been such a good idea to invite Dan, she realised. It would just be more embarrassing when they learned the truth.

'But isn't this the one you've been mooning over for ages?'

Cher laughed. Only her mother could have thought that people like Michael Hunter acted like Dan. 'No, Mum, I can assure you that Dan Rickman is not Michael Hunter.'

Her mum coughed and turned away, blushing.

'What's wrong?' Cher asked. 'You've gone as red as a ripe cherry.'

'Umm… Cher, we'd better be off now,' Dan said from the doorway with a face like thunder. Cher looked to her mum and back again, realising how that must have sounded. A shameful flush coloured her cheeks.

'It's Jamie – he's tired,' he explained, looking at Cher's mum. Jamie seemed quite content playing catch with Jeremy.

'But you haven't had dessert yet,' offered her mum, trying desperately to save a humiliating situation.

Cher vaguely heard Dan thank her for a lovely evening, but his exact words were obscured by the blood rushing through her ears.

She grabbed her handbag, cursing her own tactlessness. Clever old her had succeeded in opening her mouth to change feet, which explained the sinking feeling that had settled on top of the burger she'd eaten. At least she would get the opportunity to explain herself in the car.

Dan bid goodnight to everyone and thanked her father for the invitation. Her mother smiled warmly at him and shook her head sadly at Cher as they left.

Dan was silent in the car, taking great lengths to dodge the traffic and drop her off as soon as possible. She didn't dare speak to him. She wanted to put things right, but the rage that played on his face stopped her.

'I'll see you tomorrow then,' Dan grated as he pulled up in front of her flat. He didn't turn the motor off. She got out and turned back towards him. She had to try and make herself understood. She opened her mouth.

'Don't say anything, Cher. You've said enough,' he murmured. The hurt in his eyes pierced something inside her. He shoved the car into gear and drove away.

She threw her handbag in the corner, cursing her insensitivity, and left the light off, taking comfort from the enveloping darkness. The evening had started so well. He had fitted into her family with the ease of an old distant cousin. Why should this bother her? It wasn't like he was ever going to see them again.

She remembered her previous boyfriend, who had tried to win her mother's affections with bunches of flowers and boxes of Quality Street. The memory of his presents had been obliterated when, on his second visit, he'd placed one foot idly on the coffee table. Her mother abhorred bad manners and no amount of sucking up ever erased that feeling of dislike.

It was as clear as a perfumier's nostril that they'd loved Dan to bits, and it wasn't as though he'd put on any exaggerated performance with them. He had been the Dan that she knew: relaxed, friendly and cheerful. The only performance had been his treatment of her. Just the thought of it made her cringe with embarrassment. Not that he hadn't acted well. He'd been marvellous; the humiliation was due to the fact that she'd let herself believe in it, just for a short while.

'Stupid, stupid, stupid,' she cursed, throwing off her clothes. She turned up the temperature on the shower. Maybe that would rid her skin of the memory of his tender fingers caressing her shoulder.

'Bollocks to it,' she screamed, launching the shower gel across the room. It hit the cistern and started spewing out shiny, green puss. The red-hot needles of water pounded her skin. She lowered her head, partly to soak her hair and partly in shame. What the hell had she been thinking, dragging her boss to her parents' in an effort to pretend someone found her interesting?

She viewed herself dispassionately through the steaming droplets. She wasn't obese, for God's sake, and her feet were sort of cute. Her knees did look a little like baby grapefruits and her legs had a sort of lampstand look about them, but they were covered most of the time. Her breasts were still firm and hadn't reached the point where they disappeared into her armpits when she lay on her back. Christ, who was she trying to kid? Who the hell would want this package anyway?

She turned, startled, as the doorbell sounded continuously. It was almost eleven and too late for double-glazing salesmen.

'Who is it?' she asked, pulling her dressing gown tightly around her. Wet patches welded the light cotton garment to her.

'It's the man who's not Michael Hunter.'

Shit, what now? Was he going to fire her for being a horrible person? She opened the door. He barged past her.

'Where's Jamie?' she asked, looking behind him.

'With his grandparents. He doesn't need to hear this.'

'If it's because of what I said about Michael Hunter, I'm sorry,' she said honestly. 'I didn't mean it like that.' Maybe it was better to sort it out now. An atmosphere at work would be very uncomfortable for them both.

'You just have no idea, do you?'

'I've said I'm sorry,' she muttered weakly.

She sat opposite him, hating the tension between them. It was unnatural. They'd always been able to laugh together.

'You just can't see it, can you? Your mother can, even your father can, for fuck's sake, but not you!'

'I don't know what you mean,' she cried. She just wanted the animosity to go away.

He stood and yanked her to a standing position. 'This,' he growled as his lips came down onto hers. Shock paralysed her and prevented her from responding.

He pulled away, looking tortured. She stared at him, trying to imprint the image of Dan onto the man who had just kissed her.

'For weeks now we've been growing closer, spending hours together at work. Talking, laughing, getting to know each other. All that time I hoped you were starting to feel the same way as I do, but I'm nothing but good old Dan to you.'

She continued to stare but she wanted him to carry on.

'Even that day at the park, we connected and I relaxed around you the way I never have around anyone. For the first time I was with someone who didn't spend every minute worrying about their hair and make-up, and who could actually just be themselves. And then when I get the courage to ask you out on a date, you assure me that it isn't a real one and nothing more than a practice run for when Michael Hunter eventually asks you out,' he raged as his eyes burned into hers. 'And then you invite me to meet your family, just to show that you can get a man.' He paused, looking sickened. 'And you did get a man, Cher, and it was your boss, but it was the wrong one, wasn't it? You hanker after a man that will never see how special you are, because you'd hide it. If you ever get what you want, it won't be what you deserve. But you just can't see that, can you?'

See it? She couldn't even remember her own name. Her mind was numb with shock.

She felt the aching start in her throat again. She saw what a total bitch she'd been. Her heart reached down towards her toes at the pain she'd inflicted on him.

'Christ, it makes me sick. You've shared everything with me in the last few weeks. I've seen your amazing talent for quick, logical thinking. I've seen you trying to find the person you want to be when there's nothing wrong with the person that you are. You've told me things that have drawn me closer to you every single day.' He stood and walked over to the door. She could see him moving, she could hear him speaking, but her mind wouldn't process the information.

'You've even seen parts of my life that cause me great pain and still I don't have a chance, because I'm not Michael fucking Hunter,' he said with his back to her.

His hand rested on the door handle. 'And that's not even the worst of it,' he said quietly, in a voice that had lost the rage but gained something far worse: despair. 'Can you imagine how I felt when my son ran into the arms of the woman I love? She cradled him in her arms, whispering soothing words to him, about five minutes before she ripped my heart out.'

'The woman you what?' she screeched.

Like a woman drowning, she recalled the ease of conversation with her family. The absent yet sensual way that he'd caressed her arm, and the sly wink when he thought no one was looking. They hadn't been acts for a captive audience, as she'd assumed. They were real, evoked by true emotion, and how had they made her feel? Loved, treasured, warm, secure and excited. And when she'd realised that that excitement had nowhere to go, she'd stifled it and ignored it. She'd entered into his charade with the knowledge that that was all it was, and she'd enjoyed it, wanted it, craved it from him and then told herself that it was for the benefit of others, not her.

'I thought you were acting,' she whispered.

'Why do you find it so hard to believe that someone could love you, Cher?' he said, turning.

She shrugged, feeling a heat building from the tips of her toes and reaching up towards the frenzied excitement that was growing in her stomach. She looked at him and saw the man instead of the boss. The intensity of his gaze was reaching out to her, but she remained frozen in place.

'I've always liked you. I tried at least three times to ask you out, but you never heard me. When I was promoted, I even wondered if God was on my side. And then I saw you vacuuming for Nellie and I was lost,' he admitted.

She laughed loudly. 'You are joking.' The smile refused to leave her face.

He shook his head. A wave of hope lit his eyes and died again. 'It's true,' he whispered. 'I'd always loved your sense of humour, but when I saw you doing that I just fell head over heels.'

Without realising what she was doing, she moved towards him.

He stepped back, frowning. 'I don't need your pity, Cher. I understand that you're in love with someone else, but I had to let you know how I feel, and then maybe it'll go away.'

She felt the stirrings of real panic. She didn't want it to go away. She leaned forward towards Dan and placed her hands against his chest. The feel of his body against her fingers ignited the passion that was waiting to burn. He viewed her a little unsurely and, in that instant, she realised what she'd known for ages: she loved this man, had loved him since the day at the park, probably before. The white-hot anger that had coursed through her when she'd seen him with another woman returned to her now, just thinking about him opening the door for *her* the way he had for her.

She placed her lips against his and left him in no doubt as to her feelings.

'Cher,' he protested.

'Daniel Rickman, I can assure you that the last thing I'm feeling for you right now is pity.'

He took one look at her eyes and the passion that mirrored his own before pulling her gently towards him.

CHAPTER NINETEEN

No one ever asked Sarah to work Saturdays due to her constant refusal. They had always been special to her. She had loved to sleep in for an hour before donning her dressing gown and preparing for David's arrival in the afternoon.

Damian had gasped with surprise when Sarah had offered the previous day to fill in for Dora, because those mornings had ceased to exist. They were now spent vacuuming and polishing ready for the weekly visit of David's daughter, and she was often up earlier than if she was due to go to work, and so the prospect of a full day away from them both had been an opportunity to grab with both hands, feet and any other clawing instrument.

Sarah pulled up in front of her flat and wished for the old magic to return. She remembered arriving home to the warm, comforting feeling of her own home: a space that protected and cherished her from the outside world; a place that was hers and felt like hers with its scatter cushions and scattered books, magazines, strewn clothes. Now it seemed ominous and frightening, like something out of a horror movie. The front door looked like a mouth that was waiting to gobble her up and chew the life out of her.

She pictured the night ahead: she would go in the house and play would stop for about ten minutes while David chatted with her about her day, and then Chelsea would find some ploy to bring his attention straight back to her. Annoying as it was, Sarah couldn't blame Chelsea for her behaviour. She had no idea what was going on. David still hadn't explained the true nature of their relationship, so the child still wondered why he'd left her to sleep on someone else's sofa.

It was only because of her concern for Chelsea that she continued every week to make the effort to reach the child.

'Hiya, I'm back,' she called into the ominous silence that greeted her from the doorway.

The lounge looked like a primary school playroom with felts, crayons and finger paints all over the floor. Several colouring books were lying open, and a small doll was wedged into the DVD player. Sarah sighed and began to pick up the mess.

'Hello, love, I thought I heard you. You're back early,' David said, coming out of Chelsea's bedroom. Chelsea followed behind him and threw herself onto the sofa, clutching a doll that ate, drank and urinated, and was one of the foulest things Sarah had ever seen. David looked a little pensive, and Chelsea stared up at her with a slow smile playing around her mouth.

'Have you had a good day?' he asked, squeezing her shoulder. He looked tired and agitated.

Sarah put her handbag on the chair. 'Fine. Are you okay?'

He nodded and grimaced. 'We've… umm… had a little bit of a problem. I don't think it's anything too serious: it still works okay – well nearly okay. I've been trying to fix it before you got back but it refuses to recognise…'

'David, what are you talking about?' she asked, smiling. He looked no older than Chelsea. She half expected to look down and find him wearing knee-length trousers and white socks.

'Well I was just downloading some software for Chelsea to play with and my mobile rang—'

Sarah felt her hands begin to shake. 'What have you done?'

'It was an accident, love. She didn't mean to do it. She was just trying to find out how to play the bugs game that I bought for her. It was just an accident.'

Sarah's stomach began to churn. 'How bad is it?' she asked quietly, not daring to look at Chelsea.

'It's wiped your hard drive.'

'You must be fuck—'

'Sarah, please.' He nodded towards Chelsea.

She looked towards him and almost exploded then turned and rushed into the bedroom. The screen was covered in dancing zigzags. She switched it off at the plug and switched it back on again. The laptop chuntered for a few seconds and then stopped, sending the screen into an epileptic fit.

David followed her and closed the door. 'Sweetheart, it was an accident. She didn't mean to do it. She just pressed the wrong button.'

Sarah didn't turn to face him. He knew enough about computers to know that it took more than one button to crash a computer and wipe the hard drive.

'Everything I've ever written was on there,' she whispered, staring at the jumping screen. Sarah's head fell into her waiting hands.

'I'll get someone to fix it.'

'It's ruined, David,' she said, feeling the tears gather in her throat. Every single word that she'd dragged out of her mind, every single emotion that she'd managed to record, every word, every sentence that had developed inside her head, her own heart was gone. More than ten years of pictures that she'd painted with words had been destroyed.

'I'll buy you another one.'

'You can't replace the work, David. It took me years to produce those stories, those poems, and now they're gone.' She turned to face him and the tears rolled over her cheeks and slid off the end of her chin.

He came towards her. 'Sweetheart, don't cry. I'll find a way to make it bet—'

'I'm not fucking Chelsea,' she screamed. 'Don't speak to me as though I'm a child, and don't touch me.'

'You can write it again,' David said sharply at being rebuked.

'If you understood anything about me, you'd understand what a pathetic comment that is,' she yelled.

'But you didn't do anything with it anyway,' he snapped at her refusal to be pacified.

'What the fuck has that got to do with it? It was mine, it was me. It was every feeling I've had for the last ten years. It was every idea that I've been excited about. It was everything I had.'

She felt the heat infuse her face as she realised the truth behind the words spoken in anger.

'You can't mean that surely?' David asked.

'Just go out and take Chelsea with you,' she said, turning her face towards the window. She didn't know if she meant it. She only knew that she couldn't bear to look at him right now.

David stood motionless for a minute. 'I'll take Chelsea for ice cream and drop her off at home. It's probably not a good idea for her to stay tonight, is it?'

It infuriated Sarah that he thought there was any question. She shook her head.

Once the front door closed behind them, the floodgates opened and Sarah sobbed loudly. She seemed to have lost so much and wasn't sure what she was crying for. Her whole history seemed to have been deleted, the sense of loss overwhelming. She had recorded every thought, emotion and idea onto that machine, which now winked maliciously at her.

She switched it off; the gentle whirring like a heart monitor stopped. She sat back and wondered where it had all gone wrong. Her house was no longer her home; David was no longer the man she'd fallen in love with, turning instead into a guilty, apologetic excuse for a father. She tried to find someone to blame, but she had no one but herself. She had wanted this. She had ached to have David with her all the time; she had dreamed of the life that they would lead and her dreams had turned into this nightmare. Her place of solitude, which had once been an office with a spare bed, was now a girl's bedroom with a desk and useless computer, with teddy bears and overflowing toy boxes that hadn't appeared all at once but sort of grown over the weeks. Now Sarah felt that she shouldn't be in her own study. She felt like the interloper in her own room.

She dragged herself from the chair and showered. A fatigue had settled on her body, making it almost too much effort to reach for the shower gel. She stood and let the water wash over her then dressed in leggings and a baggy T-shirt, with a towel wrapped around her head, and began to tidy up the mess in the lounge. The post lay discarded on the dining table with pen marks and asterisks all over them. Sarah felt again the mild irritation that her things were being messed with without her permission. The first two were glossy leaflets offering her credit cards, which she threw in the bin. The third was the electricity bill, and the fourth was handwritten. She turned it over and examined it. There was something strangely different about receiving an envelope that was handwritten. The envelope was thin, as though it contained nothing.

She opened it frowning, thinking it was a chain letter stating that if she didn't send it on to ten people, she would incur bad luck for seven years. *Yeah, right*, she thought.

She pulled out a compliment slip and something else fell to the ground. Sarah read the slip with an open mouth.

Dear Ms Dunn,

We herewith enclose a cheque for the purchase of the story entitled 'Supermarket Sweep'.
Please do not hesitate to send further material for our attention.

Sarah read the words three times before the message would sink in. She'd been checking her emails almost hourly since submitting the story to the magazine. The absence of any kind of response had convinced her that the story had been sent to an electronic 'to be read' pile and that she might receive a standard rejection email sometime in the future. Never had she expected to receive an actual cheque and a handwritten note. She had no idea people did that anymore.

Her trembling fingers reached for the cheque that had fallen to the ground. It was real. This was not a joke. Someone was actually paying her for something that she'd written. She looked into the envelope to see if there was a piece of paper that said 'GOTCHA', but the envelope was empty. She stared at the compliment slip and the cheque and started to laugh. Someone had bought something of hers. Her idea, her words, her sentences had been paid for and were going to be published. The very idea was just too good to be true.

She shook her head disbelievingly. Many times she'd lain in bed and prayed for a sign. Just a hint that she had some minute smidgeon of talent on which she could build – anything that would show that the words and feelings that came from her own mind were not just a collection of words that made no sense to anyone else. She held the cheque tightly. She had asked the question and it had been answered, and the message it brought was clear.

When David returned it was after nine o'clock, and Sarah was ready. She was dressed in cream slacks and a short-sleeved cotton shirt. Her hair had been blow-dried onto her face, and the wonders of Bobbi Brown had been applied.

'You look nice. Are we going out?' he asked brightly, obviously hoping that the episode with the computer had been forgotten.

'Sit down, David. We need to talk.'

'Okay,' he said affably, looking her up and down. He gave a low whistle.

'David, one of the letters that your daughter had scribbled on earlier today was a cheque from a magazine that's bought one of my stories. What do you think?' Sarah cocked her head for his response. It was important.

He frowned slightly. 'How much did they pay?' he asked.

Sarah sighed. He had answered her question with resounding clarity. He saw the disappointment on her face.

'I mean, that's wonderful, darling,' he enthused, rising to hug her. She moved out of his reach. 'So are we going out to celebrate?' he asked, backing away from her.

'One of us is going to buy her two best friends a few drinks to celebrate, seeing as they saw fit to congratulate me on what they know is an achievement and what they know is very important to me.'

'Of course I'm pleased for you, sweetheart. I know how much you love—'

'David, please sit down,' she said, summoning the courage of her earlier convictions. 'There are a couple of things I'd like to ask you.'

'Sure,' he said, sitting on the sofa and crossing his legs. He looked cocky and arrogant and more like the man that Sarah had fallen in love with. His mouth was twisted sardonically, as though he was ready for anything.

'Why was Chelsea using the computer without my permission?'

'I've told you. I wanted to download this game for her. You know she loves bugs and things like that so I tried to—'

'You've missed the question, David. I said without *my* permission.'

David looked genuinely perplexed.

'It's my computer and I did not give permission for it to be used. You knew what was on there but, at that moment, it became nothing more than a plaything for your daughter. You had no right to use it without asking me first.'

'For God's sake, Sarah, these things happen with children. It was a bloody accident.'

'But she's not my child, David, and purely because you have such strong feelings of love and devotion for her doesn't mean that I will develop them by proxy. The point is that my things were used without asking and I don't like it.'

'You're being very territorial. You're not usually like this.'

Sarah became frustrated with trying to make herself clear. 'David, I understand that you would let your daughter have anything that her heart desires. That's only natural because you're her father, but you shouldn't let her have things that don't belong to her or to you.'

'But we live together, so how can you be so…?'

'No, David, that's the whole point: we don't live together and we never have. You have moved into my home and treated it like a hotel. You have made demands for the comfort of your daughter that I have gone along with because I wanted to please you, but I have bent over backward so far that I'm in danger of snapping into two pieces. I watch the only joy on your face when you go to collect Chelsea: I sit and watch you play together for hours; I wait for you to discipline her when she's rude or obnoxious; and then I comfort you when you have to take her home again.'

Sarah could see a muscle jumping in his neck and colour flooding his face. She spoke quietly. 'This is not what I expected, David.'

'What did you expect?' He looked searchingly at her.

'I expected us to still be in love.'

'So you're saying this is my fault?'

Sarah shook her head. 'If anyone's to blame it's me, not you, but you have to agree that you haven't made a great deal of effort either.'

His eyes pierced hers. 'I left my family for you,' he said accusingly.

She smiled at him sadly. 'But that's the whole point. You never left them. You moved out physically but you never left them psychologically and, if I'm honest, I don't think you ever really wanted to.'

'How can you say that?'

'Oh, David, it doesn't take a detective. You didn't unpack for weeks; you go to see Bianca and Chelsea almost every night after work—'

'I have to work late—'

'David, don't lie. I'm the mistress, remember. I know when you're lying. I tried to phone you a couple of times at work and you weren't there.'

He opened his mouth to protest and then closed it again. He looked lost and confused.

Sarah sat beside him and took his hand. 'You even forgot your shaver. What type of man who's leaving his home forgets to take his shaver?' she asked.

'But I wanted to be with you.'

Sarah nodded. At the time, after that one night, maybe he had wanted to be with her. Maybe her plan had worked initially, but the thrill had worn off. The lust that had carried them through the last five years had worn off in the space of a few weeks and left David what he appeared to be now: a stranger in her home.

'So what do we do now?' he asked, running his fingers through his hair.

Sarah took a deep breath. She wondered if she would ever regret her next words, but it felt right.

'You go home and beg Bianca for forgiveness.'

He opened his mouth to protest, but she placed her finger onto his lips. Her throat was constricting and she wasn't sure how long she'd be able to hold back the tears. She knew it was right, even as the last five years of her life were slipping away from her.

'It's where you belong. Maybe if we'd met first things would be different, but they're not, and you should be at home with your family.'

David tried to take her in his arms, but Sarah deftly moved away. She would welcome any excuse to backtrack. Any sign of the David she'd once known and she would crumble in his arms.

She moved away from him and stood in front of the fireplace. 'Everything is packed ready.' She swallowed and blinked rapidly.

'Sarah, I…'

She walked towards the door. 'Please, David, don't say anything else. We both know it's the right thing to do.'

She opened the door to the hallway and took a last look at the face that had lived in her dreams for five years. She ached to throw herself into his arms and beg him to make it how it used to be. She longed to feel his arms around her, soothing her, and whispering in her ear about how their life together would be. But she had made the decision and she had to be strong.

'Take your time and post the key through the letterbox,' she murmured from behind him. Her throat ached with the effort of holding back the tears.

He nodded without looking at her, and she closed the door silently behind her.

CHAPTER TWENTY

'But what if I'm making some huge mistake and he's not the one I'm destined to be with? I mean what if I've just become used to being around Mark but I don't really love him? What if he's a habit I've formed over all these years? What if my real destiny is wandering around the planet looking for me, and he'll be destined to be alone forever, because I've married the wrong person? What if—?'

'What if you shut the hell up and let me get this tiara in your hair,' said Sarah, with a mouth full of grips.

Deb turned to face her. The sharp movement pulled out the section that she'd just fixed. Deb could feel it sitting askew on top of her head. 'But when you think about it, you can never be totally sure that you're with the right person, can you?'

'Yes, you can,' Cher breathed, fingering a stem of baby's breath on the bridal bouquet.

Sarah smiled towards Cher, who sat at the dressing table. Deb detected a little sadness. The night that Sarah had finished the relationship with David had been spent alternating between great celebration at the prospect of her story being published and tears at the break-up of her relationship.

The more glasses of wine they'd poured down her, the quicker the mood swings had altered, so that within seconds, hysterical laughter had turned to wrenching sobbing and vice versa. Both she and Cher had held her hand through the rollercoaster of emotions that had finally ended when she'd passed out.

Cher had offered to stay at home with Sarah, to which she'd refused, but when Deb's phone had rung at three in the morning, she'd listened as Sarah talked and cried for an hour then eventually fell asleep. In all honesty, Deb was pleased that the relationship had broken down. Her friend deserved more and, although she'd tried not to judge, she'd often wondered about the effects of the affair on David's wife. As far as Deb was concerned, David was where he should be, providing he'd been lucky enough for Bianca to take him back and, if it had taken this episode to make Sarah come to her senses, then so be it.

Deb thought Sarah had recovered remarkably well in the short time since. She'd enrolled in a correspondence course and was due to attend her first writers' circle on Monday night.

'But I feel like a fraud, like I'm pretending to be something I'm not,' Sarah had said the previous night over countless Bacardi Breezers.

'But the only person who didn't have faith in you was you,' they'd both assured her.

'You can tell if you're with the right person – you just feel it here,' Cher said, slapping her chest.

'And if we hope to get any sense out of her today, we'll be bloody lucky,' Deb observed with a smile.

Cher had recounted in detail the events of the night Dan had accompanied her to her parents' barbecue. Deb had been surprised to find herself in tears by the time Cher reached the part where she'd returned Dan's kiss. Only Cher hadn't realised that she'd been slowly falling in love with the man who'd once been her friend.

Cher smiled serenely. 'I will perform my bridesmaidly duties to perfection.' She clamped her right, gloved hand to her mouth. 'Oh God, what if I fall and make a complete fool of myself in front of Dan and Jamie?'

'You'll be able to join my club,' Sarah offered. 'But at least you'll have clothes on.'

'Hey, hold it. Isn't it me who's supposed to be worrying about this sort of stuff?' Deb interrupted.

'Keep still,' Sarah ordered.

'But what if marriage serves as a catalyst and suddenly we don't get on anymore and soon we'll be arguing all the time? We'll both spend all our time at work, and then we'll start arguing in front of the children, traumatising them for later in life, and then he'll have an affair and before you know it we'll be divorced.'

'Bloody hell, Deb, I shouldn't worry about traumatising kids until you've actually got them.'

'You don't understand,' Deb exploded, sending the precariously balanced tiara tumbling to the ground. 'Maybe this is all wrong. Your wedding day is supposed to be perfect, like a dream, a fairy tale, and we can't even rustle up one parent between us. Doesn't that say something?'

'It says more about your parents than it does about either of you two,' Cher offered.

'But maybe it's a sign,' Deb insisted. 'And then when you think about the two cancelled attempts, it's like I've been blind to what someone has been trying to tell me. How much more proof do I need?'

Deb stood and moved to unzip her dress. 'Contact Mark and tell him it's off. I can't go through with it if I have this many doubts. It's not fair to him.'

Cher placed her hand on Deb's to stop her pulling the zip down. 'Don't be ridiculous. Sit down a minute and answer these questions for me. Just one word and don't think about the answer. Take a couple of deep breaths.'

Deb sat down, and Sarah removed the hair grips from her mouth.

'Now remember, don't think about your answers. Just say the first word that comes into your mind. How is the sex?'

'Hot, steamy, sensu—'

'One word, I said. How does he make you feel after sex?'

'Hmmmmmm…'

'I'll take that groan as a sign of satisfaction. What's the first word that comes into your head when you lay eyes on him each morning?'

'Yummy.'

'What's his best point?'

'He's tender and loving…'

'And what's his worst point?'

'The way he sometimes eats really quickly, but even that's quite endearing once you—'

'Christ, total bastard, dump him,' Sarah cried, throwing her hands out expressively. 'Now get your head back over here so I can finish this damn headdress.'

'Need I say more?' Cher asked.

Deb sighed. 'I know all that, but what if it doesn't work out?'

Cher rolled her eyes. 'Then make sure you get half of everything. You're just getting the jitters, for God's sake. Everyone has them.'

Deb leaned across to her bedside table and retrieved the piece of notepaper. She'd spent the previous night alone after a few drinks with her friends and a couple of people from work then crawled into bed in a state of cheery stupidity that just preceded being shit-faced. The envelope had been lying on her pillow with a single red rose. She read again the note that Mark had left her.

Although I'm not with you, I am. Wherever I am you're with me, and tomorrow I will look into your eyes and vow to love and protect you forever. I have loved you since that day on the steps when we met and will never stop. You are my heart, my love and my life.

Deb felt the tears gather in her throat as they had done the night before. He wasn't poetic, he wasn't eloquent, but he was honest, and he was hers. If only Margie was here to see her only son get married.

'Don't even think about it,' Sarah ordered, removing the paper from her grasp. 'We don't have time to take you back to the salon to get your face repaired.'

'It'll be okay, won't it?' Deb asked in a small voice.

Cher came to sit beside her, and Sarah stopped fumbling with her hair.

'It'll be perfect,' Cher said, clasping her hand.

'It'll be everything you could wish for,' Sarah said, squeezing her shoulder.

'Yeah, like that night we were throwing herbs around Cher's bloody garden and a fat lot of good that did us.'

Cher tipped her head thoughtfully. 'Hang on, think about it – you wished for Margie to disappear and, well, has anyone seen her in over a week?'

'Don't be bloody stupid – that's just coincidence,' Deb snapped.

'Well what about me?'

'What about you?'

Cher's voice became excited. 'I wished for my boss to fall in love with me, and he did. Only it was the wrong one.'

Deb frowned. 'You're just trying to make things fit now. What about Sarah – things didn't work out for her, did they?'

A slow smile spread on Sarah's face. 'Now you just wait a moment.' She paused and held the comb aloft. 'I wished for David's child and I certainly got that.'

Deb looked at them both before howling with laughter. 'You can't be serious?'

'But you've got to concede, it's a little bit weird,' Sarah said, still wielding the comb.

'It's just the natural conclusion of things that were already in progress. It's nothing to do with throwing herbs around in the dark. We didn't even perform it properly, for God's sake. If you recall, Cher got bored halfway through and started making up her own spell. Even if there was something in it, that could never have worked.'

'How do you know?' Sarah asked, putting the last clip in place. She stood back to admire her handiwork.

'Because it's just not real. If you're saying that you think we've all arrived at this point in our lives from what we did that night, then I'm not sure I want either of you opening your mouths at my wedding. You'll be carted away to the loony bin.'

'So it's still on then?' Sarah asked with a lopsided grin.

Deb saw in the mirror that Cher and Sarah smiled at each other across her head.

'Okay, I get it. Deb has now been distracted from all her lunatic ramblings.' Even so, she couldn't help wondering at what they'd said. She tried to remember exactly what had happened that night, but the cheap wine and time in between had dimmed the memory. Were mystic forces responsible for the things that had happened in her life or were they down to her?

Were mystic forces responsible for her professional situation as well? Was all that due to some idiotic, drunken caper? she wondered as Cher handed her the bouquet. No, that had been all her own hard work. She had put the effort in and reaped the rewards.

'And talking of bosses, I'm not sure Michael Hunter is going to be one for much longer.'

'Ooooh, do tell?' Sarah asked, giving Deb's hair one last check over.

'Well it would appear that he was trying some underhanded way to get rid of his last assistant, Letty, after his amorous advances were rejected, and she has threatened a wrongful dismissal suit. A very worried human resources lady interviewed me and asked if I had anything to offer, clearly hoping I was going to say no.'

'And?' Deb asked, remembering Cher's account of his cruel response to an invitation to her home.

'It's fair to say she wasn't thrilled when I produced Michael's handwritten notes from my handbag. A check of the dated Word documents proved he was trying to backtrack the disciplinary action that had never taken place, and he was suspended within the hour.'

'And Letty?' Sarah asked.

'Will be settling out of court from the rumours I heard.'

'Sounds fair to me,' Deb said, taking one last look in the mirror.

'Ready?' Sarah asked as the car horn sounded outside.

Deb took a deep breath. 'Ready.'

Deb caught sight of Mark's back as his figure disappeared into the church and her heart lurched. She was about to commit herself to that man for the rest of her life. She took a deep breath and nodded to the other two.

'Get me in there before I change my mind.'

Sarah straightened her dress while Cher fussed with the flowers. Passers-by stopped and tipped their heads. Deb smiled awkwardly, unable to do anything else through her chattering teeth.

Milton's round, shining head popped around the side of the wooden doors.

'You look beautiful,' he gasped as she approached. 'I'm honoured to be a part of this,' he said, coughing slightly.

Deb smiled and looked away, sure she would begin blubbering at him. Her senses seemed to have become emotionally charged, heightened, like a current of electricity buzzing behind a socket, waiting for someone to put their finger in. She wanted to laugh. She wanted to cry. She wanted to run down the aisle and throw herself into Mark's arms, for him to tell her that everything would be okay and they would love each other forever.

'What time is it?' Deb murmured.

'Ten minutes after two.'

Deb took a deep breath. 'She's not coming, is she?' she asked, defeated.

Sarah and Cher looked at each other. She wasn't angry with Margie, just disappointed for Mark. She hoped this was going to be the only wedding either of them were going to have, and neither of their parents were here to witness their marriage.

She'd thought about picking up the phone to Margie during the last week, but her pride hadn't allowed it. The harsh words had stuck in her mind and wouldn't let her make the first move, but now, thinking about Mark at the other end of the church, she almost wished she had. For herself, she wasn't as hurt. If she was completely honest with herself, she hadn't expected her father to attend. It would take a lot more than his daughter's wedding day to have him surgically removed from the armchair.

Cher placed a hand on her arm and squeezed. 'Come on – this is your day. It's your fairy tale. Now it's time to meet your prince.'

Deb smiled and nodded. Milton offered his arm and Deb took it. She had raised her head to signal that she was ready when the sound of tyres screeching echoed into the entrance of the church.

A familiar voice reached them before they saw the cause of the commotion.

'Look, I told you we'd be late if you insisted on searching for that blasted blue shirt, and it still doesn't match that tie as well as I'd have liked, and I'd have thought your shoes would have been already polished, but no, I had to get the old black shoeshine out myself and give them—'

Deb's heart jumped into her mouth as she turned and saw Margie, resplendent in lavender, nudging her father forcefully up the pathway towards the church. He looked sheepish and a little intimidated.

'See, if you'd have ironed your suit last night, we wouldn't have kept your daughter waiting, would we? Not coming to her wedding, I've never heard anything like it.'

Suddenly, he was there, in front of her. Red-faced but smiling. He took her hand, his trembling as much as hers. 'You look…' He shook his head. She felt Milton step away from her. Her father saw it too.

Fear shadowed his eyes. 'Love, I don't want— I mean, if you'd rather…'

Deb smiled widely at him. It was enough that he was here. It was more than she'd hoped for. 'It's okay, Dad. I'm just pleased that you've come.'

He stepped back, visibly relieved. He moved aside to reveal Margie.

'I told him I wasn't having such nonsense. Today is about you two, not us, and things just have to be put aside and forgotten about. Sometimes you say things you just don't mean, and sometimes you regret the hurtful things you said, but you just don't know how to say sorry.'

Their eyes met and Deb nodded her agreement.

'I told him that if he didn't get dressed, I'd—'

Margie's words were cut short as Deb leaned forward and hugged her tightly. Deb felt a small sob against her shoulder. 'Thank you,' she whispered against Margie's full brimmed hat.

'Oh now stop it, you silly girl, you'll have me blubbering before I'm even in the church and how would that look?'

Margie reached out with her right hand and brushed away a single tear from Deb's cheek. 'You look like a princess.'

Deb smiled tremulously, dangerously close to losing her composure.

Margie smiled at Sarah and tipped her head at Cher. 'You look like you've lost weight, dear. You both look lovely.' She turned her attention to Deb's father and whacked his forearm with her handbag. 'Come on – you can walk me down the aisle, seeing as we're both going to the front, and then I can keep my beady little eye on you,' she said as they disappeared through the double doors.

'Shit, I think I'm gonna cry,' Cher said, sniffing.

Milton once again offered his arm and Deb took it.

'Ready?' they all asked.

'Yes,' she breathed. 'I'm ready.'

A LETTER FROM ANGELA

First of all, I want to say a huge thank you for choosing to read *If Only*, a departure from the adventures of Kim Stone and the team. If you'd like to keep up to date with all my latest releases, just sign up at the website link below.

www.bookouture.com/angela-marsons

Many years ago I had the idea for a light-hearted story of three friends casting a drunken spell in the garden in an effort to change their lives and make their dreams come true. Over time the characters of Cher, Deb and Sarah became clearer in my head, as did the things in their lives that they wanted to change.

During the writing of the book these three women found a special place in my heart as they journeyed towards their happy ever after and the challenges they faced along the way.

If you enjoyed it, I would be forever grateful if you'd write a review. I'd love to hear what you think, and it can also help other readers discover one of my books for the first time. Or maybe you can recommend it to your friends and family…

I'd love to hear from you – so please get in touch on my Facebook or Goodreads page, Twitter or through my website.

Thank you so much for your support – it is hugely appreciated.
Angela Marsons

www.angelamarsons-books.com

angelamarsonsauthor

@WriteAngie

ACKNOWLEDGEMENTS

As ever my first and foremost thanks go to my partner, Julie. She encourages me to write whatever I want to, even if it's an idea that I think will fizzle out halfway through. This book was no different to the Kim Stone books, and Julie was with me during the early mornings and late nights as I explored the idea that was in my head. No book gets written without her.

Thank you to my mum and dad who continue to spread the word proudly to anyone who will listen. And to my sister Lyn, her husband, Clive, and my nephews, Matthew and Christopher, for their support too.

Thank you to Amanda and Steve Nicol who support us in so many ways, and to Kyle Nicol for book spotting my books everywhere he goes.

I would like to thank the team at Bookouture for their continued enthusiasm and willingness to publish something a bit different from Kim Stone and her stories. Special thanks, as ever, to my editor, Claire Bord, who encouraged this standalone project and offered invaluable input to making this story the best it can be.

To Kim Nash (Mama Bear) who works tirelessly to promote our books and protect us from the world. To Noelle Holten who has limitless enthusiasm and passion for our work, and Sarah Hardy who also champions our books at every opportunity.

Thank you to the fantastic Kim Slater who has been an incredible support and friend to me for many years now who, despite writing outstanding novels herself, always finds time for a chat. Massive thanks to Emma Tallon who keeps me going with funny stories and endless support. Also to the fabulous Renita D'Silva and Caroline Mitchell, both writers that I follow and read voraciously and without whom this journey would be impossible. Huge thanks to the growing family of Bookouture authors who continue to amuse, encourage and inspire me on a daily basis.

My eternal gratitude goes to all the wonderful bloggers and reviewers who I hope will take Cher, Deb and Sarah to their hearts as they have with Kim Stone. These wonderful people shout loudly and share generously not because it is their job but because it is their passion. I will never tire of thanking this community for their support of both myself and my books. Thank you all so much.

Massive thanks to all my fabulous readers, especially the ones that have taken time out of their busy day to visit me on my website, Facebook page, Goodreads or Twitter.

Printed in Great Britain
by Amazon